Bride's Bay Resort

WEDNESDAY
Conference registration

THURSDAY
Cocktail party for conference attendees

FRIDAY
Afternoon press reception
Sunset beach cookout

SATURDAY
Frisbee-throwing contest
Dinner and keynote speech by two-time
Olympic gold medalist Steve Lantz

LOST BABY!
SEE CONCIERGE/BABY-SITTER
JOANIE GRIFFIN IF YOU HAVE
ANY INFORMATION

GUEST REGISTER

Mrs. Frances Flannagan

Phoebe Claterberry

Dennis Wright

Steve Lantz

Baby Emily

Joanie Griffin, *your concierge*

Cathy Gillen Thacker

MATCHMAKING BABY

Harlequin Books

TORONTO • NEW YORK • LONDON
AMSTERDAM • PARIS • SYDNEY • HAMBURG
STOCKHOLM • ATHENS • TOKYO • MILAN
MADRID • WARSAW • BUDAPEST • AUCKLAND

ISBN 0-373-16613-3

MATCHMAKING BABY

Copyright © 1996 by Cathy Gillen Thacker.

This edition published by arrangement with Harlequin Books S.A.

® and TM are trademarks of the publisher. Trademarks indicated with ® are registered in the United States Patent and Trademark Office, the Canadian Trade Marks Office and in other countries.

Printed in U.S.A.

Dear Reader,

Imaging a warm ocean breeze blowing gently over your skin...the heady scent of flowers mixing with the salty tang of the sea air.

Imagine warm, sunny days filled with love, passion and excitement...strong, sexy heroes and beautiful, spirited heroines. And you are ready to step into the romantic world of Bride's Bay.

Created by seven authors and a team of eight wonderful editors led by Marsha Zinberg, Bride's Bay Resort is located on a fictional island off the coast of South Carolina. Working together, we strove to create a romantic world you would never want to forget and, indeed, would want to visit again and again.

We hope you enjoy reading the Bride's Bay books as much as we enjoyed writing them for you.

With best wishes,

Cathy Gillen Thacker

P.S. Don't forget to catch all seven books!

ABOUT THE AUTHOR

Cathy Gillen Thacker believes that love and laughter go hand in hand. Not surprisingly, her warm family stories and fast-paced romantic comedies are very popular with readers. She's written forty-four novels and numerous nonfiction articles, and her books frequently appear on the Waldenbooks bestseller list. Cathy is originally from the Midwest, but now makes her home in North Carolina with her husband and three children.

Books by Cathy Gillen Thacker

*Too Many Dads miniseries

Prologue

"You're here about the envelope, aren't you?" the attorney said.

"It's time. I wish it wasn't." The woman cast a look at the towheaded toddler beside her. Taking her by the hand, she led her over to the sofa and watched as she climbed unassisted onto the seat. Taking the envelope from the attorney, the woman sat down beside the little girl and waited until she was settled comfortably, with her back against the sofa and her legs stretched out in front of her.

"But I have to do what is best for Emily," the woman continued.

At the mention of her name, eighteen-month-old Emily perked up. She watched as the woman carefully loosened the flap of the envelope with the tip of her finger and removed the enclosed instructions. As the woman read, Emily mimicked her and "read" the paper, too.

"Oh, my," the woman said at last, tucking the paper back into the envelope and clasping a hand to her heart. She looked at the attorney, her glance startled. "What if this doesn't work?"

The attorney smiled at Emily, taking in her sturdy little body, curly golden blond hair, fair skin and long-lashed blue-gray eyes. She was every parent's dream.

"It will," he said confidently. "After all, who could resist such a precious little girl?"

The woman watched as Emily removed the letter from her lap and tried to work the folded paper out of the envelope again. "You have a point there. Emily is an adorable child."

"Besides—" the attorney gestured to the letter "—we have a legal and moral obligation to at least try it that way first." He paused. "We both promised that when the time came we would do what was requested of us."

"You're right of course," the woman said, sighing. "And I will keep my word. I'll just have to trust that the plan is a good one and that everything will work out in Emily's best interests."

"Here's something that should help." The attorney handed over a video cassette marked simply, "For Emily."

The woman accepted the cassette gratefully as Emily finally managed to clumsily pull the letter from the envelope and open it. Again the little girl pretended to read. "Oh, my," she said, clasping a hand to her chest.

The woman and the attorney chuckled softly at Emily's mimicry.

"She certainly is growing up fast," the attorney said, gazing at the toddler fondly.

"Too fast, I sometimes think," the woman said with another sigh.

Sensing something was going on, Emily studied the attorney and then the woman beside her. Abruptly losing interest in the letter and envelope she tossed them aside and scrambled onto the woman's lap.

"Kiss!" she shouted enthusiastically, determined, it seemed, to make her guardian feel better. Wreathing her tiny arms about the woman's neck, she kissed her cheek and hugged her fiercely.

The woman hugged and kissed her back, wishing she didn't have to let Emily go. Yet she knew she had no choice but to follow the instructions she'd been given. She'd move heaven and earth to see that Emily had the wonderful home and caring parents she deserved. And if this was the only way to get those for her, Emily's guardian thought determinedly, then so be it.

"Are you ready for this?" she asked Emily thickly.

Emily gurgled in response. She drew back to look at the woman's face, waved both her arms and smiled again. Then, tinkering with a gold pin on the woman's blouse, Emily said, "Geh Mama."

Chapter One

"This can't be right," Joanie Griffin moaned.

It was early Wednesday afternoon, and she was reading the memo Elizabeth Jermain had sent to all staff members. As concierge, Joanie thought she knew everything that was going on at the prestigious Jermain Island resort. Apparently not.

"What can't be right?" Liz Jermain, Elizabeth's granddaughter and the hotel manager, asked, stepping into Joanie's office behind the front desk. As always, Liz was dressed chicly, today in a short lavender sheath, her long, brown hair was drawn back in a chignon.

Joanie pointed to the memo bearing the Bride's Bay Resort logo. "Do you know anything about this?"

"Sure," Liz said, crossing her arms and resting a hip against the built-in credenza opposite Joanie's antique cherry desk. "I recommended Steve Lantz be hired as keynote speaker for the mentoring conference this week. You know, the one where college students learn how to mentor underprivileged kids and help them stay in school. Why that look? Do you know him?"

All too well, Joanie thought. "I think the question is, since his shaving-cream commercials started airing on television almost two years ago, who *doesn't* know him? The man is reportedly a lady-killer extraordinaire.''

"And a two-time Olympic gold medalist," Liz added. "Besides, those stories about him bedding every woman he meets are greatly exaggerated."

Joanie glanced heavenward. She knew the lust Steve Lantz could inspire. "I suppose he gave you his word on that?" Joanie returned, doing her best to hide the torrent of confused feelings welling up inside her.

"As a matter of fact, he did." Liz paused. She stepped closer and peered into Joanie's face. "But you don't believe it, do you?"

"I think where there's smoke, there's fire. And in Steve Lantz's case, there's plenty of smoke," Joanie said decisively.

"Sounds to me like you're the one with the fire," a deep voice said from the doorway. Joanie turned to see Steve Lantz leaning against the portal.

It had been two years, three months, four days and six hours since she'd last seen him. And he hadn't changed a bit. At six foot six, he still had the honed-to-perfection body of a champion swimmer and the heart-stopping good looks of an all-American, all-around good guy, which was, she supposed, what had made him so popular as a motivational speaker and celebrity spokesperson for a variety of products. Since the Olympics, he had spoken at gatherings nationwide and sold everything from chicken noodle soup to suntan lotion, swim gear and designer warm-ups to shaving cream. And why not, with his knowing glances, burnished gold hair and dazzling white smile, he was every woman's fantasy man. Every woman's except hers, she thought.

"Hello, Joanie," he said, his eyes moving over her. He smiled and took another step closer. "Nice to see you. Again."

"SO YOU TWO KNOW each other?" Liz asked.

"No," Joanie said quickly. She'd just thought she knew him, which was, in retrospect, utterly ridiculous after just one week. "We don't."

"Yes," Steve said simultaneously, his gaze sweeping Joanie's pink-and-gray checked jacket, pale pink silk blouse and slim gray skirt approvingly. "We do."

Liz looked from one to the other. "So which is it?" she asked. "Do you two know each other or don't you?"

"We met several years ago, when Steve was on vacation in Myrtle Beach and I was working at a hotel there," Joanie said, knowing Liz would find out sooner or later if she didn't fess up now. "I wouldn't say we were anything more than casual acquaintances, however, if even that."

"But we would have been, if you hadn't run off in a temper," Steve countered.

Joanie stood and stepped from behind her desk, planting her hands on her hips. "If you don't mind, I'd rather not discuss that."

"I'm sure you wouldn't," he agreed mildly.

"I wouldn't mind hearing," Liz interjected. "I'm always in the mood for a good story."

"There's nothing to tell," Joanie said, but her cheeks flamed as she made her denial.

Liz looked at Steve for confirmation. "Joanie and I never did see eye to eye," he said by way of answer.

"Meaning?" Liz asked Steve pointedly.

His eyes still on Joanie, Steve shrugged his broad shoulders. "I think the two of us have plenty to talk about, or at least we would have," he said, "if Joanie hadn't overreacted and run away."

"Well, Joanie, now I understand why you're upset, anyway," Liz said.

"I am not upset!" Joanie snapped. With a swift about-face she marched into the lobby, her mane of hair billowing behind her, Steve and Liz both hard on her heels. "I just have a lot to do today," Joanie said as she stepped behind the check-in counter and cast a look at the spacious lemon yellow lobby, with its gleaming wood floors. Bright spring sunshine streamed in through the floor-to-ceiling windows flanking the front doors. She bent beneath the counter, rummaged around and came up with a three-foot blue-and-white rope with a loop on the end. "We have a group of college kids checking in today for their annual Mentoring At-Risk Children seminar. A woman from Kansas—Mrs. Frances Flannagan—whose reservation was mysteriously lost, needs to be put up in one of the guest cottages until a room here in the hotel becomes available. And there's a lost puppy, roaming the grounds."

Liz nodded, knowing as did Joanie that all this was par for the course. "Joanie, would you get Steve his key?"

Joanie forced a nonchalant smile. "Where are you putting him?" she asked Liz.

"I haven't decided. Would you prefer a suite on the first or second floor?" Liz asked Steve.

"Actually I'd prefer to be housed away from the main hotel and guest cottages so I won't be overwhelmed by convention guests. Perhaps you have something in the staff quarters?" he suggested affably.

"Unit 108 is available," Liz replied.

"Perfect." Steve smiled.

It was all Joanie could do not to swear. She was in unit 110, which meant they'd be side by side. Trying hard not to imagine how difficult that was going to be, seeing Steve coming and going at all hours of the day and night, Joanie used her front desk key to open the drawer beneath the counter. Inside were keys to all the rooms in the hotel, guest cottages and staff quarters arranged by number in little trays. She picked up the key marked 108 and handed it to him. "Here you go," she said, making an effort to sound polite.

His hand grazed hers as they transferred the key; his palm was as warm and strong as she recalled, her reaction to his touch just as potent.

"Would you mind showing Steve to his quarters?" Liz asked.

"There's no need to trouble Joanie," Steve said. "I can see she's very busy."

Joanie's breath lodged in her throat. He was up to something; she knew it. There was no way his taking a speaking job here was a simple coincidence, because unlike her, he hadn't seemed the least bit surprised to see her. So he must have known she worked at Bride's Bay and come, anyway. What did that mean? What did she *want* it to mean?

Joanie slid a trembling hand into the pocket of her blazer. The last thing she needed was to have her heart broken by Steve again. "If you'll excuse me, I've got a puppy to track down." And avoiding what she was certain was Steve's assessing look, she turned and strode out of the hotel.

"SORRY ABOUT THAT," Steve said to Liz after Joanie left. He'd known his appearance would shock and perhaps even irritate Joanie initially. But maybe it was good they'd gotten it out of the way. Maybe when Joanie calmed down they would be able to talk reasonably again. At least he hoped so.

Liz Jermain pulled a map of the resort from beneath the counter and handed it to Steve, then led him down a long hall and out the back way. They paused a moment, letting their eyes adjust to the brightness of the sun. The sharp salt tang of the Atlantic lent an invigorating crispness to the early-spring air, while the absence of traffic and crowds added to the overall tranquillity of this island paradise off the coast of South Carolina.

They walked across the veranda of the two-story white brick mansion, which was, in fact, an old plantation home. Black wrought-iron railing and white Corinthian columns edged the porches on both floors. On either side of the gracious rectangular home was a half-circle wing. Long black-shuttered windows overlooked the immaculate lawns.

"You didn't mention you knew Joanie," Liz said.

"If I had, would it have kept you from recommending me?"

"It wouldn't have influenced me one way or the other," Liz responded, as they walked down the half-dozen steps that led to a path.

Passing a beautiful formal garden and a swimming pool, they finally reached the converted stables that housed the staff. A low wall and flower beds surrounded the two-story building, adding to the quaint, homey appeal of the staff quarters. Sea gulls swooped and circled overhead.

"We consider all our staff, including relatively new employees like Joanie, to be part of one big family. But in the final analysis I do what's best for the resort." Liz turned onto the sidewalk that led straight to Steve's door on the main floor.

"I won't let you down," Steve said, shortening his step to keep pace with her.

Liz gave him a contemplative look as she paused in front of the covered portico with its latticework sides. The door behind her bore the gold-plated number 108. "But you have let Joanie down in the past," she guessed.

Steve didn't mind Liz's question; he knew she was only protecting her friend. He dropped his head, knowing he should never have let Joanie go. "She just *thinks* I did. It's a misconception I intend to correct," he stated firmly.

And he'd known the moment he saw her today, sitting behind that desk, that he'd done the right thing in tracking her down and coming after her at long last.

And it wasn't just because she was gorgeous in her breezy, girl-next-door way, or because she had the loveliest golden hair and the most incredibly beautiful, long-lashed baby blue eyes he'd ever seen. Or because she'd greeted him like a duchess greeting a lowly serf. He was drawn to her for reasons that went beyond her soft, kissable lips and her high cheekbones and her flawless skin. He was drawn to her for how she made him feel.

She might want to believe what they'd felt was ordinary; but after two-plus years of looking high and low to replace the passion and excitement he'd felt with Joanie, he knew what they'd shared was anything but ordinary. Maybe Joanie hadn't realized that, but she would one day soon, he promised himself silently.

Liz tilted her head to study him as Steve unlocked and opened the door to his quarters.

"Is Joanie dating anyone now?" Steve asked, leading the way into the small but comfortably decorated two-room suite. He had the feeling if anyone knew what was going on in Joanie's heart and mind, it was Liz Jermain.

"Not since her engagement ended."

Steve tensed. Joanie had been engaged?

Liz paused. "You don't know about Dylan?"

Steve shook his head and wondered what else he didn't know about Joanie.

"Well, perhaps one day she'll tell you about it." Liz opened the window next to the door, letting in the breeze. "Do you need help with your bags?"

Steve shook his head. "I'll walk back and get them." He wanted to be settled as soon as possible so he could continue with his plan.

THE WOMAN WATCHED Steve Lantz leave the staff quarters with Liz Jermain at his side. As soon as the coast was clear, she pushed the stroller out into the sunshine. Beneath the ruffled pink-and-white canopy, little Emily slept on, blissfully unaware of what was about to happen.

Her gloved hands shaking, the woman parked the stroller by the latticework-sided private entryway of unit 110 to keep Emily safely out of sight for the moment. Making sure the envelope was still taped to the toddler's sweater, the woman tiptoed nervously to unit 108. *Please be open*, she wished fervently.

It wasn't.

Frowning, the woman stepped to the left and gazed inside the open window. It was set low, two feet off the ground. She had no idea if any of the staff rooms connected, never mind units 110 and 108 specifically, but if she could remove the screen, she could get inside 108, just by stepping over the windowsill....

"C'MON, PUPPY. Stop playing games with me. Just come here and let me pet you," Joanie coaxed, hiding the leash she'd brought with her in the pocket of her blazer and getting down on her knees.

The golden retriever, stolen beach sandal clamped between his teeth, danced back and forth playfully, staying just out of Joanie's reach.

Joanie leaned forward. The puppy jerked back and took off running full speed in the direction of the main building of the hotel. Joanie scrambled to her feet and dashed after him, her heels sinking in the soft grass. Irritated, she pulled off her gray suede shoes and, with one shoe in each hand, raced across the soft, manicured lawn. But the faster she ran, the faster the puppy ran.

Realizing the futility of trying to outrun the wily little creature, Joanie stopped at the edge of the formal gardens to catch her breath. As much as she wanted to go for help, she didn't dare, for fear she would lose sight of the puppy again. Jermain Island was three miles long and five miles wide. There were dozens of places he could disappear to and tons more mischief he could get in. He'd already knocked over fifteen flowerpots on the front porch of one of the twelve private estates, taken a dip in the surf, chewed up someone's towel on the beach and, last but not least, stolen someone's sandal.

The puppy, realizing he was no longer being chased, swung around and headed back her way. Tail wagging playfully, he approached her, but again, stayed just out of reach.

With one hand on the leash in her pocket, Joanie dangled a shoe in front of him with the other. "Isn't this pretty?" she said softly, wishing the pup hadn't managed to lose his collar, too. If he still had a collar, it would have been a lot easier for her to grab hold of him. "Wouldn't you like to chew on this for a while?"

The rambunctious pup dropped the sandal he was carrying. Joanie started forward. He danced back. She held her ground. He eyed her cautiously and started to approach her again when, out of the corner of her eye, she saw a woman in a white trench coat, scarf and sunglasses taking off the screen of a staff-quarters window. Joanie didn't have to be hit over the head to know a burglary in progress when she saw one.

Forgetting the puppy, she yelled, "Hey! You!" Slipping her shoes back on, she started toward the prowler, who was still a good fifty yards away. "What do you think you're doing?" she shouted.

The woman dropped the screen and took off around the side of the building. Joanie swore and broke into a run. No sooner had she gotten up to speed than she heard panting behind her. The puppy snatched playfully at her skirt, got a piece and held on tight. Joanie groaned as she felt the fabric rip. The puppy danced off, a mouthful of fabric held tight in his jaws, and much to Joanie's chagrin, disappeared around the corner after the burglar.

Not sure what to do first, Joanie headed for the screen lying on the ground. She was not surprised to see the room being broken into was unit 108. Steve Lantz's. Of course. If they had a celebrity on the premises, they would have the problems that came with celebrities, like overzealous fans and tabloid reporters. Or at least, she knew that was how *he* would define this. Just as he'd once—

No! Joanie stopped herself firmly. She was *not* going to think about that. Not again.

She hiked up her ripped skirt and stepped across the threshold of the window and into the room. Nothing seemed to be disturbed, she noted, as she strode across the floor, reached for the phone and dialed. "Security? We've got an emergency. Staff quarters, unit 108."

"I KNEW YOU WERE MAD at me, but isn't ripping my window screen out just a bit excessive?" Steve asked, dropping his duffel bag in the doorway. It hit the floor with a soft thud.

Joanie whirled to face him. At five eleven, she was accustomed to physically holding her own with most men. Steve was one of the few men who could make her feel dwarfed. "I just caught someone trying to break into your room," she said.

"Uh-huh." Steve folded his arms on his chest and looked around. His glance tracked the spill of tousled golden curls falling from a side part over Joanie's shoulder before returning to her long-lashed blue eyes. "So where is he?"

"It was a she," Joanie specified, refusing to become flustered by him. With a straight back, she stalked closer. "She was wearing a trench coat. She's not here because she ran off."

His silver-gray eyes gleamed with mischief. "That how your skirt got ripped—from chasing her?" he questioned.

"No." Joanie bristled and moved around Steve, so she was standing in the portal and he was inside the room. "The puppy ripped it with his teeth."

"What puppy?"

Joanie leaned against the latticework wall and glanced around, irritated to find that the grounds outside the staff quarters were perfectly quiet. "He was here just a minute ago."

"Uh-huh." Steve strode into the unit to check out the bedroom and bath. When he returned to the main room, he cast her an even more skeptical look.

"Don't look at me like that," Joanie said, stepping into the unit. "I'm not making this up."

He lifted one broad shoulder, let it fall. "Did I say you were?" he asked.

He didn't need to, Joanie thought furiously. "It's in your eyes," she said.

"Ah." He nodded at her with mock gravity. "So now you know what it's like to try and give a highly improbable but true explanation to a disbelieving third party."

Joanie flushed and found it necessary to turn her back on him again. She crossed her arms. "If you're talking about that night I caught you..." she began in a strangled voice.

"What else?" An edge of irony in his voice, he came up behind her and rested both his hands on her shoulders.

Joanie drew a shaky breath. Trying not to notice how gentle and right his hands felt on her, she whirled to face him. "This is hardly the same thing."

His eyes filled with unrepentant mischief, and he dropped his hands. "Looks exactly the same thing to me—because I don't see a burglar nor any real evidence of one, except for that screen being off, and I don't see a puppy, either."

Joanie started to push her heavy fall of hair away from her face, but found the ends curled around the hotel-employee badge pinned above her left breast. Looking down, she tried to untangle it and, though her fingers were unbearably clumsy, finally managed. "You heard me say at the front desk a few minutes ago that one was on the loose," she said.

Steve leaned forward. "For all I know you could have been making that up as a cover."

"Honestly!"

His glance narrowed. "Doesn't feel good, does it, to have someone thinking the worst of you," he taunted softly.

Joanie blew out a weary breath. He was reminding them both of a night best forgotten. She regarded him with all the passion and temper of a woman betrayed. "Will you please stop this?" she said.

One corner of his mouth tilted up. "If that's the way you want it."

"It is."

"Hm." Steve's glance traveled over her slender legs, then slowly, impertinently, returned to her face. "So. What happened to your shoes?"

Joanie flushed again. Noting the soles of her shoes were covered with mud and blades of grass, she'd taken them off upon entering his quarters to avoid soiling his freshly vacuumed carpet. "They got muddy when I was chasing the puppy."

"Right," Steve said disbelievingly. "Of course. I don't know why I didn't think of that."

"There was a puppy. I mean there is. He's been causing havoc on the island all morning."

Steve grinned, looking pleased he'd gotten her so riled.

"Honestly, I don't know why I even bother talking to you," Joanie muttered, then to her relief, saw reinforcements were on the way.

"Got a problem here, Ms. Griffin?" Howard Forsythe, the chief of hotel security, stepped in. Howard was tall and lean, with gentle, assessing eyes and receding dark brown hair. A former customs officer, he had been with the resort for five years.

"Yes." Joanie quickly explained what had happened.

Howard examined the quarters front to back, then returned to ask, "Anything missing?"

Steve shook his head. "Not that I can see," he said. "I guess the person didn't get inside."

Suddenly the three of them heard what sounded like the giggle of a very young child. They looked at one another in surprise. There were no children in the staff quarters. The giggle came again. It was followed by a little bark.

"There's the puppy now." Joanie said.

She stepped outside and looked in the direction of the sound. The golden-retriever pup was lying on the walk in front of her unit with a mangled blue envelope clutched between his jaws.

"Oh, no," Joanie groaned. Now the pup had gotten into someone's mail.

"Help me, guys," she said to Howard and Steve. Then stopped. Stared. The puppy wasn't alone. There was a beautiful little girl in a pink-and-white stroller on her front doorstep. The child was grinning happily, watching the puppy. She had a crumpled blue piece of stationery in the other hand. To Joanie's consternation, there wasn't an adult in sight.

"I'm going to check around for that woman," Howard said, already moving on. "What did you say she was wearing, Joanie?"

"A long white trench coat and scarf."

Howard nodded and moved around back, out of sight.

"Puppy!" the little girl announced, pounding the shiny silver rim of her stroller seat emphatically. "Me d'ink!"

"What'd she say?" Steve frowned.

"I'm not sure." Joanie stared at the little girl with the halo of golden blond curls and pretty gray-blue eyes. Try as she might, she couldn't place her. Not with any one family, either those that were guests at the resort or island residents. And after nearly a year and a half on the job at Bride's Bay, Joanie was sure she knew just about everyone on Jermain Island.

Aware that the precious little girl was waiting for some reaction to her demands, Joanie looked at Steve. "I think she's either telling us there's a puppy who needs a drink or telling us there's a puppy and *she* needs a drink." She watched as the golden retriever jumped up unexpectedly and ran across the lawn toward a group of unsuspecting hotel guests. Joanie could tell by their youth and their attire that they were the college students checking in for the mentoring conference.

"In any case, I have to wonder where her mama is," Steve said, in Joanie's ear.

"Me, too," Joanie murmured, concerned.

The little girl held out her hands to Joanie. "Up!" she said.

Joanie wasn't sure if she should pick up someone else's child, and she didn't have a lot of experience with babies. But this child's parents didn't seem to be around at the moment, so...

The toddler made the decision for her by sliding a foot up onto the seat and turning around. Afraid she would fall, or at the very least tip over the stroller in her attempt to crawl out if left to her own devices, Joanie held out her arms to the little girl. "Honey, let me help you."

The little girl stopped in midclimb, turned her face up to Joanie's and regarded her with huge blue-gray eyes. Wordlessly she handed Joanie the crumpled piece of blue notepaper she had in her hand. Joanie took it, hoping whoever had lost this mail would understand that both a puppy and a baby had gotten to it first. The little girl held out her hands. "Em-lee up!" she demanded again.

Joanie picked her up. Steve, his expression as captivated as Joanie's moved closer. Emily reached out and patted his shoulder, as if testing the hardness of the muscle beneath her fingers.

Joanie's heart raced at his nearness. And the knowledge that the crisis had caused her to drop all the defenses she'd erected between them, at least for the moment. And that, in turn, left her feeling vulnerable—and breathless.

"What's on the notepaper?" he asked curiously.

"I don't know." Joanie shifted the toddler onto one hip and shook out the paper with her free hand. She turned it so she could see it and read the elaborate calligraphy aloud:

Because there was no other way, I cared for Emily and was glad to do it. But now at eighteen months she needs so much more than I alone can give her. I know this isn't what you expected, but trust me when I tell you that Emily belongs with you. So give it your best shot, and remember to keep her blankie and teddy close at hand. I'll be in touch to work things out as soon as I can. Until then, Fiona.

"Fiona," Joanie murmured. *Who the heck is Fiona?* Completely mystified, Joanie looked at Steve.

He plastered a hand across his broad, muscled chest and stepped slightly away. "Don't look at me. She wasn't in front of my door," he said, then pointed to the number 110 on the door directly behind Emily's stroller. "Who's unit is this?"

Joanie bit her lip. "Mine."

"Well, well. And no one else lives here with you?"

"No."

His eyes lasered hers. "Then . . . ?"

"Obviously there's been some mistake," she said.

"I would guess so, if someone abandoned this little girl."

Joanie shook her head in confusion. "Let's not jump the gun here. She may not be abandoned. Maybe this note was meant for someone else and someone just expects me to baby-sit while the real parent is located. It wouldn't be the oddest request I've ever had as a concierge."

Although it was one of the most heartless, Joanie thought. Emily was obviously at the climbing stage. Who knew where she would have run off to or what she would have gotten into if Joanie hadn't come along? She could have been seriously hurt. Kidnapped. At the very least, seriously frightened.

Steve lifted a brow. "Surely if someone left her with you, Joanie, he or she must trust you."

Joanie blushed and felt, oddly, even more inept. She didn't know why, but when she was around Steve, she wanted to be completely self-possessed and in control. "Not a clue," Joanie admitted.

"You're saying you've never seen this child before?"

Joanie studied the toddler again. "No. I haven't."

"Then it doesn't make sense," he said, clearly exasperated.

"You're telling me," Joanie replied, feeling all the more baffled in the face of his impatience. She looked down at the toddler, who was happily fingering the delicate lacy edges of her Peter Pan collar and the gold pin she'd pinned to the throat of her silk blouse.

Joanie tucked her finger beneath Emily's chin and lifted the cherubic face so they were eye to eye. "Honey, who brought you here?" Joanie asked Emily softly. "Where's your baby-sitter or whoever was watching you? Can you tell me, honey?"

Emily regarded Joanie solemnly, clearly not understanding.

"Who was pushing you in the stroller?" Joanie tried again, pointing to Emily's stroller. "Who was pushing Emily?"

Suddenly Emily grinned, as if she now understood Joanie's questions. She rested both chubby little hands on Joanie's shoulders, then pointed at the gold pin at Joanie's throat. "Geh Mama," she said.

Stunned, Steve looked to Joanie. "Is this your baby?"

Chapter Two

"No, this is not my baby!" Joanie snapped, looking as confused as Steve felt.

He towered over her. "You're right. This baby is not yours alone. It's our child. Damn it, Joanie, how could you not have told me we'd had a child together?"

Joanie shook her head at him in mute admonition. "I didn't tell you because Emily is not our child."

"Then who's the father?" Steve demanded, his glance traveling from Joanie to Emily and back again. "Dylan?"

Joanie's soft lips curved in a smile. "If I didn't know better, I'd think you were jealous," she taunted.

She was right about that, Steve thought. He *was* jealous. He couldn't bear the thought of her with another man, any more than he could imagine himself making love with another woman. Since the two of them had broken up, he hadn't been tempted once. "You didn't answer me. Is Dylan the father of your baby?"

"You're on the wrong track, Steve."

"Meaning?"

"Unless it was the Immaculate Conception, that would be impossible."

It took a moment for her words to sink in. "You're telling me that you and he...didn't..."

Joanie held up a hand. "Don't look so smug."

"You were engaged to him."

Joanie shrugged and went back to smoothing Emily's hair. "So?"

"This proves you're not over us any more than I am," he asserted.

"No, Steve," Joanie said, angling her head up at him, "it proves I learn from my mistakes. Allowing myself to be seduced by the wrong man once makes me a fool. Allowing it to happen again with someone else makes me plain stupid, and I am not stupid. Besides, as you will undoubtedly find out if you investigate the matter at all, the timing isn't right. I met Dylan just before I came to Bride's Bay a little over a year and a half ago."

"Then she *is* our child."

"No—" Joanie rolled her eyes with exasperation "—she isn't!"

"Then how do you explain Emily's being left on your doorstep with this note?" Steve returned calmly. "Is this why you were so furious with me? Why you didn't return any of my calls and sent back all my letters unopened? Because you didn't want me to know about our child? Or was it because you didn't think I was up to the task of rearing a child with you?"

"Are you?"

"Yes. And I'll show you."

Joanie lifted a brow. "And then what?"

"And then I'll have to understand why you never told me about something this important and forgive you your mistake."

"Suppose I don't want to be forgiven?" Joanie asked hypothetically, as she speared him with another frank look.

Steve studied her, his frustration growing by leaps and bounds. "You're not making this easy, are you?"

"I suppose I'm not." And for that she offered no apology.

They stared at each other in silence.

"There's something I need to know," Steve said finally.

Joanie kept her eyes on his. "And that is?"

Drawing on every ounce of compassion he had, Steve asked, "Why did you give Emily to Fiona, rather than raise her yourself? Why didn't you give her to me?"

Joanie paused in the act of smoothing Emily's tousled blond curls and gave him another wary look. "Listen to me, Steve, and pay attention. I did *not* abandon Emily."

He regarded her incredulously, watching as Emily cuddled against Joanie contentedly. "Then everyone here knows you're a single mother?"

A pale wash of color, the same pink as her blouse, highlighted Joanie's cheeks. "Of course not! Everyone here knows I am both single and childless."

Steve knitted his brow, his patience gone. "And yet...Emily just called you Mama."

The wash of color on Joanie's cheeks deepened. "She doesn't know what she's saying," Joanie protested, but even as she spoke Emily was softly crooning her delight at being held and rubbing her face against the silk of Joanie's blouse.

Steve knew Joanie wanted him to back off. He wasn't about to, not until he knew the truth. "She could identify a puppy. She knows how to tell us she wants to be picked up. She pointed to you and said what sounded like

'Goo' Mama.' Sounds to me like she knows what she's talking about," he said plainly.

"Obviously she was trying to tell us something else," Joanie said. "Here, I'll show you." She ran her thumb gently across Emily's cheek to get the little girl's attention. "Emily, honey, where is your mommy?"

To Joanie's obvious dismay, Emily said nothing and rested her head on Joanie's shoulder. She wreathed both her arms around Joanie's neck and clung tightly.

Steve studied the two of them. Never had there been a more perfect mother and child. Pictures like this didn't lie. Nor did genetics or heredity. "You even look alike," Steve said quietly, his heart swelling with joy at the possibility that he and Joanie might share a child. "You've got the same naturally curly golden blond hair, same long eyelashes, same stubborn chin and rosebud lips."

For a moment, Joanie's eyes seemed to light up at his description of both of them, but to his disappointment, she quickly reined in her feelings. "You're being ridiculous!"

Was he? Steve wondered. Emily's eyes were blue-gray. His were gray. Joanie's were blue. Of course any child they had would have blue gray eyes and blond hair. And those curls—just like Joanie's.

Howard Forsythe, the security officer, came back. "No sign of anyone in a trench coat. Maybe if you could give us a better description. Hair color, build. Something else to go on," he suggested.

Steve noted dispassionately that Howard didn't seem to find it unusual at all to see Joanie holding a baby in her arms.

Ignoring Steve, Joanie looked at Howard. "The woman was of medium height. I think she had a medium build. The scarf covered her hair, but I could see her skin was very fair—I think. But again, it was at a distance.''

"D'ink!" Emily demanded, tugging Joanie's sleeve. "Em-lee, d'ink!"

"All right, honey, we'll get you something to drink," Joanie said, patting the toddler on the back.

"Em-lee hungee!"

"And something to eat, too," Joanie said. She looked at the security chief. "Do you have any idea what kids this age like to eat?" Joanie asked.

Howard shrugged. "My wife, Catherine, always handles the menu selections for our kids. But someone in the hotel kitchen is bound to know."

What was going on here? Steve wondered. Was Howard in on this, too? Or just completely out of the loop of information?

"All right, I'll take her over there," Joanie said purposefully. She shifted Emily to her other hip, then turned to face Steve. "Would you please leave a note on my door for this Fiona, telling her where I've taken her baby?"

Steve grinned. "Determined to play this out until the bitter end, aren't you?"

"Just do it," Joanie advised.

She headed briskly toward the main building, Emily babbling all the while. Steve watched longingly until they were both out of sight.

"WELL, WELL, what have we got here?" Columbia Hanes, the head chef said, as Joanie and Emily entered the hotel kitchen a few minutes later.

At the stoves, half-a-dozen cooks were busy preparing the evening banquet for the mentoring conference. The fragrant smell of roast pork and corn-bread stuffing hung in the air. Homemade applesauce simmered on the stove, loaves of bread baked in the oven, and a variety of vegetables were being cleaned and chopped in preparation for cooking. In the glass-fronted refrigerator were several elegant desserts. Ice tea was cooling in large glass pitchers. Emily regarded all the activity with wide-eye amazement.

Joanie looked down at the little girl. "This is Emily."

"And where did she come from?" Columbia asked, closing the distance between herself and Joanie.

Emily shyly regarded the statuesque African-American woman. Noticing the miniature orchid pinned on the brim of Columbia's tall white chef's hat, she pointed to it and muttered something indecipherable.

"A woman named Fiona seems to have left a baby in my care temporarily," Joanie said. And that act had caused her all sorts of grief with Steve Lantz, because now he was making all sorts of assumptions. Assumptions that were bound to lead to even more trouble. Doing her best to hide her uneasiness over what Steve's next move might be, Joanie handed the note to Columbia, figuring if anyone could help her make sense of it, Columbia could.

"Who is this Fiona?" Columbia asked after she'd read the note and returned it to Joanie.

Joanie shrugged as she shifted Emily to her other hip and pocketed the note. "I haven't a clue. I was hoping you might have an idea."

But Columbia shook her head. "Sorry."

Emily smiled and gurgled as Steve came up behind Joanie. He was pushing the stroller, which had a diaper bag slung over the back of it. "I thought you might need that," he said by way of explanation.

Joanie regarded Steve stoically, hoping he'd given up the notion that Emily was her daughter. "Did you leave a note on my door?"

"Yes, ma'am." He chucked Emily on the chin, and the toddler looked at him and smiled happily. Columbia led them into the employee cafeteria, which was adjacent to the kitchen, and brought out one of the high chairs. Joanie tried to put Emily into it, but Emily clung to her neck and held her legs out stiff as boards, which made seating her impossible.

"C'mon, honey," Joanie coaxed. "Help us out here so we can get you something to eat." With Steve's help she managed to get Emily settled into the high chair. "Now. How about some milk?" Joanie asked, bending down to the lively toddler's level. "Do you like milk, Emily?"

Eyes huge, Emily nodded.

While Joanie found a plastic cup and poured two inches of milk into it, Steve knelt down in front of Emily and kept her amused by walking his fingers across her tray.

"I'll fix her a grilled cheese sandwich," Columbia said. "In the meantime, maybe she'd like some applesauce or tapioca pudding."

Joanie handed Steve the milk, then got out the applesauce. She put some in a bowl, then sat down in front of Emily's high chair and offered her a teaspoon of applesauce. Emily clamped her lips shut and shook her head.

"You don't like applesauce?"

"Me do!" Emily pushed Joanie's hand aside and reached for the spoon.

"I think she wants to feed herself," Steve said.

Joanie met Steve's eyes. She wasn't sure that was such a good idea, but seeing as how Emily wasn't going to let herself be fed, it didn't look as if there was much choice.

Reluctantly Joanie handed Emily the spoon and the bowl.

Emily clutched the spoon in her right hand. She dug it in, brought it up to her mouth, spilling applesauce all over the tray and herself in the process, and got just a smidgen of what she had started out with into her mouth. Too late, Joanie realized what they'd forgotten. "I don't suppose there's a bib in that diaper bag," she said.

"I'll look." Steve swiftly retrieved the bag and rummaged through it. "Nope," he said finally. "Just clean clothes, diapers, sunscreen and a hat. Plus a blanket and a teddy bear."

Seeing her bear and blanket, Emily dropped the spoon. It clattered as it hit the tray. "Blankie!" she shouted. "Bear!"

Joanie knew a godsend when she saw one. She wet a clean cloth and wiped Emily's hands, face, the front of her clothes and the tray, then handed over the bear and blankie. "Would you like to hold these, Emily?" Joanie asked, pulling the tray forward, to give Emily a little more room.

"She's going to get food all over them," Steve predicted as he pulled up a chair, turned it around and sank onto it.

"Not if I feed her while she holds them, she won't," Joanie said.

Steve grinned. "Good point." He folded his arms across the back of the chair as Joanie draped the blanket across Emily's lap and placed the teddy bear next to her.

Emily clutched her blanket with one hand and cuddled up to her teddy bear, looking as if she was in seventh heaven to have her things so close. Joanie got a clean teaspoon, since the handle on the first one was all sticky, and dished up another bite of applesauce. With both her hands full, Joanie figured Emily would not mind being fed. Wrong again.

"No," Emily said, dropping her stranglehold on her bear and blanket. "Me do!"

"Emily, I'm going to feed you the applesauce," Joanie said firmly.

Emily shook her head.

Joanie held the spoon to her lips.

Emily batted it away with an earsplitting screech.

The spoon clattered to the tray and then fell on her blanket, spraying applesauce everywhere.

"Told you so," Steve whispered in Joanie's ear.

Joanie's pulse picked up as the familiar scent of Steve's cologne tantalized her senses. She drew a stabilizing breath and turned to face him, just as Columbia Hanes swooped in to the rescue with a perfectly prepared grilled cheese sandwich, cut into tiny pieces. She set it in front of Emily. "Here you go, lovey. Grilled cheese."

Emily smiled. Obviously, Joanie thought, they'd hit on something familiar to the little girl. Forgetting for a moment about the applesauce, Emily scooped up a bite of sandwich and brought it clumsily to her mouth. She chewed on it, then grabbed another, happy at last. "Looks like we got a hit on our hands," Steve said.

"Thanks, Columbia," Joanie added.

The chef grinned. "If you all don't mind, I'm going back to the kitchen and my dinner preparations."

"No problem. I'm sure we can handle it," Joanie replied. Columbia bustled off.

Silence fell. Joanie noted that although their chairs were facing different directions, she and Steve were sitting side by side, directly in front of Emily's high chair—close enough for Joanie to feel the heat emanating from him. It was a disturbingly intimate sensation.

Steve turned to look at Joanie. "Once she's fed, then what?"

"I don't know." Joanie shrugged, wishing she knew more about children; she'd have liked to be able to show off for him. Instead, she'd never felt so at a loss. "My duties as concierge here have included a lot of unusual things..."

His grin was enough to light a thousand inner fires. "Such as?" he prompted.

Joanie shrugged, surprised to find herself feeling a little shy. That wasn't like her at all. "I once walked a guest's peacock on a leash at two every morning for the week he was here."

"I hope he tipped you well."

"He did."

Joanie watched as Emily accidentally knocked a square of grilled cheese off her tray. She reached down to get it, then found, as her fingers closed around the piece of food, that her face was only inches from his knee. She moved back slowly, trying not to notice how snugly his jeans fit his long, muscled legs.

"What else?" he asked after she'd tossed the piece of sandwich into the trash.

Aware that her skirt had hiked up well above her knees, Joanie tugged it down. "I arranged for a flower sculpture of wedding bells for a couple's honeymoon, and then had to come up with a flower sculpture every day thereafter to commemorate each day of their honeymoon."

Steve smiled. "Do you like your job here?"

Joanie looked at Emily, who was still munching contentedly on her sandwich. "Very much. All the other hotels I've worked at have been much bigger, but the staff here feels like family."

Liz strode in from the doorway of the cafeteria. She wound her way through several tables and chairs to their side. "Is what security told me true, Joanie? Someone named Fiona abandoned this little girl on your doorstep?"

Joanie showed her the note. Liz perused it carefully, her expression perplexed.

"Maybe Fiona thinks this falls within my duties as concierge," Joanie said. "You know how some people push the limits."

"Maybe." Liz frowned. "Do we have someone named Fiona staying with us now?"

"Not now. In fact, I can't recall any Fiona at all, in the year and a half I've been working here," Joanie said. "Though I'd have to check the computer records to be sure."

Emily had finished her cheese sandwich and was gesturing for her applesauce again. Joanie cleared away the empty plate and handed Emily her bowl and spoon.

"Howard also said Emily was pointing to you and calling you Mama," Liz continued.

"I think she was just admiring my gold pin and talking about or asking us for her mama," Joanie theorized.

"You have a point there," Liz mused. "I've been around my nieces and nephews enough to realize that at this age kids don't have much of a vocabulary."

Steve nodded. "No doubt there's a lot Emily would like to tell us."

Realizing full well what Steve was implying, Joanie shot him a sharp look. Liz glanced from Joanie to Steve and back again, probably putting clues together rapidly, Joanie thought. Unfortunately those clues would be leading her to the wrong conclusion.

Joanie needed to prevent Liz from making any assumptions. "Look, it's obvious that Emily has been well cared for. Because if she hadn't been, well, we'd see signs of it. Therefore, I have to believe in my heart that this Fiona, whoever she is, will be in touch with me as she promised in the letter, and that she'll come back for Emily as soon as she can. In the meantime, I'll just wait to hear."

"So you don't want to call social services just yet?" Liz asked.

"Oh, no. Heavens no," Joanie said quickly. Just the thought of turning cute little Emily over to some nameless, faceless bureaucrat alarmed her. "We don't want Emily shuffled around from place to place unnecessarily. Particularly if Fiona does come back soon, as I suspect she will."

"Well," Liz said with a sigh, "if you don't mind taking care of her until the woman does show up..."

"It'll be no problem," Joanie said, meaning it. She loved children, always had.

"Then I'll talk to your assistant and ask him to see that the concierge desk is covered the rest of the evening. Jerry'll take care of it, I'm sure. In addition, I suppose we better get a crib over to your quarters," Liz decided. "Steve, since you aren't busy, if you wouldn't mind..."

"No problem," Steve said, getting to his feet before Joanie could make even a token protest. He grinned down at Emily and caressed her cheek with the back of his hand. "If you'll just show me where—"

"Shampoo!" Emily said merrily, smearing applesauce in her hair before anyone could stop her.

"Oh, no," Joanie murmured as Emily got a second glob, added it to the first and swirled it around her halo of curls. Giggling, she picked up her spoon and flung it around. Applesauce flew off, hitting both Joanie and Steve, as well as her tray and face. Amused by her antics, Emily giggled again.

"You know, Joanie, I think our little Emily here is finished eating," Steve remarked, using a napkin to wipe some of the applesauce off the front of his jeans.

Joanie wiped her cheek. She looked up at Steve. "I think you're right."

"HAVE YOU EVER given a child a bath?" Joanie asked as Steve wheeled the hotel crib into her unit.

In layout, the place was identical to his. A living room furnished with sofa, easy chair, television and small beverage refrigerator in front, a bathroom and bedroom to the rear. Both were fully carpeted in soft beige, and several pastel seascapes adorned the walls. But Joanie had added many feminine touches. Throw pillows in assorted pastels decorated the sofa. She had brought her own linens for the bedroom and added a rolltop desk.

Now she was sitting on the living room floor sorting through the half-dozen outfits and diapers that had been packed in Emily's bag. Emily was sitting cross-legged on the floor, busily taking off her one remaining sock and shoe.

"No, never have," Steve said. "You?"

"I have no experience in that regard whatsoever," Joanie said with a sigh. "But it can't be all that hard. I stopped by the gift shop on the way over and picked up a small bottle of baby shampoo." She showed it to Steve, then bit her lip. "I wonder if I should put some bubble bath in her bathwater."

Steve shrugged. "I guess it'd be okay. Unless..."

"What?"

"Well, if she splashes a lot and the bubbles are ordinary soap, it could sting her eyes."

"Oooooh," Joanie said, imagining the worst. She rose to her feet. "Good point. We wouldn't want that. Plain bathwater it is, then."

"Bath," Emily repeated.

Joanie smiled as Emily tugged and tugged on the toe of her sock until it came all the way off. Delighted to be minus her socks and shoes, Emily wiggled her toes, then got carefully to her feet, apparently testing the feel of the carpet.

"Emily, are you ready for your bath?" Joanie asked. She knelt and held out her arms.

Giggling uproariously, Emily turned and ran in the other direction.

Joanie looked at Steve, glad he was here, glad they had something else to talk about besides their past. "Get the feeling she likes to play chase?" Joanie said.

"Just a little." Steve grinned, watching as Emily played peekaboo with him from behind the corner of the sofa. He turned back to Joanie contemplatively. "Want me to stay and lend a hand, at least until you get her to sleep?"

"I think you mean if I *ever* get her to sleep," Joanie muttered. She picked up a pair of yellow-and-white floral pajamas from the stack of clothing. "And yes, I would appreciate it if you could stay a little longer."

As Joanie approached Emily, Emily giggled and ducked even farther behind the sofa.

Joanie straightened in exasperation. A consoling hand on her shoulder, Steve pointed her in the direction of the bathroom and suggested, "What do you say I keep an eye on her while you get her bath ready? Then I'll bring her in and fetch and carry whatever's needed."

Joanie felt the warmth and the gentleness of Steve's touch. And yet she knew, because of what happened between them before, he was the worst man in the world for her. Was there no justice?

"I notice you're not volunteering to shampoo the applesauce out of her hair," Joanie observed, crossing her arms.

"But it looks so cute," he said teasingly.

Joanie wrinkled her nose at him, then, pivoting on her heel, headed through the bedroom into the bathroom. The minute Joanie disappeared from sight, Emily gave up her game of hide-and-seek and toddled after her, waving her arms in the air. "Bye-bye!" she shouted. "Bye-bye!"

His laughter low and enticing, Steve followed the toddler toward the bathroom. He watched as Joanie slipped off her blazer and rolled up the sleeves on her silk blouse. While she knelt down to adjust the bathwater, Emily stood on tiptoes and peered over Joanie's shoulder.

"Bath?" Emily asked hopefully.

"Yes. It's time for Emily's bath," Joanie announced as she unhooked Emily's overalls and unsnapped the legs, slipping them down and off. "Is that all right with you, Emily?"

Emily just smiled and lifted her arms so Joanie could take off her matching knit shirt. Undershirt and diaper soon followed. Joanie made sure the temperature was right, then lifted her into the water.

Emily looked down, her disappointment apparent. "Toys?"

"I think she expects some bath toys," Steve said.

"And I don't have any." Joanie frowned. "Oh, dear."

"Maybe there's something you could use." Steve cast a glance around. "We could try these." He grabbed a plastic water cup next to the sink and a clean, folded washcloth.

"These might work," Joanie said, handing them to Emily. "And underneath the sink are some old-fashioned plastic rollers."

Steve dug out a box of jumbo rollers. "Somehow I can't see you in these." He chuckled.

"I use them to straighten my hair from time to time," she explained self-consciously.

"Why would you want to do that?" Steve seemed genuinely perplexed.

"Sometimes I like my hair straight. If you have naturally curly hair, that's how you straighten it. You set it on big rollers and let it dry that way."

"Oh."

"I don't do it often. Only when I want to wear my hair in a chignon or something." Joanie dropped a bunch of rollers in the bathwater.

They floated. Emily loved them.

"Now that she's otherwise amused, maybe it's time we used the shampoo." Joanie dampened Emily's sticky hair with the washcloth, then put a dollop of golden shampoo in her hair. As soon as Joanie began to lather it gently, Emily got into the act.

"Em-lee help," she said, pushing her fingers through her halo of suds.

"Emily's a big help," Steve agreed.

"Em-lee out!" Emily demanded.

"Oh, honey, we haven't rinsed your hair yet," Joanie said.

"Em-lee out!"Emily tried to scramble to her feet.

Joanie held on to Emily's waist, so she wouldn't slip and fall. "Now what?" she said over her shoulder, glad she had put aside her feelings toward Steve temporarily and allowed him to stay. This was one of those times when two baby-sitters were better than one.

"Now it's time for Super Steve to come to the rescue," he said. He pushed up his sleeves and got down on his knees beside Joanie so close their shoulders were touching. He dunked the plastic cup into the water, filling it to the brim. "You hold her and try to distract her for a moment, and I'll rinse."

"Look up there, Emily," Joanie said, pointing to the shower nozzle. She didn't want soapy water getting in Emily's eyes. "See that?"

Emily looked. Steve rinsed. Joanie continued, "What is that thing up there, Emily? Is it a shower?"

Steve rinsed again. And again and again, as Emily babbled nonsensically. Somehow they managed to get the suds out of the toddler's hair without getting either shampoo or water in her eyes. Joanie lifted her out of the tub and Steve handed her a towel. Minutes later they had Emily dressed and in pajamas.

"Goo' Mama," Emily said, circling Joanie's neck with her arms. She snuggled closer. "Goo' Mama."

Joanie hugged Emily back. "The way she keeps repeating that...I think she's trying to tell us something," Joanie said with a puzzled frown.

"Maybe that she thinks you're a good mother," Steve said.

"But I'm not," Joanie replied, embarrassed again as she lifted her face to his. "Her mother, that is."

Steve gave Joanie a skeptical look, but said nothing more. "How are we going to get her to sleep?" he asked casually, hanging up the towel and collecting the "toys."

"I doubt just putting her down in the crib would work."

"I doubt so, too." Steve sighed. "Driving babies around in a car is supposed to work. I mean, I've seen it on TV."

"Only one problem there," Joanie said, gathering up Emily's blanket and teddy. She walked over to the sofa. Emily climbed up beside her and scrambled onto her lap. "I don't have a car."

"We could try a golf cart," he suggested, knowing he was loathe to leave.

A knock sounded at the door. Howard Forsythe appeared, a rocking chair in his arms. "Liz told her grandmother about the baby, and Elizabeth sent this over."

"How nice of her." Joanie made a mental note to call and thank Elizabeth. "Thank you for bringing it over, Howard."

"Everything okay here?" Howard asked Joanie protectively.

It was all Joanie could do not to grin. Howard was acting like a father whose daughter was on her first date, but then, maybe that was because he had children of his own.

Joanie nodded. "Everything's fine."

"Rock?" Emily asked, tugging Joanie's sleeve. "You rock?" she asked plaintively.

"Yes, I'll rock you, honey," Joanie said softly, able to see at once how tired Emily was. Emily laid her head on Joanie's shoulder and hugged her fiercely, her blanket and teddy caught up between them.

Howard looked at Steve and then the door. It was clear to all that the men's presence was no longer needed.

Steve headed for the door with Howard right behind him. "I'll be nearby if you need anything," Steve promised.

"You can call me and Catherine, too," Howard offered.

Joanie smiled, aware there was something very sweet and fulfilling about holding a baby in her arms, even if she couldn't claim Emily as her own. "Thanks, guys, but I think she'll fall asleep as long as there's nothing much going on here, so if you'd just turn off that lamp next to the door on your way out, I'd be much obliged."

After they'd left, Joanie rocked Emily for several minutes. Emily kept repeating the phrase "Goo' Mama," or sometimes "Geh Mama." Joanie knew Emily was probably asking for Fiona, and it broke her heart.

"Sing," Emily said sleepily, cuddling closer. "Sing 'mit-sog.'"

"Mit-sog, mit-sog, mit-sog," Joanie murmured, trying to make some sense of Emily's words. "Oh, Em, how about this one, instead?" She launched into the only song she could think of at the moment—"It Had to Be You."

STEVE SAT on the steps outside his quarters listening to the melodious sound of Joanie's voice singing, of all things, "It Had to Be You" to little Emily. He couldn't help but shake his head at her selection. Was she trying to tell him something? Or just admitting to herself what he had finally concluded—that after two years, three months and too many days and even more hours apart, there was no one else for either of them. And never would be. It didn't matter what Joanie had done. Or what she still evidently thought he had done. He could see she loved Emily. She probably even loved him, though she'd be damned if she'd admit it. All he had to do was figure a way for everything to work out for the best for everyone.

EMILY WAS ASLEEP. Joanie could hear it in the slow, steady meter of her breath and feel it in the motionless weight of her body. Whether or not she could actually put the toddler in the crib without her waking, she didn't know, but she was determined to try.

Still singing softly, she got up carefully and glided over to the crib. One hand behind Emily's head, the other beneath her bottom, she lowered her ever so gently down onto the mattress. Emily whimpered slightly but otherwise didn't stir as Joanie tucked her teddy beneath her arm and covered her with her favorite blanket. Only as she backed away, did Joanie realize she was perspiring. This instant-motherhood business was taking more out of her than she'd expected, even if it was only temporary.

Deciding a little fresh air would do her good, Joanie stepped outside onto the front stoop, shutting the door quietly behind her.

The scent of roses floated on the soft island breeze. Cicadas chirped in the silence of the evening, and farther away a lone bullfrog croaked.

Just then Steve headed across the narrow grassy rectangle between their two front walks. "Emily asleep?" he asked.

Aware her heart had begun pounding at breakneck speed, Joanie nodded. "For the moment, anyway." Now she wished she hadn't come outside. She didn't need to see Steve in the moonlight, didn't need to see the moonlight glinting off his burnished gold hair or illuminating the handsome features of his face. She didn't need to feel a resurgence of all those old, romantic feelings that she'd tried her hardest to put away for good.

"I thought you'd left," she said.

Steve shook his head, and as he did, Joanie saw there was something different in his silver gray eyes, something she'd have one hell of a time reckoning with.

"Well..." Joanie backed up toward her door, intending to go back in before she forgot herself and what had happened in the past and let this moment turn into something she'd regret. She tucked her hands in the pockets of her skirt to hide their trembling. "I'd better go back in. Emily—"

"Not so fast," Steve said gruffly as his hand shot out to encircle her wrist. He tugged her close, the warmth of the island night nothing compared to the warmth of him. "We have to talk."

Chapter Three

"Is Emily's appearance the reason you were so unhappy to see me today?" Steve demanded. He clasped her arms lightly and looked down at her, his eyes intense.

"Is that what you think?" Joanie shook free of his grasp. Was that why he'd been helpful? she wondered, upset.

Steve jammed his fingers through his hair. "I don't know what to think."

Joanie breathed in the sea air. "I have good reason to hold you in very low esteem. Furthermore, if you remember," she replied, moving away from him, "the one and only time we were together, we took precautions."

Steve followed her to the edge of the portico. He leaned against the post, his eyes alight with desire. "Precautions sometimes fail," he said softly.

Joanie had made a complete and utter fool of herself by trusting him once. She wasn't about to do it again, no matter what he said. "I know the time frame fits, Steve, but I repeat—Emily is not your child."

Steve hooked his thumbs through the belt loops on either side of his fly and lifted a brow. "Was there someone else besides Dylan, then?"

"I do not sleep around!"

He watched her through narrowed eyes. "And you're implying I do?"

Anger roiled inside Joanie. She shrugged, wanting to hurt him the way he had hurt her. "If the shoe fits—"

"It doesn't."

"But you have been known to have naked women in your bed," she asserted. Joanie recalled very well finding one there.

"I told you," Steve returned with exaggerated patience, "that was not my fault. That was just some groupie."

Joanie wrinkled her nose in disgust. "Right."

"I was expecting you that night," Steve continued.

"Not until much later," Joanie reminded Steve in a scathing voice. She shook her head grimly, recounting in a low, strangled voice, "The worst part is, if I had gotten off work on time that night, I never would have known you'd had another woman there, in your bed, before me."

"I didn't know she was in the room."

Joanie clenched her hands into fists. "Then how did she get in?" she demanded, the old hurt and humiliation welling up out of nowhere.

"Beats me." Steve shrugged. "I was in the shower, getting ready for our date."

Trying desperately to ignore how good he looked with the moonlight gilding the handsome contours of his face, Joanie folded her arms in front of her and assumed a contentious stance. "You're denying you ordered room service and asked for champagne and strawberries?"

"It was supposed to be served later," he explained reasonably. "Just before you arrived."

"Until you called down and asked it be sent up early," Joanie corrected, gritting her teeth.

"I told you." He blew out an exasperated breath. "I did not do that. The woman...in my bed...must have."

"How did she know you had placed the order?" Joanie asked impatiently.

Steve rubbed a contemplative hand across his jaw. "She probably read the notepad beside the phone. I had jotted down a list of things to do that evening before you arrived. Placing that order was one of them."

Joanie turned away, reminding herself Steve had had a good two years and three months to come up with a reasonable explanation. It didn't matter that this all made sense now in a convoluted way, at least to him. She knew what she had seen then and it wasn't pretty.

Steve grasped her shoulders and turned her back around. "I wanted to be with you that night, Joanie," he swore passionately. "I was waiting for you. I don't know how that woman got in there, but she did. She got undressed and got into my bed while I was in the shower. She let you in while I was still in the shower. The first I knew of either of you being there was when I heard voices and stepped out."

"I remember that all right," Joanie said. Steve, dripping wet, shampoo still in his hair, a towel around his waist. The stunned expression on his face as he regarded the voluptuous redhead, wrapped only in his bedsheet, and Joanie, her face white and enraged all at once.

She'd felt like such a fool. Like such a stupid, stupid fool. Falling head over heels in love with a man in just one week. When she, as a hotel employee, had been warned repeatedly by co-workers and superiors not to indulge in a vacation romance with a hotel guest for just this very reason.

"If you'd only stopped to listen—"

"I saw what I needed to see."

"No," Steve corrected, leaning defiantly close. "You saw what you wanted to see. You saw enough to give you license to walk away."

Joanie tipped her head back, but didn't move away. "You didn't come after me."

"I didn't see any reason to until I got that other woman out of my suite and got dressed." He scowled. "By the time I made it across town to your apartment, you were long gone."

Joanie shrugged insouciantly. "I had vacation coming."

Steve studied her, clearly annoyed. "You mean you ran," he said.

So what if she had? Joanie blinked back hot, angry tears. "I didn't want to listen to any more of your lies."

He grimaced. "And I didn't want to waste my breath, which was all it would have been at that point."

Joanie blew out a tremulous breath. "So, the best happened," she continued, recounting the end of their brief, heartbreaking liaison. "You went on to win your second Olympic gold medal the following summer. And you cleaned up in endorsement contracts after that and spent the next two years chasing beautiful women all over the world."

At her recitation, he lifted an interested brow and regarded her with a satisfied smile. "I see you kept up with me."

Not because she'd wanted to, Joanie thought. After the way he'd hurt her, she'd wanted only to forget him. And until he'd taken the job at Bride's Bay, she almost had. "I try not to read the sports page," Joanie responded coolly to his assertion, "but I do read *Personalities* magazine, and unfortunately you were in it from time to time." *Usually with a princess or famous model,* she added silently.

He knew without her saying what she was thinking. "Those women meant nothing to me."

His assurance was no comfort. "That makes me even gladder I wised up early," Joanie said, looking away.

"Is that why you didn't return my calls?" he asked.

"I didn't return your calls because I saw no reason to do so," Joanie said coldly. Restlessly, she walked to the open screen door and back again to the edge of the porch. "What I'd felt for you was over."

"Sure about that?" Steve taunted.

"Yes!" Joanie flushed, then said, not too proud to admit it, "Sad to say, to you I was just another groupie in love with a famous athlete."

"Now hold on there a minute," Steve said. "My memory isn't *that* bad. You couldn't have cared less about my celebrity status. You weren't the least bit starstruck when we met."

Joanie swung around to confront him. What he'd said was true. She'd fallen in love with Steve Lantz the man, not Steve Lantz the star.

"That's what I liked most about you," he continued, "the fact my celebrity didn't blow your mind."

Joanie strode forward until they were standing toe-to-toe. Hands on her hips, she glared up at him contentiously, heat flooding her senses as she recalled the uninhibited way she'd given herself to him. "I told you then and I'll tell you again," she said. "I'm not looking for someone rich and famous. I am looking for a regular guy with a regular job. Someone who could build a life with someone like me. Someone who will be content to live an ordinary, low-key life here on Jermain Island."

A muscle worked in his cheek as he stared down at her in obvious frustration. "How do you know that's not me?" he demanded.

Joanie rolled her eyes. "Get real."

He gave her a searing look. "Why do you think I took this job?"

Joanie shrugged. "To torment me—probably because I'm the one who got away."

He stepped a little closer, so that their bodies were now less than half an inch apart. He regarded her for a long, thoughtful moment. "How do you know I don't still have feelings for you?"

They were so close Joanie could feel undulating waves of heat from his body. "Because you don't love me," she retorted, stubbornly holding her ground. "You didn't then and you don't now." She arrowed a finger at his chest. "And furthermore, I don't love you anymore, either," she asserted boldly.

"Oh, really?"

"Really."

"Well, we'll just see about that."

The next thing Joanie knew, she was in his arms and he was delivering a kiss that took them both back in time. She could feel the hard length of him pressed against her, the pounding of his heart against hers, the firmness of his mouth. This was no gentle request, she thought as his tongue plundered her mouth, creating a storm of desire. He wanted her desperately, and he wanted her to want him, too. Before Joanie knew it, she was clinging to him. Shuddering in reaction and kissing him back madly as a flood of longing swept over her as effortlessly and timelessly as the tides. Even as she knew they were going too far too fast again, she could feel the proprietary quality of his kiss. The knowledge that somewhere, deep down, she was already his. And always would be. Only the sound of rapid footsteps on the walk stopped them. They drew apart, Joanie quickly, desperately, Steve slowly. Their eyes met. His told her that this was just the beginning. Joanie's breath hitched in her chest. She felt some of the strength leave her legs. This was how it had happened before. Like magic. Out of nowhere.

"Uh...sorry to interrupt, Joanie," Shad Teach said.

With an effort, Joanie pulled herself together. "Yes?" she said curtly, pushing her hair back into place. Ignoring the tingling of her lips, she turned and faced the hotel's bell captain with as much self-assurance as she could muster. It wasn't easy. At sixty-five, the darkly tanned Shad Teach was still every bit as wily, eccentric and mischievous as he had reportedly been in his youth. A descendant of Blackbeard the pirate, Shad wore a gold hoop in his left ear. Besides being famous for his tall tales and colorful expressions, Shad knew everything that went on at the hotel. And now he knew about her and Steve, too, Joanie thought miserably. Which meant the list of people who had witnessed the tension and the sparks between her and Steve was growing.

Shad ran a hand across his mustache and he regarded her with his piercing blue eyes. "Liz wondered if maybe you could come up and work until midnight. With all the college kids roaming the resort, we really need you at the concierge desk. But she'll understand if you can't on account of Emily."

Joanie looked back at her quarters, where inside all was quiet and Emily was still apparently sleeping soundly. "Go ahead," Steve said. "I'll stay with Emily."

"I'll be gone quite a while," Joanie warned.

"No problem. I'll be here when you get back," Steve promised.

Joanie knew he would be. That was what worried her.

LIZ WAS SEATED at the concierge desk when Joanie entered the lobby. "I heard you called a truce with Steve Lantz." At Joanie's look, Liz explained, "Columbia Hanes said you were quite congenial when the two of you fed Emily her supper."

Joanie tried to brush that off as inconsequential as she slipped behind the desk. "That's no surprise. We were united in a common cause."

"And what a cute little cause she is," Liz murmured.

"A cute little cause without a mama or a daddy," Joanie added. She had hoped to hear from the mysterious Fiona by now. The fact that she hadn't worried her. This was beginning to appear to be more than a simple if unorthodox baby-sitting job.

Liz frowned. Apparently she was thinking along the same lines. "Any further word from the woman who left her on your doorstep?"

"No, not yet. But at least Emily is asleep and Steve is watching her."

"I told you he was a good guy," Liz said.

Joanie was saved from having to respond by a woman approaching the front desk. "I've got some errands to run," Liz said, "so I'm going back to lock up my office and then I'll be out of here." Liz scooted away just as the woman, white-haired with kind blue eyes, reached the desk. She looked to be in her late sixties and was wearing a buttercup yellow jogging suit and sneakers. "My, you all are busy tonight," she said.

"Yes—" Joanie noted the college kids roaming the lounge, restaurant and lobby "—we are, aren't we? How may I help you?"

"I heard there was a bridge tournament going on this week. I'd like to sign up, if I may."

"And you are?" Joanie brought out the list.

"Mrs. Frances Flannagan, in cottage 3."

Joanie wrote it out. "I've got you down. It starts the day after tomorrow."

"Thank you." Her business done, Mrs. Flannagan seemed reluctant to leave. Joanie thought she knew why. Mrs. Flannagan had checked in alone. According to their records, this was her first time at the resort. She seemed to be having a little trouble adjusting, which was probably intensified by the fact that, due to a glitch in her reservation, she'd been put in one of the cottages at the other end of the resort, instead of the hotel room she'd requested.

"Is there a place to buy groceries on the island?" Mrs. Flannagan asked.

"Yes." Joanie smiled. "There's a general store in the village that's open every day from nine to nine. Whenever you're ready to go, call the front desk and we'll send a minivan over to get you."

"Thank you. Although I may just take all my meals in the hotel." Mrs. Flannagan paused. Seeing no one behind her, she continued in a more gossipy tone, "Over dinner tonight I heard the most amazing thing. Is it true a baby was abandoned here this afternoon?"

"Yes. I'm afraid so."

"Where is he now?"

"It's a she," Joanie said. "And she's in my room . . . with a friend."

"Poor little dear." Mrs. Flannagan put her hand over her heart. "She must be so upset."

"Actually," Joanie replied, "she's not hysterical at all—which surprised me. I mean, she's been asking for her mama periodically, which is normal under the circumstances, but she also ate a nice supper and let Steve and me give her a bath before I rocked her to sleep. Steve is with her now."

"Steve?"

"Steve Lantz."

"The Olympic athlete?"

"Yes. He's staying with us through the weekend, too. Now, is there anything else I can do for you?"

"No," Mrs. Flannagan said reluctantly, "I think I'm going back to my cottage and try to relax."

"You have trouble taking vacations?" Joanie said sympathetically.

Mrs. Flannagan admitted this was so, then added, "I've never really had one all by myself before. I'm finding I don't really know what to do with myself now that I have so much free time on my hands."

That was a common problem for people with very busy lives. They were so used to going full speed ahead they didn't know how to slow down. Hence, vacations made them more tense, instead of less. The only way to calm them down, Joanie knew, was to fill up their days with pleasurable activities. As long as they had a schedule, they were usually content.

"Do you play golf? No? If you want, I could set you up with some lessons with our pro. He's really wonderful. And the course is beautiful—championship quality, in fact."

Mrs. Flannagan smiled. "Well, I imagine it'll be some time before I'm a champion player, but yes, golf lessons would be very nice."

No sooner had Joanie finished setting that up and said goodbye to Mrs. Flannagan than one of the college kids walked up to her. The conference badge pinned to his polo shirt said his name was Dennis Wright and he was a student from Yale University. "I'm looking for a girl from Cornell, Phoebe Claterberry," he said. "We meet every year at this conference. Has she checked in yet?"

Joanie checked the computer. "No, I'm sorry, she hasn't. But we're holding her bags, so that means she's here somewhere. She probably didn't want to stand in line earlier and then got caught up in the initial conference activities."

"But that's just it. No one's seen her this evening," Dennis said, looking worried.

"Maybe she's having dinner somewhere else."

"And maybe something happened to her," he said.

Another young woman came up. Her badge said she was Rhonda Wayne, from Cornell. "Phoebe's fine," Rhonda told Joanie frankly, then glared at Dennis. "Phoebe said she wanted time alone to think. She'll see you tomorrow. Now stop worrying and come back to the conference," Rhonda demanded, linking arms with Dennis.

"I'll tell Phoebe you're looking for her if I see her," Joanie promised Dennis.

He nodded, looking only slightly less worried. "Thanks."

"Boy, there must be something in the air around here," Liz remarked from behind Joanie. "I've never seen so many hopelessly lovesick people in my life. And that tally includes you and Steve," she teased.

Joanie flushed. "Will you stop making presumptions?"

"Maybe you're right," Liz said, rummaging through her purse. "Maybe I should concentrate on my own life."

Joanie raised an inquisitive brow. "Is there one?"

"Like I could keep a secret on this island," Liz said. Evidently finding what she wanted, she smiled and closed her purse without removing anything.

Joanie noticed Liz had taken her hair out of its usual chignon to let it fall loosely to her shoulders. She was also wearing a new perfume and earrings Joanie had never seen before. "Well, I'm off," Liz said.

"Have fun," Joanie murmured, watching the manager dash out the front doors.

Before Joanie could wonder where Liz was going—she was too dressed up to simply be running errands, and besides, what kind of errands got done at ten o'clock at night?—a mother and and her teenage son stepped up to the desk. Joanie recognized them both as longtime residents of the island. "Hello, Mrs. Remmington, Chuck. What can I do for you?" she asked.

"We want to report a lost puppy," Chuck said. He pulled a photo of a golden retriever out of his shirt pocket. "We put Sigmund outside in the backyard this afternoon, and he dug a hole under the fence and got out."

"We noticed Sigmund was missing this evening around dinnertime and we've been looking for him ever since," Mrs. Remington said. "We were hoping maybe he'd turned up here."

Joanie admitted that he had. "We saw Sigmund. We haven't caught him yet." Joanie wrote down the puppy's name. "We'll do our best to find him for you."

"Thank you." The Remingtons looked vastly relieved as they walked away.

Elizabeth Jermain and her second husband, retired judge Cameron Bradshaw, walked into the lobby. Just back from an evening out with friends, the elderly couple was dressed in elegant evening clothes. In a stunning designer dress, her silver hair expertly coiffed, Elizabeth looked particularly beautiful. The couple stopped by the front desk.

After greeting Joanie graciously, Elizabeth asked, "Is my granddaughter working this evening?"

"She just got off a little while ago," Joanie said.

"Did she go back to her cottage?" Elizabeth asked.

"I'm not sure."

"I'll call and see if she's in." Cameron walked over to use the house phone.

Elizabeth turned back to Joanie. "How's the little one you found this afternoon? Any word on her parents yet?"

"None," Joanie said. "Oh, and thank you for the rocking chair. You're very thoughtful."

"Don't mention it, dear."

Cameron returned a moment later, frowning. "No answer. Liz must be out with friends or something."

His wife appeared puzzled. "Must be. Although I would like to talk to her this evening, so Joanie, if you run into Liz...?"

"I'll tell her you're looking for her," Joanie promised.

As soon as they left, Joanie settled down to check the records. As she'd feared, she found no Fiona listed anywhere.

She sighed her disappointment and then wondered about Steve. She definitely still had feelings for him even after all this time.

Surely by now she should have gotten over him, but she hadn't. Exhaling heavily, she looked at the clock. Eleven p.m. Another hour to go before she got off work.

STEVE SAT in Joanie's living room at midnight absently flipping through the pages of the monthly report from his broker. But his mind wasn't on the status of his investments. His mind was on Joanie and the toddler sleeping in the next room, who might or might not be his.

A knock at the door interrupted Steve's thoughts. To his surprise, Liz, not Joanie, was at the door. "I'm going to stay with the baby awhile," she whispered.

Steve noticed that Liz's hair was mussed, her clothing rumpled, her eyes unusually bright. If he didn't know better, he'd think by her slightly guilty expression that Liz was having a clandestine love affair. "Where's Joanie?" he asked.

"She went into the hotel kitchen to fix something to eat. I guess she missed supper." Liz gave Steve a closer look. "Did you have a chance to eat?"

"No, not yet." Steve stood. "I think I'll head over there, too."

When he caught up with Joanie, she was in one corner of the kitchen making a sandwich. Columbia and three cooks were rolling out large squares of yeasty dough, spreading them with butter and topping them with an assortment of cinnamon, nuts and cooked fruit. "Rolls for breakfast?" he asked.

"That's right," Columbia confirmed. "We make cinnamon rolls every day. They'll rise overnight and be baked at dawn."

"In that case, I'll be sure and stop by first thing," Steve said with a smile.

"You do that," Columbia returned warmly, "because they'll go fast."

Steve walked over to where Joanie was busy layering lettuce and tomatoes on top of sliced chicken, cheese and bread. Making use of the ingredients she'd brought out of the refrigerator, he began building a sandwich for himself, too. He noted Joanie didn't look any happier to see him now than she had when he'd first arrived.

"Liz sent you here, didn't she?" Joanie guessed.

Steve nodded, knowing that Joanie probably hadn't forgiven him for stealing a kiss earlier. He was still glad he had, because that one kiss had told him that Joanie still had feelings for him—in spades.

"I gather that wasn't the plan," Steve said. "You weren't expecting me to join you?"

Joanie's shoulders stiffened. "No. I was going to grab something quickly, take it back to my quarters and then send you back here to fend for yourself, *by* yourself," Joanie whispered, so just he could hear.

Columbia sent the two of them an interested look. "Hurry up, you two," she said loudly as she made shooing motions with her hands. "My staff and I have a lot of preparations to make for the conference breakfast tomorrow and little time to do it in."

Joanie and Steve hastily packed their sandwiches in carryout containers and took chilled bottles of flavored water from the fridge. The employee cafeteria was being cleaned. "We could take it back to our rooms," Steve suggested.

"And eat separately," Joanie stated.

"Together," Steve said firmly. "Preferably in my place. We still need to talk and we don't want to disturb Em."

Joanie looked as if she felt that his place sounded a little too cozy.

"I don't want anyone getting the wrong idea about us," she said. "There's enough talk already."

Steve paused, thinking about where they were least likely to be observed. "What if we walk down toward the beach? There are some picnic tables scattered among the trees overlooking the shore."

"All right," Joanie said after a moment, falling into step beside him. "Though what we have left to say to each other," she continued as they headed out the doors and down the back steps, "is beyond me. But I suppose for the sake of the hotel, we should call a truce."

He flashed her a pleased smile. "Now you're talking."

"But no more passes," she stipulated.

"No more passes," Steve agreed. *At least not tonight.*

They were silent as they strolled toward the beach. He grasped her elbow when she slipped on the damp grass. She responded to his touch, trembling slightly even as she leaned into him, then immediately pulled away. Moonlight shimmered on the water, the waves lapped gently on the shore, and a balmy breeze whispered through the trees.

Steve breathed in the salty air. "It's beautiful down here," he said.

"Yes, it is," Joanie agreed, as she sat down at the picnic table facing the ocean and tucked her skirt around her knees.

"But the beauty of the island is only part of the reason I took the speaking job here," Steve said, sitting sideways on the bench beside her and unwrapping his sandwich.

Joanie took a long drink of her water. "And the rest is?"

"I want you back," he said.

Joanie sighed, but to Steve's pleasure did not look all that surprised or unhappy about his revelation. "Why is it I suddenly feel like you've just set your sights on a seemingly insurmountable, Olympic-level goal that you are determined to achieve come what may?" she asked.

"I am not in this just for the challenge," Steve vowed.

"No?" Joanie queried as she set her half-eaten sandwich down in front of her.

"No." Steve said. His own sandwich, though made of the finest ingredients, suddenly had all the appeal of sawdust.

Joanie rested her elbows on the redwood table in front of her and stared out at the ocean. "I suppose next you're going to tell me that in the two years and three months we've been apart you haven't had eyes for anyone else," she said. "That all those dates you had with beautiful women all over the world meant nothing to you."

"No, I'm not," Steve said.

Joanie turned to look at him.

He drew a long breath and gathered his courage. "When you left the way you did that night and wouldn't at least hear me out, I was angry and hurt. To be honest, I've tried like hell to forget you during my training for the Olympics and the twenty months I've spent on the road doing product endorsements since. But no one has measured up to you, Joanie. No one can even make me feel anything close to what we had—for that one week— and so I knew I had to come back and find you, and when I did I had to give it my best shot. All I'm asking, all I want from you is to let me try."

He leaned toward her passionately, knowing he was wearing his heart on his sleeve and not caring. "Don't you see, it doesn't matter what's happened in the interim on your side because I've made mistakes, too."

Joanie moistened her lips. "What are you saying?"

Steve took her hands in his and clasped them tightly. "Just that...I understand if...in the aftermath of what happened...what you thought you saw in my hotel room that night...if you went out and tried to even the score."

He didn't like the idea of her being with anyone else since they'd made love, particularly as he hadn't been with anyone else—in the biblical sense—in all that time. But he figured if they were going to have any kind of relationship in the future, they'd both have to forgive and forget on some level. Because it was obvious that mistakes had been made.

Unfortunately, Steve thought as he studied the expression on her upturned face, Joanie didn't feel that his willingness to forgive and forget was a magnanimous gesture on his part. She saw it as anything but generous and noble.

"You mean you forgive me if I slept with someone I barely knew while on the rebound from you?" she asked.

"Right."

"What if I knew the person well?"

That, Steve thought, was a little harder. Still, he knew it was unfair of him to judge anything she had done or not done. "That, too."

Joanie swore and looked as if she wanted nothing more than to deck him then and there. "Honestly, Steve," she grumbled as she tried to pull her hands away.

Steve only tightened his grip. "Hold on a minute, Joanie. I'm *trying* to be understanding here."

And he was. He was trying to figure out why she hadn't told him she was going to have a baby when he was clearly in the running for said baby's father. He was trying to understand why she'd elect to have this baby on her own, especially if that meant she had to give up care of Emily altogether. And the only possibility he could come up with, other than the idea that Emily had been fathered by someone else, was the notion that she hadn't told him about her pregnancy because she'd been trying to punish him for his alleged dalliance by depriving him of his child. But that didn't make sense, either. Joanie had a temper. She wasn't vindictive.

"Well, understand this," Joanie shot back, wresting her hands from his and vaulting to her feet. "Emily is not the result of my liaison with another man, and even if she was, I wouldn't tell you."

Now they were getting somewhere, he thought with satisfaction. "Just as I thought," he said, crossing his arms. Joanie had kept the seriousness of her situation from him for reasons that probably seemed noble at the time. Now she was just plain scared. Scared and hurt. And that meant she needed him now more than she knew or perhaps was willing to admit.

Joanie paled as she continued to study his face. "But she isn't," Joanie said, looking all the more defiant and flustered. "My child, I mean."

Maybe she thought he wouldn't want the child. Maybe she still felt that. If so, Steve knew he had to rectify that.

His heart going out to her, he took Joanie in his arms and, ignoring the flailing arms she threw up between them, gathered her to him. She felt good there. Very good.

"You could have come to me, you know, if you'd needed help," he said, threading his fingers through her golden hair. "I would have given you anything. I would've married you right away had I just known about the baby."

Joanie looked at him, her expression stunned and disbelieving.

Why not? It seemed only right, especially now that they had Emily's well-being to think about. And their own happiness at stake. He clasped her shoulders gently. "Joanie, I want you to be my wife."

Chapter Four

"You're kidding! You're not kidding. Well, get this straight." Joanie wrenched herself from his embrace. "I would not marry you if you were the last man on earth!" Particularly, she thought, after that ridiculously inept proposal.

Steve crossed his arms again, the muscles of his chest bunching beneath the thick cotton knit of his long-sleeved shirt. "Look, maybe that didn't come out right."

"You're damn right it didn't," Joanie said furiously, whirling away from him.

He took off after her and grabbed her arm, forcing her to face him. To her irritation, he became calmer as her emotions rose. They stood as they were a moment, studying each other, forming their next moves. Finally he smiled down at her confidently and spoke in a voice as smooth as silk, "Nevertheless, if you and I have a child together, Joanie, we owe it to each other to get married."

Owe it, she thought. Not *want to. Owe it,* as in *have to.* Well she was not about to get married because she had to, and on that score, she didn't care what anyone else thought.

"And suppose you and I don't have a child together?" Joanie replied, her pulse racing at his nearness. "Do we still *owe* it to each other to get married?"

She raked her hands through her hair, clasped the length of it against the nape of her neck as she fought for calm.

"What do you mean?" Steve asked.

"I have no intention of explaining myself further to you," Joanie said. Deciding that trying to keep her hair from blowing around in the soft ocean breeze was futile, she dropped her hands to her sides.

His expression gentling, he slipped his arms around her. "I meant what I said, Joanie. I think you and I belong together. And Emily certainly needs us."

Joanie stiffened at the almost unbearable tenderness in his touch. "Emily needs her own family," she said in a strangled voice.

"Right." Steve pulled her closer.

She felt the iron hardness of his thighs and torso, and shivers of desire coursed through her body. She wedged her forearms between them, hoping that would halt the flow of sensation. All it did was remind her of the warmth and solidity of his swimmer's body and how it felt to be held against that tensile length, skin to skin. She turned her head, and felt his lips skim her temple, softly, seductively.

"We're not her family," Joanie whispered.

He ran a fingertip down her cheek, slipped it beneath her chin and guided her face back to his. His mouth lowered inexorably toward hers.

Joanie knew if he kissed her again, she really would be lost. It was hard enough not to give into what he wanted. What at one time she had wanted, too.

"I mean it, Steve," she said. "Emily is not our child."

Her words served only to inflame him more. "Keep saying it and maybe you'll end up believing it," he murmured, letting his lips brush her cheek and then the shell of her ear.

Joanie gulped in air as she began to tremble. "Honestly!" She moaned, exasperated, then paused at the sight of a puppy running full speed down the beach. Spurred into action, she used her forearms to push out of the circle of Steve's arms. "I don't believe it. There's Sigmund, the Remington's golden-retriever puppy."

Momentarily diverted, Steve peered after Sigmund. "You're sure he's the one?"

"Positive! Come on! We've got to catch him before he does any more damage." She grabbed what was left of her sandwich and dashed after the pup.

"How long has he been on the run?" Steve caught up with her easily and jogged beside her.

"All afternoon," Joanie puffed, struggling to keep up with Steve's longer strides.

"And what's that he's got in his mouth?" Thoroughly involved in the chase, Steve edged on ahead.

"Looks like the remnants of someone's towel, doesn't it?" Joanie pumped her arms and legs and increased her speed to stay even with Steve. Unfortunately so did the puppy.

"That little son of a gun must've had a nap," she complained as Sigmund dashed along the water's edge, kicking up water as he ran.

"Think we should split up?" Steve asked, when the pup had managed to outdistance them once again.

"Absolutely," Joanie replied. While Steve dashed off in the direction of the grass, Joanie knelt down in the sand and whistled for the pup. Nothing. She clapped her hands. Still no effect. She whistled and clapped at the same time, then followed it with her shout, "Sigmund. Here Sigmund. Come here, boy."

At the sound of his name, Sigmund came to a dead stop. Tail high, he turned around and faced Joanie. Afraid to leave her place in the sand for fear the puppy would take off again, Joanie wiggled her sandwich in front of him. "Here Sigmund. Time for supper, Sigmund...."

Ears cocked, the puppy looked at Joanie. He lurched forward, then midstride did an about-face that landed him right in Steve's arms. Steve held on to him, despite the lack of collar.

He lifted all thirty pounds of squirming wet puppy in his arms. They made a ridiculously cute sight, Joanie thought.

"Now what?" he said, as she closed the distance between them.

"We need to get him back to the Remingtons."

Joanie spied a lone young woman on the beach, clad in jeans, sneakers and a Cornell sweatshirt. She wondered if that was the student Dennis Wright had been looking for earlier. "Listen, would you mind taking Sigmund here up to hotel security by yourself? I'll clean up our picnic and check on that guest."

"No problem. Sig and I'll walk you over." They headed for the young woman who was sitting, hands clasped around her knees, staring listlessly out at the ocean.

Before Joanie had a chance to speak, the young woman bounded to her feet. "Steve, hi!"

Steve paused. "Hi." It was obvious he couldn't place her.

"I'm Phoebe Claterberry. We met at a regional mentoring conference a couple of years ago." She beamed, her joy at seeing him again spilling over. "I told every-one how great you were that weekend. In fact, I chaired the committee that nominated you for this year's na-tional conference. Remember? We even spoke on the phone a couple of times? I told you I had talked to Liz Jermain."

"Oh. Right." Steve nodded as a squirming Sigmund licked his face. "I'm sorry I didn't recall you right off the bat. It's been a confusing night."

"That's okay," Phoebe said a little shyly. "It *has* been two years..."

"Well, I better get Sigmund on over to security. Phoebe, nice to have seen you again. Joanie, I'll see you later."

Joanie and Phoebe watched Steve saunter off, a madly squirming Sigmund in his arms. Joanie turned back to Phoebe.

"I'm Joanie Griffin, the hotel concierge." She paused. She didn't want to intrude. She did want to be of ser-vice, and a moment ago, before Steve's celebrity had gotten in the way, this young woman had looked as if she very much needed a friend. Joanie gave her an encour-aging smile. "Is everything okay with your stay so far?"

Phoebe shrugged, her expression guarded. "I guess. I mean, my bags are being held by the bellman, but I haven't formally checked in yet."

"I know." Joanie nodded. "Another conference goer mentioned that to me."

Abruptly Phoebe looked peeved. "Let me narrow that down even more. Dennis Wright sent you to find me, didn't he?"

"You guessed right, no pun intended."

Looking down at the sand clinging to her legs, Phoebe dusted herself off with a frown. "Yeah, I figured." Then her expression became worried. "There's no problem with my room reservation, is there? I mean, I had that guaranteed arrival—"

"There's no problem with your room. It'll be ready whenever you are, Ms. Claterberry. I just wondered why you were out here all alone."

Again Phoebe withdrew into herself. "I just have an awful lot on my mind. I wanted to be alone, to think about things, before I dealt with people...you know?"

Joanie did indeed. There were times she needed to be alone, too. "Well, if there's anything I or the hotel staff can do, please let me know." Determined to let the young woman have her privacy, Joanie turned to go.

"Ms. Griffin?"

Joanie turned back.

Phoebe stuck her hands in the front pockets of her hooded sweatshirt. "About that baby that was found today..." she began. At Joanie's look of surprise, she elaborated, "The news was all over the resort almost as soon as it happened. Of course, that's to be expected. I mean, it's not every day a baby is left on someone's doorstep."

"No," Joanie said slowly, wondering for the first time if Phoebe had had anything to do with Emily's sudden appearance at the resort, "it isn't."

"Anyway." Phoebe looked anxious. "Is the baby okay?"

"Yes. Emily's fine. In fact, she's sleeping right now."

"Have you found her folks?"

"We're working on it."

"Good." Phoebe seemed relieved.

"You wouldn't happen to know anything about this, would you?" Joanie asked.

"No. Why would you ask?"

"Well, Emily was left about the same time that all the college kids hit the island and were starting to check in."

"Sorry, I didn't see anything." Phoebe changed the subject. "Listen, about my friends. I'll face them tomorrow, but not tonight. Promise me you won't tell anyone—especially Dennis Wright—where I am."

"I promise," Joanie said reluctantly.

Leaving Phoebe on the beach, she gathered up the remains of the meal at the picnic table, then headed back toward the hotel. Halfway between the beach and the hotel, a security van pulled up. Steve was in the front seat, Sigmund still in his arms. Howard Forsythe was driving.

"We're headed for the Remingtons," Steve said. "Want to tag along?"

Joanie shook her head. "No. I want to get back to Emily. Liz'll be wondering where I am. And I think I'm going to turn in. It's been a long day, and who knows when Emily will wake up tomorrow morning?"

"Okay. Let me know if you need help during the night," Steve said as Sigmund continued to snuggle up to him.

Joanie nodded agreeably, though she had no intention of taking Steve up on his offer. Howard waved and the two men drove off.

Liz was watching a rerun of *An Affair to Remember* when Joanie walked in. "Hi," she said softly, her eyes alert and searching. "How'd it go with Steve?"

Joanie rolled her eyes and motioned Liz outside, so the sound of their voices wouldn't wake the sleeping Emily. "The man's an idiot," she confided.

Liz smiled. "Meaning?"

Joanie stalked back and forth, her indignation rising as she recalled the audacious yet matter-of-fact way Steve had gone about it. She'd never known bluntness could hurt so much. "He proposed to me! Can you believe it?"

"Well, honestly, Joanie, what did you expect?" Liz asked.

Joanie did a double take at Liz's reaction. "Wait a minute. I told you. Emily is *not* my baby."

Liz nodded agreeably. "So you've said today, numerous times."

Joanie paused, her heart pounding as she got a glimmer of what she was going to be up against until the situation with Emily and Steve was resolved. "But you don't believe me, do you?" she asked softly.

"And neither, apparently, does Steve. Which is why, of course, he did the absolutely right thing and offered to marry you right away."

Joanie considered trying to explain one more time that this situation was not her fault, then decided the heck with it; no one was listening to her, anyway, so why waste her breath?

Evidently realizing Joanie wasn't going to say anything else on the subject, Liz prodded, "What did you tell him?"

"No, of course."

Liz looked appalled. "Joanie, for heaven's sake. Hasn't he suffered enough?"

"Not by half," Joanie muttered, and meant it.

"But if Emily...I mean..."

Joanie held up both palms to ward off the lecture she was sure was coming. "Now, Liz, don't you start."

"I know how it is to be in love and not want anyone to know about it. I'm not sure why anyone would want to keep a *baby* as precious as Emily hidden but...well, I'm sure there are reasons. Good reasons. I mean, she was obviously loved and well taken care of."

Joanie thought so, too. And that was a comfort to her. The conjecture about her was not thrilling, though. Figuring if she couldn't defeat the talk, she'd join it, she speculated in a deadpan voice, "Perhaps I did it to save my reputation."

Liz pressed her lips together solemnly. "Perhaps."

Joanie flushed. "I was kidding."

"Well, I wasn't." Liz's voice dropped a persuasive notch. "Look, Joanie, I know you haven't been here that long, but in the time we've known each other we've become good friends. You know if you needed help, I'd give it."

Liz's efforts to help were sincere, if misguided. "I know. And right now, I need you and everyone else to back off," Joanie replied, standing her ground.

"All right, I will," Liz agreed, "but not before I say one more thing. I know better than anyone how my grandmother feels about any scandal becoming attached to Bride's Bay. And I also know there's a morals clause in your contract with the resort that says you could be dismissed for conduct unbecoming, but this situation does not fall into that."

Joanie thought about Elizabeth Jermain's desire to run a squeaky clean, family-oriented resort. Licentious affairs and secret illegitimate children did not fall into that category. "Steve isn't just anyone, Liz. He's a public figure, one who's graced the cover of many a national magazine. If even the suspicion got out that he was suspected of fathering an illegitimate child, we'd have tabloid reporters on the island in no time."

And Joanie couldn't imagine what a nightmare that would be, particularly if the mere mention of the island reignited the previous scandal involving Rafe Jermain.

Unable to hide her nervousness, she said, "If that happened, I'd lose my job for sure."

"Not if the scandal had somehow been defused by then, an agreement between Emily's two parents reached."

Joanie groaned softly, sure where this was heading. "You mean marriage, don't you?"

Liz nodded. "I'm sure my grandmother would prefer it. But if that didn't happen, you could stay here and be a single mother, you know. I feel sure my grandmother would agree to that if you just went and talked to her."

Joanie admitted silently that prior to Emily's appearance on her doorstep, she wouldn't have imagined that marriage to Steve Lantz was even in the realm of possibilities. Now she knew it was so. All she had to do was go along with Steve and Liz's view of things... But that wouldn't be fair to Emily.

"I think it's premature to discuss all this," Joanie said, even if the idea of marrying Steve *was* a little tempting.

"I just wanted to lay out the options for you," Liz said.

"I appreciate your concern," Joanie said, working to keep her emotions in check. "But to be honest with you, I am more concerned with locating Fiona than working out my love life." Or lack of it.

"Of course. You must be very upset with the woman. Leaving Emily on your doorstep the way she did."

Joanie deliberately misunderstood what Liz was implying. "Of course I'm angry, but that doesn't change the fact that I can in no way shape or form lay claim to Emily as either my child or my familial responsibility," Joanie said.

"Are you sure about that?"

Unable to take any more, Joanie exploded, "Of course I'm sure! Why can't anyone believe me when I tell them that Emily is not my child? And you, Liz. You're supposed to be my friend. Surely you, better than anyone, know I would never abandon my child."

"I know you wouldn't want to—"

"No," Joanie corrected. "I wouldn't, period. Now if you don't mind, this discussion is over. I really need to get some sleep."

Then, remembering her earlier conversation with Elizabeth Jermain and the judge, Joanie told Liz her grandmother was looking for her.

"I know," Liz replied coyly.

After her friend left, Joanie couldn't help but wonder what she was up to, but quickly lost interest when she walked in to check on the sleeping child.

Oh, Emily, where did you come from?

An ironic smile crossed Joanie's face when she thought about how everyone mistakenly believed Emily was hers—even Steve. And now this little bundle of joy had unknowingly brought her and Steve together again. Just like a little matchmaker. But Joanie wasn't so sure she and Steve would have an ending any happier than their last. Even with Emily in the picture....

"JOANIE, DEAR, may I speak to you for a moment?" Elizabeth Jermain asked at six o'clock Thursday morning as she stopped by Joanie's table in the employee cafeteria.

"Certainly." Joanie stood and held out a chair for the woman. When the elegantly attired Elizabeth was seated, Joanie pushed in her chair for her, then resumed her seat.

"I assume there's been no word from Fiona as of yet?" Elizabeth questioned.

"No, none," Joanie said. "I called the authorities. There've been no reports of a missing child. The police won't be coming to the island for several days. Until then, I offered to take care of Emily. They agreed that'd be fine for two reasons. One, there's a temporary shortage of foster care. And two, there's still a chance Fiona will turn up to reclaim Emily at any moment."

"What if she doesn't?" Elizabeth asked. "If it turns out Emily has been abandoned to you, do you still intend to turn the child over to the foster-care system? Or will you continue to take a more personal interest in her?"

Joanie glanced at Emily, who was messily attempting to eat oatmeal and toast with jelly all by herself. She knew that relinquishing all responsibility would be the quickest way to demonstrate to one and all that Emily was not her child. But she couldn't do that, not without putting Emily at risk of being caught up in endless bureaucratic red tape and placed in a less than ideal situation.

"Actually," Joanie told Elizabeth frankly, "I'm hoping it won't come to my making a tough decision like that. In any case, I'd like a few more days to try and straighten the situation out, if I may."

"Yes," Elizabeth said softly, her glance drifting from Joanie to Emily and back again, "I can see where you might want to do that. After all, every child needs his or her mother, and darling Emily is no exception."

Joanie looked at the matriarch of the Jermain family and knew that Elizabeth suspected Emily was Joanie's child, too.

Joanie cupped her coffee cup with both hands. "The problem with that plan, however, is twofold," Joanie

continued. "One, I don't know very much about toddlers at all."

"No new mother does," Elizabeth consoled Joanie
gently. "But in time they all learn. Just take it one day at
a time."

"Yes. Well, that leads us to the second problem,"
Joanie said, working hard to rein in her exasperation. "I
still have to work, and managing both Emily and my job
is going to be difficult, to say the least."

"Don't worry, I'll be glad to lend a hand," Steve Lantz
said from behind Joanie. Without waiting to be invited
to join them, he pulled up a chair. "And so will a few
others. So you should still be able to work, Joanie."

"Good morning, Steve," Elizabeth said, regarding him
assessingly. "You're up bright and early."

"I had planned to help Joanie with the baby this
morning," he said. He leaned sideways and planted a
good-morning kiss on top of Emily's head.

Emily chortled happily and grinned at Steve.

Joanie flushed.

Elizabeth continued to study Steve and Emily both.
"You know," she said after a moment, "I believe that
little girl has your profile, Steve. In fact, I think she looks
remarkably like you, now that I see the two of you side
by side."

"Really?" It was Steve's turn to flush self-consciously.
But unlike Joanie, he looked delighted by Elizabeth's
implication, as if that proved what he had been saying all
along.

Elizabeth tapped her hand on the tabletop. "I suppose it wouldn't hurt to wait a few more days for this situation to be straightened out," she said finally as she
smiled and rose with regal grace. "Steve, I expect you to
give Joanie all the help she needs."

"No problem," Steve said, his low voice radiating with satisfaction.

Elizabeth left them alone.

"I think I'll get some breakfast from the buffet," Steve said, rising energetically. Freshly shaved and showered, he was handsome in tan deck pants and a long-sleeved polo with the hotel logo. "Can I get you anything?"

Joanie shook her head. She noticed how soft and touchable his hair looked in the morning sunlight streaming through the windows, but resisted the thought. "I'll just finish my coffee."

He returned moments later with a plate of food and a damp cloth for Emily's face and hands. "Guess what they're talking about in the kitchen?" he said, straddling his chair like a jock.

"Us."

His teeth flashed white against his suntanned face as he grinned. "You got it."

Joanie watched him dig into his breakfast with the same uninhibited gusto he did everything else.

"Columbia says that Desmond is taking bets that we'll be married before all is said and done," Steve continued.

Joanie wasn't surprised to learn that Desmond was in on the gossip about them, too. Working behind the hotel bar made the middle-aged black man privy to a lot of talk, and he was an excellent listener. Still, it irritated her. "That's ridiculous!" Joanie fumed.

Steve gave a sidelong look at Emily, who was now playing merrily with her food. "And Elizabeth isn't the only one who's noticed the familial resemblance between Emily and you and me." Steve paused to wipe a spot of jelly off Emily's chin. She smiled back at him, delighting in the attention.

"A lot of babies have curly blond hair."

Steve wiped the stickiness from Emily's hands, then handed her pieces of a corn muffin from his plate. "For the record, I am not enjoying being gossiped about, either," he said flatly, his own irritation surfacing at last. He leaned toward Joanie conspiratorially, engulfing her in the tantalizing woodsy scent of his cologne. "But there is a way we could put all this to rest. And soon."

Joanie concentrated on breathing evenly as she looked away. "By getting married?" she said a great deal more nonchalantly than she felt.

Steve covered her hand with his. Skin tingling, she tensed. People were staring and he seemed loathe to let go of her. He gave her a penetrating look. "My offer still stands."

Joanie thought he only wanted to marry her because he felt he *had* to marry her. In her book that wasn't nearly good enough. She withdrew her hand from his and cast him a wordless look that told him precisely what she thought of his proposal.

"Shampoo!" Emily said. She dug into her cereal bowl and lifted oatmeal-covered fingers toward her hair. Steve and Joanie reacted simultaneously, each of them rescuing one of her sticky hands before it reached its target destination. Emily giggled.

"Emily fun-nee!" she said.

"Oh, very funny," Steve agreed in amusement. With his free hand, he reached for the damp washcloth and cleaned Emily's hand. Still holding on to her playfully, he handed the cloth to Joanie. She washed Emily's other hand, and her face, but there wasn't much she could do about Emily's jelly-stained outfit.

"Looks like I'm going to have to change her clothes again," Joanie said with a sigh. This mothering business was hard work.

Steve frowned. "Did you bring the diaper bag?"

"It's in my office."

"Then let's go." Steve carried Emily in his arms. Joanie led the way.

For lack of a better place, Joanie cleared off her desk and stood Emily in the center of it. Steve shut the door while she unsnapped Emily's overalls. He studied Joanie's unhappy expression. "Don't look so down," he said finally.

As if that was possible when her whole life was falling apart around her, Joanie thought. "I can't help it," she grumbled. "I don't like being the center of so much talk."

"I'm used to being the center of attention, both good and bad, so it doesn't really bother me," Steve admitted as he took charge of the jelly-smeared overalls. He turned them inside out, then folded them and placed them back in the diaper bag. "But it's the first time, for you, hm?"

Joanie coaxed Emily into a clean shirt. "Not really."

Steve edged closer, his shoulder brushing Joanie's as he took Emily's other hand. "This has happened before?"

Joanie nodded. "When I was growing up. My parents quarreled constantly. Their fights were loud, dramatic and usually in front of the whole neighborhood. Everyone talked about them and made fun of them, and usually me, too."

"It must have been hard on you," Steve said.

"I was thoroughly humiliated, and at the same time I was helpless to do anything about it." Joanie finished snapping Emily's clean overalls. Emily rewarded her with a smile that showed all eight of her teeth. Joanie sat down on the edge of the desk. Emily tumbled into her lap and cuddled close. "I suppose that's why I like solving people's problems now," Joanie admitted, smoothing Emily's curls with her hand. "As concierge, I can often do something to make people's lives more enjoyable, at least for a little while."

"And you're a very good concierge," Steve said, his tender glance and low voice reminding her of the time they had first met, when he stayed in the Myrtle Beach hotel where Joanie worked, and Joanie was doing her all to make his stay as blissful and problem-free as possible.

"Unfortunately I'm afraid all this has tarnished my image," Joanie said as Emily held out her hands to Steve.

Obliging, Steve picked Emily up. Emily laid her head on his shoulder.

"Not in terms of your work," Steve disagreed.

"No. In terms of me," Joanie corrected. "And darn it all," she whispered, her frustration with the situation evident, "I promised myself this would never happen. I promised myself that when I grew up I would always lead a very proper life. That I would never be caught screaming at my husband or making a spectacle of myself for all the neighbors to see, and I haven't, yet here I am—the victim of innuendo and talk. And poor Emily, who's done nothing to anyone, is now the brunt of it, too."

"Don't forget me," Steve said.

"Believe me, I haven't." As their gazes clashed, there was a moment of sizzling awareness.

Forcing back her turbulent emotions, Joanie dropped her eyes. "I'm just glad Emily isn't old enough to understand what's going on. But one day she will be old enough—" Joanie sighed "—and what then?"

"You talk as if you plan to keep her," Steve said, a glint of approval in his eyes.

Joanie told herself she neither wanted nor needed his approval. "It has occurred to me that the person who left her with me might not come back," she retorted as Emily continued to cuddle against Steve's broad swimmer's chest.

"And if that happened and you took Emily in, then everyone would see you as kind of a heroine, right?" Steve said as if for him, everything had just snapped into place. "And not the heartless mother who let her own child be raised by a stranger for the first year and a half of her life?"

"Wait a minute!" Joanie straightened. "I'm not the villain here."

"I know that." He towered over her, Emily still in his arms.

"Do you?" Joanie's heart thudded at his nearness. "Sometimes I wonder."

His glance roved her upturned face, his desire for her evident. "Well, you needn't," he began. "Because—"

Emily broke the spell. She touched Steve's face with her hands, putting her nose to his nose. "Down!" Emily demanded with toddler sternness, pointing at the sofa. "Down!"

Steve looked at Joanie. "Is it all right?"

She nodded, aware now there'd be no little girl in his arms to keep him from touching her or taking her in his arms again, if he wished.

Noting a spot of jelly on her blazer, Joanie frowned and slipped the blazer off. She pulled a bottle of club soda from the drawer and blotted a little on the spot.

"I care about Emily." Steve watched the little girl begin to untie her shoes.

"I know that, too," Joanie said, relieved that Emily would be busy for the next few moments. Backing up so her hips were against the desk, Joanie laid her drying jacket aside. Doing her best to avoid the quiet challenge in his eyes, she sat on the desk and folded her arms. ''I just don't like the gossip.''

''I know how much you want to protect her.'' Steve's gaze dropped to her silk blouse before returning to her face. ''And in that regard, my heart goes out to you, Joanie,'' he said. ''I want to protect Emily from any hint of gossip or scandal, too.'' He took a step nearer. ''As for her being born out of wedlock, as I am guessing she was, I don't have a problem with that. Most people here probably wouldn't, either. But apparently you do mind the talk. So we'll need to work around it.''

Joanie sighed in exasperation. The situation was driving her nuts. Everyone assuming the worst about her, none of them knowing all or even part of the facts.

Steve shifted one hip onto the desk beside her. He took her hand in his, entwining their fingers. ''I'm sorry my being here has made us the brunt of so much gossip, Joanie.'' His thigh nudged hers. ''I thought coming here...after you was the right thing to do. But because of all the talk I can see now that it was a mistake for me to arrive without contacting you in advance.''

Neither resisting nor leaning into his grip, Joanie looked pensively down at their joined hands. ''Perhaps if I hadn't reacted so emotionally to the news, people wouldn't be talking so much now.''

With his free hand, he lifted her face to his. She didn't know what it was—the smallness of her office, the intimacy of their conversation—but he seemed larger than she remembered, stronger and more resolute.

''I never meant to hurt you, Joanie.''

Her gaze dropped to the masculine curve of his lips before returning to the seducing brilliance of his eyes. ''I know that," she murmured, feeling herself moving ever toward him. Emotionally, physically...

He rubbed the pad of his thumb across the top of hers, making her feel gloriously alive for the first time in months and months. "I can also understand your not wanting Emily to be the brunt of any scandal or linked to whatever was between us in the past."

Joanie drew a steadying breath and, because she couldn't think when Steve was touching her, withdrew her hand from his light grasp. Struggling to hold on to the threads of their conversation, she looked at their young charge, who was now down to just one sock and shoe.

"I don't want Emily hurt the way I was when I was growing up, Steve," Joanie said, feeling her heart thud heavily against her ribs.

"I know. And I agree with you that Emily should be protected from conjecture about the past." He got to his feet. "It doesn't mean I'm going to stop helping you with the baby," he specified, leaning close and causing another jittery jump in Joanie's pulse, "only that I'll try to go about it in a less scandalous way."

Joanie flushed but refused to be drawn into yet another quarrel with him. "Thank you," she said, slipping off the desk, too. She faced Steve equably, her innate graciousness intact. "I would really appreciate it if you could do that, at least until we get this straightened out somehow."

"Right." Steve reached around her to help her slip her jacket back on.

He watched as she buttoned it and adjusted the slim rope of pearls around her neck. "So to that end," he continued casually, "I am going to do the only gallant thing..."

Here it came, she thought, the determined, unflappable, fathomless Steve she dreaded. The Steve who always, *always* met his goals, no matter what Olympic-size obstacles had to be overcome.

"...and spread the news high and low around the resort that, regardless of the way it first may have appeared, there is no scandal in our past, Joanie," Steve continued with set jaw, his voice a little rough around the edges but otherwise as calm as ever. "I'm going to tell them that we were—and are—just friends."

Chapter Five

"Friends," Joanie repeated in a shocked tone of voice.

"Yes," Steve said, delighted to see that the idea of them going backward in terms of their relationship didn't appeal to Joanie any more than it appealed to him. Now all he needed to do was buy them some time and space so Joanie could realize this was so—and admit to herself that she wanted, more than anything, for the two of them to pick up where they'd left off.

Confident, he edged closer. Determined to play it cool, he kept his hands in his pockets. "I firmly believe that if everyone stops trying to conjure up what we were or weren't to each other way back when, then they'll stop trying to link you and I to Emily, at least in a biological way. When that happens, the scandal, at least the majority of it, will die down."

Steve paused to peer down into her upturned face. He took in the tenderness of her lips and the new flush of color in her cheeks. It was all he could do not to draw her into his arms and kiss her until she went limp with longing.

Keeping his eyes locked on hers, he drew a calming breath. "That is what you want, isn't it?"

Joanie's lips parted. Everything about her softened. Then realizing she was inviting a kiss, she straightened abruptly and edged away, around the corner of her desk. "Of course. Absolutely," she said, keeping her face averted.

She didn't look convinced, Steve thought. "Or would you rather we went the other way and told everyone we were lovers?"

Joanie smiled down at Emily, who was still sitting on the sofa, trying to figure out how to put on the socks she had just taken off. Joanie crossed her arms. "It was just one night. I don't think one night allows us to call ourselves lovers."

"Then suppose we say it was a one-night stand," Steve suggested.

Joanie whirled to face him, brisk color flooding her cheeks. "That will *not* help."

He studied the new brilliance in her blue eyes, even as he shrugged off his own suggestion. "I suppose you're right."

"Besides, then they'd want to know why we didn't continue, and then we'd have to tell them all about that last night and—"

"You didn't see what you thought you saw, Joanie," Steve interrupted, frustration bubbling up in him anew. He wished he could make her believe that. He wished she trusted him enough to believe in him with all her heart and soul. But she didn't. And he couldn't change that, not easily. Maybe not at all.

Still, he wanted to try. He knew before even coming to the island that seeing Joanie again, being with her, would either make or break her hold on him. So far, all it had done was intensify his feelings, both good and bad. She was the one woman he'd ever really wanted. The one woman he'd ever really loved.

She turned away. "I've got to go to work."

Steve paused. Despite her lack of faith in him, they still had a child to protect and nurture, hopefully together. And because they had Emily to think about, he swallowed his pride and let her lack of belief in him go unchallenged, at least for the moment.

"Do you want me to watch Emily?" he asked, knowing more than anything that he wanted to be part of his child's life, no matter what happened with him and Joanie in the end.

Joanie looked up at him, surprised but wary. Irritation flooded him. He wished she wouldn't continually act so astonished by every decent or kind thing he did.

"Aren't you supposed to have tea with Phoebe Claterberry to talk about the speech you intend to give at the closing banquet Saturday evening?" she asked.

"Yes. In about fifteen minutes. But I can reschedule," Steve allowed. Unlike his own father, he knew what was important. Emily was important and so was Joanie.

"No, I don't want you to reschedule," Joanie said. She sat down beside Emily on the sofa and began to help her put on her socks and shoes again. Not content to just sit beside Joanie, Emily stood and scrambled onto Joanie's lap, hiking her skirt up slightly in the process.

With effort, Steve turned his glance away from the sight of Joanie's slim, nylon-covered thigh. Remembering how those thighs had felt beneath his hands, it was all he could do not to groan out loud.

"Why not?" Steve persisted, picking up the thread of the conversation. "I'm sure Phoebe would understand if I wanted to reschedule."

Joanie didn't look as sure of that as he was.

"Besides, the conference committee already has a general outline of my speech," Steve added.

Again Joanie shook her head, nixing his suggestion. "Emily's presence has thrown the resort into enough turmoil as it is. I promised Elizabeth this morning that I could handle working and simultaneously watching over Emily, and I intend to prove that." She smiled as Emily wreathed her arms about her neck and delivered a smacking kiss to Joanie's cheek.

It sounded to Steve as if Joanie was setting herself up for failure. Plus, she was taking on a lot more than she had to take on alone. "And how, may I ask, are you going to do that?" he said.

Joanie kissed Emily's head and smoothed her tousled curls with a gentle sweep of her hand. "By putting a crib next to the concierge desk. Hopefully Emily will be entertained just watching all the activity."

"And if she's not?" Steve felt frustrated to be continually held at arm's length. Whether she meant to or not, Joanie was shutting him out of Emily's life—and her own—again.

Joanie shrugged. "Then I'll ask for help."

Steve reminded himself that gaining Joanie's trust again was going to take time. "From me?" he asked, knowing he wanted to be there for her if she'd let him.

Joanie gestured blandly. "If you're there to give it."

"THIS LOOKS GREAT, Steve," Phoebe said as he filled her in on specific details of his speech and the slide show of his own work with kids that would accompany it. "If you want, I can arrange for a run-through in the dining room after hours, with the mike and projector."

"Thanks, but it won't be necessary." It was all Steve could do to keep from looking at his watch. "I've spoken enough to feel comfortable in any situation. I'm sure it'll be fine. And if anything's not, we'll fix it on the spot.''

"Well...okay, but if there's anything I can do for you between now and then..." Phoebe said, looking reluctant to let the meeting end.

Steve stood. "I'll let you know," he promised. But he didn't expect to call her. Instead, he wanted to spend all his spare time with Joanie and Emily.

"In the meantime, you have your schedule for the next three days," Phoebe said. "You know where you're supposed to be when."

Steve nodded and patted his blazer pocket. "It's right here." He noted she still looked stressed, which, considering this was the first time she had chaired a national conference committee, was probably to be expected. "Don't worry," he said, reassuring her. "Everything's going to be fine."

Phoebe forced a smile. "I hope so."

They said goodbye. And because Steve had a few hours before his next appearance at the conference, he quickly got his own mission under way.

"I know there's been a lot of gossip about Joanie and me," Steve told the bell captain, Shad Teach, as they got a second crib out of storage for use in the lobby.

"Sure has—you two must go way back. That was some kiss I saw the other day," Shad replied as they headed down to the lobby with the crib.

So much for diffusing the gossip through Shad Teach, Steve thought, striding out of the hotel and heading for the greenhouse.

"I know there are a lot of stories about us going around," Steve said to Cameron Bradshaw, who was here working on his new hybrid tea roses.

"Son, you got that right!" Elizabeth Jermain's husband replied.

"But I'm here to set the record straight," Steve continued, watching as Cameron snipped off one perfect red rose and carefully removed the thorns from the stem. "The truth is that Joanie and I were friends once. We think—hope—we can be friends again."

"Friends or more than friends?" The judge smiled as he handed Steve the rose.

Steve had no answer for that. He was hoping Joanie and he could go from friends to more than friends in short order.

"Just as I thought. Do yourself a favor, Steve, and don't protest so much," the judge advised, giving Steve's shoulder a fatherly pat. "And in the meantime, take that flower to Joanie. I happen to know that red roses are her absolute favorite."

So much for fooling the judge where his own aspirations regarding Joanie were concerned, Steve thought as he headed back to the main building. The fact that he wanted to make her his must have been as clear as the nose on his face.

Thwarted but not defeated, Steve tried again, sticking as close to the truth as he dared.

"Those stories about Joanie being in love with me are untrue," Steve told Columbia, the rose the judge had given him still in his hands. "She never was." Because if she had been, she would have given him a chance to explain that night, and then she would've believed him.

"Call it what you like, Steve Lantz, but I am a woman who knows what she sees. And what I see are sparks between the two of you that couldn't be put out with a fire hose," Columbia replied, as she boxed up a light snack of fruit juice and graham crackers for Emily and sent him on his way.

Steve delivered the snack to Joanie at the front desk. Emily was standing in her crib, lobbing her shoes and socks at passersby. They were unerringly amused, but Steve knew it wasn't going to last. He stopped by Joanie's desk and handed her the rose. "Trouble in paradise?"

"In more than one way," Joanie whispered back. She looked down at the rose, her hand trembling slightly as she accepted it. "What's this for?"

"It's from the judge. He cut it specially for you, so be sure to thank him."

"I will. Although I wonder why he sent it via you?" Joanie pulled a white bud vase from beneath the desk and fit the rose into it.

Steve shrugged as she added a dash of water to the vase from the bottle beneath her desk. "I was talking to him at the time."

Joanie gave Steve a look that was at once skeptical and amused. Steve noted she was more beautiful than he remembered, and more fragile.

"I get the feeling you've been talking to a few people, at least Shad and the judge, anyway...who else?" she asked. Wordlessly she handed Emily the toddler cup of fruit juice. Emily held on to the crib rail with one hand and tipped the cup up with the other, drinking thirstily, before she sat down, cup still in hand, to munch on her graham cracker.

Because there were no guests needing attention at the moment, Steve felt free to step behind the front desk, too. "Just Columbia."

"No one believed you," Joanie guessed, turning her glance up to his face.

Steve shrugged and turned so the lobby was behind him, Joanie just in front of him. Her golden curls fell from a side part, spilling gloriously over her shoulder to her breast. "They all think there's something special between the two of us."

"And we know that's not true," Joanie replied quietly, holding his gaze defiantly.

Steve watched as she lifted a slender hand to push back her hair and tuck it behind one delicate ear. Feeling welled up inside him, fierce and undeniable.

"Isn't it?" he retorted, focusing on the pulse he could see throbbing in her throat.

A snap sounded to their left. They looked over just in time to see Emily wave the cap from her drinking cup in one hand and pour the juice down the front of her overalls with the other.

Joanie groaned. "Oh, no. Em, honey, that's your last clean outfit."

Steve was already striding past Joanie to the crib. "No problem. We'll just go dry you off, won't we, Em?"

The next few minutes were spent at the men's-room sink and the hand dryer next to it. Emily thought the whole experience hilarious. By the time he'd finished washing and drying her off, Steve was chuckling, too. "Geh Mama," Emily said, tugging on his shirt.

"We're going," Steve promised, lifting Emily into his arms.

When Steve returned, the crib was gone and Liz was standing at the front desk with Joanie. "Take the afternoon off," Liz was saying, "and just see to Emily here."

"I'm sorry she spilled her juice and lobbed her socks at the guests so many times."

Liz waved it off. "She's a baby, Joanie. She was just amusing herself."

"And speaking of amusing herself, maybe we should see if we can't find some age-appropriate toys for her," Steve quipped, "and really tucker her out."

They spent the afternoon alternately amusing Emily and rounding up toys from other employees, then finished with a boat ride around the island. Exhausted, Emily fell asleep almost immediately, then woke up as the boat pulled into the marina. She looked around once and, to Steve and Joanie's dismay, immediately began to rub her eyes and cry.

"Looks like someone didn't get her nap," Kent Prescott, the marina manager, said as Joanie and Steve disembarked, cranky toddler in tow.

"Maybe she's just hungry," Joanie said, patting Emily's back affectionately and noting it was almost six.

Unfortunately the prospect of dinner did not please Emily any more than getting off the boat had. "She doesn't look very hungry, does she?" Steve mused in the employee cafeteria as Emily grumpily used her spoon to pound the finely diced chicken and mashed potatoes Joanie had set before her.

"How about some applesauce, Emily?" Joanie offered a spoonful.

Emily clamped her mouth shut and shook her head, refusing to let Joanie feed her. "Out!" she demanded, plucking at the safety strap around her waist and struggling to stand up.

"I don't think you're supposed to try and force a baby to eat," Joanie said with a troubled sigh.

Steve frowned. "I don't think so, either."

Joanie met his gaze. "I suppose if she gets hungry later on, she'll let us know."

"Probably," Steve agreed.

Without warning, Emily rubbed her eyes and began to cry. Knowing instant action was called for, Steve unstrapped her and picked her up.

"In the meantime, maybe a bath is in order," Joanie said.

Steve nodded and headed for the door. "Can't hurt." And going back to their quarters would give him more time alone with Joanie and Emily.

Unfortunately the prospect of a bath was about as appealing to Emily as dinner had been. Nonetheless, he and Joanie were determined she should have one. "I thought these bath toys were supposed to be entertaining," Steve said, ducking as Emily hurled one of the floating rubber ducks at his chest.

Joanie winced as Emily splashed her in the face. She gently but quickly shampooed Emily's hair. Emily continued to splash her mercilessly as she rinsed her hair. "I don't think Emily is in the mood to be entertained."

Steve watched as Joanie finished washing Emily's hands and face. Joanie's blouse was completely drenched. It molded to the soft curves of her breasts. Water spots dotted her face and glistened in her golden hair. She looked deliciously tousled.

"Could you get a towel please?" Joanie asked. Not taking her eyes off her unruly charge for an instant, she reached over to unplug the drain.

Frowning at the water leaving the tub, Emily tried to replug the drain, but hadn't the strength to work the metal lever.

Steve held out a thick, fluffy towel. "C'mon Em, time to get out," he said.

"No!" Emily shouted cantankerously. She followed this with a sweeping splash of the remaining water, this one aimed at Steve. It hit him square in the face. Watching the water drip down his nose, and off his chin, Emily burst into giggles.

Joanie leaned against the tile and laughed softly, too. "Your turn to be in charge," she said to him with a wicked grin.

"Emily," Steve said gently but firmly, "it's time to get out. The bathtub is no place to horse around." He handed Joanie the towel and reached over to lift Emily out of the tub. Ignoring the way she immediately made use of an old toddler trick and went completely limp in his arms, he held her aloft so Joanie could wrap the towel around her middle. Once it was secured, he carried Emily into the bedroom and set her down on the bed. Joanie followed with clean clothes, diaper and baby powder.

"Maybe we should just put her to bed," Steve suggested. It was clear Emily was far too tired to know what she wanted. And the only cure for that was sleep.

"No!" Emily shouted. Fully clad in her pajamas, she scooted toward the pillows of Joanie's double bed. Her diaper-clad bottom up in the air, she pulled back the bedspread, then the sheets, and wiggled her way beneath the covers.

Steve handed Emily her blanket and her teddy. Emily looked beseechingly at Joanie and pointed to the pillow beside her.

"I think she wants me to lie down with her," Joanie said finally.

"I'm all for getting her to sleep any way we can," Steve murmured cooperatively. He looked at Joanie, glad they were of one mind on this. "Maybe we just need to put her in a conducive mood to nodding off."

As Joanie stretched out on one side of Emily, her skirt hiking up over her knees, Steve reluctantly got up to leave. He hated to go, but figured the quieter it was, the better. "I'll be just next door," he said.

Emily began to cry as Steve reached for the doorknob. She looked at him and pointed to the pillow on the other side of her.

"So much for a fast getaway," Steve concluded. "Seems Emily wants us all to go to sleep." He looked at Joanie, wondering if she was being hit with the same deluge of memories he was. Judging from the sudden softening of her eyes, she was. "Do you mind if I join the two of you?" he asked.

"Just dim the lights on your way over, will you please?" Steve switched off the lamp on the dresser. The bedroom was dark except for the soft yellow light streaming in from the bathroom. He stretched out beside Emily on the other side of the bed. The mattress shifted as he and Joanie got comfortable. Emily cuddled up between them, adjusting her blanket and teddy just so.

"Sing 'mit!" Emily demanded, grabbing a handful of Joanie's blouse and another handful of Steve's shirt as if to insure they wouldn't go away.

"Honey, I don't know the 'mit," Joanie said softly, gently stroking Emily's halo of golden curls, so like her own. "But if you want to sing it, I'll hum along."

"Sing!" When they didn't, Emily struggled tiredly to a sitting position and started to cry the loud racking sobs of a completely exhausted baby.

"Maybe we should just sing anything." Steve glanced over at Joanie with a shrug. "It's bound to be soothing."

"Okay," Joanie agreed with a soft sigh as she brought Emily back down to cuddle between her and Steve, "but it'll have to be something I know." And then Joanie started in again on "It Had to Be You."

His senses swimming at the magical lilt of Joanie's voice, Steve joined in, their voices blending and harmonizing softly, soothingly, in the darkness.

Twenty minutes and ten choruses later, Emily was fast asleep. They waited another five minutes, and then Steve signaled to Joanie that he was going to try to get up. Emily didn't budge as he moved from the bed.

Encouraged, Joanie tried it, too. Emily whimpered slightly as the bed shifted. In a flash, Steve leaned over and patted her softly until she quieted while Joanie crept from the room. Seconds later, after he moved the little bundle to the crib, he joined Joanie in the living room.

"Thanks for staying with me this evening," she said, sinking into a corner of the sofa.

"No problem," Steve said, watching as she curled her long, slim legs beneath her. He sank down beside her. "I was glad to help."

Joanie rested her head on his shoulder and closed her eyes. "This evening has made me realize how much I don't know about children. I was considering keeping Emily and raising her myself if Fiona doesn't return for her, but this evening has made me doubt my capacity for being a full-time mom."

Was that why Joanie had abandoned Emily in the first place? Steve wondered, reaching over to rub the tension from her neck and shoulders. Because she felt inadequate? And her parents were not the kind of people she could turn to for help and advice, at least in any peaceful way?

"I think you're doing fine," he said, realizing his anger at having been initially shut out of his child's life was fading fast.

Joanie lifted her head. In the soft evening light, her eyes were an incredible shade of blue. She seemed weary but deeply content, too.

"Yes, but you seem to know just what to do. Like having us both lie down and sing whatever we knew to her, instead of the 'mit, whatever that is."

Steve knew it was just dumb luck and sheer desperation that led him to suggest they sing whatever they knew, since they couldn't decipher what song the child wanted to hear.

"I really needed you tonight," Joanie continued softly, trailing a light hand up his forearm, tracing the light dusting of hair.

Steve's heart swelled. This was the first time Joanie had ever confessed to needing him. Knowing that her needing him was the first step to her eventually loving him, he decided that there was only one thing to do. Make it the norm.

"I was glad to help out," he said. "So, anytime you have questions or need ideas on how to better handle Emily, even if I'm not around, feel free to seek me out." If he didn't know what to do, he'd darn well find out.

"So now you're a walking encyclopedia on toddlers?" Joanie teased.

No, Steve thought determinedly, *but I will be, just as soon as I get my hands on the right baby-care book.* "Just remember I will always be there whenever, wherever you need me," he said, lifting her onto his lap.

Joanie put her arms about his neck. For a second she looked as if she wanted very much to commit her heart to him then and there. But as always, her natural wariness kicked in and her expression changed. "You don't have to make promises to me, Steve," she said. "Especially about Emily."

He shifted her position on his lap, taking her fully into his arms and gathering her soft body against the harder length of his. "Yes, I do, Joanie," he whispered as their warm breaths met and blended. Because it would be the promises made and the promises kept that would bring them together in the end.

Pausing only long enough to align their lips and noses, he bent his head to deliver a long, soulful kiss. And for once she didn't draw away, but simply let him hold her. That, too, was another step in the right direction, he thought as he brushed his lips over her hair, enchanted by the softness and scent of the unruly curls.

Her arms were tight around his neck, her head nestled on his shoulder, her thighs aligned warmly over his. With a soft sigh of surrender, she tilted her head back to look at him again. Her fragrance waltzing through his system, he brought his lips back down to hers, letting all that he felt, all that he knew, all that he wanted, come through in another long, passionate kiss. Desire seared through him as he felt her deep need. She might be saying they still had a lot to work out—and in truth they did—but he knew her mind was already made up, just as his was. They would make love again. And soon. And this time it would be even better, even more meaningful, than before.

But they had to wait until the time was right, he realized with regret, his own instinct for survival coming to the fore, and it wasn't right quite yet.

"I think I'd better go," he said. Because if he didn't, he would end up staying. And she might hate him for that in the morning. And they'd come too far today to lose it all on a whim.

"Of course." She nodded, pulling herself together. She withdrew from the coziness of his lap and stood, looking a little disoriented.

Knowing exactly how she felt, he stood, too. His whole body throbbing with passion, he said a quick good-night.

To his pleasure, Steve was aware of Joanie watching him, long after he let himself out of her quarters and strode away.

Chapter Six

Stopping briefly to say hello to the scattered groups of conventioning college kids, Steve made his way to Liz's office. She was seated behind her desk, a mound of paperwork in front of her, a frown on her face.

"This isn't a good time, is it?" he said as she looked up. Liz looked like she had the weight of the world on her shoulders.

She tossed down her pen and waved him in. "Actually I could use the interruption," she confessed as she sat back in her chair.

"Problem?" Steve guessed, wondering if he could help.

Liz sighed and rubbed her temples. "That's one way to put it."

Steve waited, not sure he should press for further details.

Apparently needing to unburden herself to someone, Liz continued, "I used to travel a lot and get bookings for conferences and tour groups while my grandmother ran Bride's Bay. But since my grandmother has slowed down and really cut back on her hours, I've had to be at Bride's Bay more and more. Hence, our conference bookings are not what they used to be. If we don't remedy the situation before the season begins, we'll be feeling the pinch by year's end."

Steve dropped into the chair she indicated. He understood why she looked so stressed out. "Sounds to me like you need to hire a marketing director to help bring business in," he said.

"I've been thinking the same thing. Do you know of anyone who might be interested in the job? I know you majored in marketing and finance when you were at Duke... Have you kept in touch with any of your old classmates? We'd need someone right away."

The germ of an idea began to form. "Let me think about it and I'll get back to you."

"Soon?"

"By tomorrow morning," Steve promised. "In the meantime, I need a favor. I want to purchase a how-to book, and all the gift shop has is a few novels from the bestseller list. Where would I find a store on the island that carries nonfiction?"

Liz made a final notation on the computer printout before her, then picked up the pages of the weekly work schedule and pinned them to the bulletin board just outside her office door. "The book section in the village general store carries an extensive array of books, since many of our guests and local residents are voracious readers. I don't know that they'd have what you're looking for, but you might check there."

"How late are they open?" Steve asked, holding the schedule in place while Liz pinned it to the cork bulletin board.

"Until nine this evening."

Steve glanced at his watch. "That only gives me fifteen minutes."

Liz returned to her office. She regarded him with calm interest and a raised brow. "It's an emergency, I take it?"

Maybe not to anyone else. "You could say that, yes," Steve replied.

"I've got to pick up a friend at the helipad in a few minutes, but I could drop you off at the general store on my way."

"That'd be great. Thanks."

"If you don't mind my asking, what kind of how-to information are you looking for?" Liz asked as she led him outside to the white Bride's Bay minivan and slipped behind the wheel.

"Child care."

When Liz slanted him another curious glance, he explained, "Joanie has been turning to me for help and advice in caring for Emily. So far it's been sheer luck that things have worked out so well. And I'm not one to rely solely on luck. I much prefer to go into a situation well prepared."

"Hence the plan to read up on the subject." Liz smiled as she backed the van out of its parking space and headed down the drive toward the main road that circled Jermain Island.

"Taking care of Emily and simultaneously romancing Joanie is a lot more challenging than I would've ever thought. I want to do right by them both. And I want Joanie to feel good about leaning on me for help." *I want her to see we can be a family, and a happy one at that.* Steve glanced out the window as they passed the island's dozen private estates, one of which was the Remingtons'. He couldn't help but notice the For Sale or Rent sign on another one, with a particularly beautiful plantation cottage home.

"So, you are in love with her?" Liz asked.

"I know she's the woman for me," Steve acknowledged. And he'd realized it the first time their eyes had met. She'd known who he was and she hadn't cared. The only thing that had mattered was the electricity flowing between them and the fact he'd been in Myrtle Beach for only one week's stay....

Maybe they would have rushed things, anyway, Steve thought. God knew their feelings for each other had been very powerful. But the added burden of knowing the time they had to make a connection was limited had made each stolen moment all the more precious.

"And all those stories you told people this morning about there being nothing scandalous between the two of you in the past?"

"They were all true." *As far as they went,* Steve added silently. The scandal had been in what Joanie *thought* she'd seen when she came into his suite that last fateful night at Myrtle Beach.

Liz frowned as she approached the village.

"But if you are in love with her now, I don't understand why you're going to such pains to make people think the opposite."

Steve frowned, his unhappiness returning. "Joanie's been upset about the gossip."

Liz slowed as she drove past the ship chandler and the gas station, the diner and the grocery. "I see."

Steve turned toward Liz as she parked in front of the general store. "I was trying to take the pressure for us to get together off Joanie. Unfortunately all my protests did was convince people that Joanie and I belonged together even more."

"Maybe you do," Liz said with another smile.

Steve couldn't disagree with that.

"Good luck with your search," Liz said as he climbed out of the minivan.

"Thanks," Steve said. Joanie might have kissed him like she meant it tonight, but he still needed all the help he could get. He also needed time to be with her. There was only one way to arrange that.

"FIND WHAT YOU WERE looking for last night?" Liz said the next morning when Steve showed up in her office, Emily in his arms.

Steve nodded. He'd been up half the night, first scanning the baby-care book for information, then planning his presentation. Elise Jennings, who ran the Bride's Bay business center, had taken his computer disk and printed and assembled bound copies of his proposal when her office opened that morning.

"Did you come up with any names for the marketing job?" Liz asked as Steve settled Emily on the sofa beside him. She had a shape sorter to keep her busy.

"Just one," Steve said. He handed over the proposal he'd pulled together on the laptop he used for writing his speeches.

"*You're* interested in the job?" she asked, amazed.

Steve grinned, excited by the prospect of doing something new. "As you said last night, I've got the background for the job."

"What about your endorsement contracts?" Liz asked.

"They're about up. I've already decided not to resign."

"Your motivational speaking?"

"I enjoy it, but after dozens of speeches to dozens of groups, I'm looking to cut way back there, too." Steve leaned forward earnestly. "I want a new challenge, Liz.

Give me six months, and if you're not happy with what I've done, you can let me go, but in the meantime let me show you what I can do. And let's start by looking at the proposal I pulled together last night to get Bride's Bay's bookings back on track." They discussed that in detail for several minutes without interruption, Emily playing contentedly at Steve's side.

Finally Liz smiled. "This all looks great."

"Thanks."

She held on to the proposal. "You understand, of course, that only my grandmother can hire you."

Steve nodded. "When can I meet with her?"

"I'll set up something right away." Liz glanced out the window, then turned back to Steve. "I'm sorry to cut this short, but I've really got to go." She snatched a tube of lipstick from her desk drawer and threw a silk scarf over her shoulder. "I'll set up the meeting with my grandmother and then you and I'll talk later?" she said, already rushing out the door.

"Sure," Steve said.

He gathered up Emily and her toys and headed out into the lobby. Joanie was behind the concierge desk giving detailed instructions to her assistant, Jerry. When she saw Steve and Emily, she smiled and stepped out from behind the desk.

"My turn to watch Emily?" she guessed.

Steve nodded. "But I've got time for a cup of coffee. How about you?"

"I'm due for one."

Together they walked to Joanie's office. While Joanie settled Emily in a corner of the sofa with a drawstring bag of toys and returned two phone calls, Steve went down to the employee cafeteria and rounded up two coffees and a milk for Emily. He returned with a tray in hand and sat down, noting how fresh and pretty Joanie looked, her hair glowing golden in the morning light streaming through the window.

Joanie frowned pensively as she stirred a lavish dollop of cream into her coffee. She sat down behind her desk, crossing her legs at the knee. As her skirt hiked up slightly, exposing a slender expanse of thigh, it was all Steve could do not to take her in his arms.

"How's your morning been?" Steve asked.

"Not so good." Joanie took a sip of coffee.

Steve noticed Joanie looked disconsolate. Her baby blue eyes, so like Emily's with their thick fringe of long, gold lashes, lifted to his.

"It occurred to me last night that Fiona wasn't necessarily Emily's mother. She could be a friend or relative. Fiona could even be an alias for someone else. So I did a global search, looking for people who had requested cribs in their rooms during their stay. And from there, I looked at the types of requests the guests made of the front desk while they were here, because we put all that on computer."

This was news to Steve. "Everything?" he asked.

Joanie nodded. "And we also keep records of any problems that occur. You know—" she waved a hand in his direction "—if someone gets careless or damages one of the rooms in some way. Or if they have a dispute about a bill or want to hire a sitter for their children while they have an evening out. It's all there, under the guest's name. Here, I'll show you."

Joanie typed in Cunningham, Bradford W. on the computer keyboard that sat on the far corner of her desk. Steve read: "October 10, 10:00 a.m. Room service request made by Marilyn Cunningham. Scones and a pot of coffee—decaf." Below that were other requests made during the Cunningham family's stay: a deep-sea fishing lesson for the son, a request for a wake-up call by the father, a golf lesson for the mother and son together and half-a-dozen other room-service requests.

"Boy, this is detailed," Steve said.

"And it's very helpful, too, because if I look at these records and see there's a big interest in deep-sea fishing, I can let them know about available charters in the area. And if there's any dispute about the bill later on—you know teenage children ordering room service or making long-distance calls their parents don't know about—then we can pin it down for them."

Steve glanced behind him to make sure Emily was okay; she was happily pulling apart some interlocking plastic blocks. "So you looked through all the records," he said, turning back to Joanie.

"Yes." She put her elbow on the desk and rested her chin on her fist as she scowled at the screen in front of her. "Only this time I was looking for any babies named Emily."

Steve reached out to untangle a curly strand of her hair that had gotten tangled in the tiny gold hoop earring she wore."Did you find anything on an Emily?" he asked, moving to sit on the corner of Joanie's desk facing her, so he could see her and Emily with equal ease.

"No, nothing." Joanie rubbed the back of her neck, her frustration obvious. "I'm going to work on requests for baby bottles and diapers next."

Steve moved around her to knead the tense muscles. "But you don't have much hope you'll find anything, do you?"

Joanie closed her eyes and, head thrown back, leaned into his touch. "No, not really."

Aware that her muscles had relaxed and that both he and the skin beneath his hands were getting entirely too warm, Steve dropped his hands. "So what next?" he said to Joanie.

"I'm not sure." Joanie stood, suddenly looking as restless as he felt. He didn't know whether it was the small size of her office or just the fact they were both so tall, but he felt hemmed in.

Joanie sighed and lowered her voice to a whisper. "The more time that passes, the more I think she has simply been abandoned to me, for whatever reason." Her voice dropped another emotional notch. "And that, in turn, means that I need to take care of her, Steve."

"Even though technically she isn't your responsibility?"

"Yes." Joanie searched his eyes. "You understand that now, don't you?"

He nodded. "I desperately wanted Emily to be ours and I just didn't . . . I mean . . ." Steve paused before going on. "But whatever the case, she's here now—with us. She needs us, Joanie." *Just like I need you.*

Joanie was silent a moment, her expression clouded with turbulent feeling. It was as if she wanted him to want her, Steve thought, and she didn't. As if she wanted them to be connected by Emily, and she didn't.

The phone on her desk buzzed.

Tearing her eyes from his, Joanie reached for it. "Hi, Liz. Yes. I'll tell him." Joanie cupped a hand over the receiver. "Liz says her grandmother can see you now in her suite."

"Great," Steve said. "Tell her I'll be right there."

At the mention of someone leaving, Emily looked up and said, "Bye-bye?" Joanie lifted Emily into her arms.

"Yes, honey, Steve is going bye-bye," she soothed in a loving voice.

Emily held out her arms to Steve. "Kiss?"

"Kiss," Steve repeated as he bent to kiss Emily's baby-scented cheek and the top of her curly blond head. Then, unable to resist, he bent and kissed Joanie's cheek and the top of her head, too. Her hair was soft, fragrant and scented with the intoxicating floral bouquet of her signature perfume. Memories of the kisses they'd shared the one night they were together hit him full force in the gut. It was all he could do to step away from her.

It pleased him to note he wasn't the only one affected by the brief, searing contact; Joanie looked a little shaken, too.

She drew a quick breath, took her own step back, Emily still held lovingly in her arms. "I'll see Emily gets some lunch and then I'll take her outside to play," she said. "You have to be at the conference luncheon today, don't you?"

Steve nodded, knowing he had to get out of there or he'd never want to leave. He touched Emily's hair one last time, smiled down at her, more love than he'd ever expected filling his heart.

He knew that Joanie was watching him, and he also knew that his action wasn't reassuring her. From the look on her face, it had hit her just the opposite way.

What now? he wondered, puzzling over her unexpectedly wary reaction. Was she bracing herself for a custody battle over Emily if Emily *had* been permanently abandoned, as they were beginning to suspect? Or just wishing that she—and/or Fiona—had never alerted him to Emily's existence? Only time would tell.

"MINE!" EMILY YELLED at the top of her lungs, grabbing her sturdy orange dump truck from the only other child on the small playground next to the swimming pool.

"No! Mine!" a carrot-topped little boy slightly older and larger than Emily shouted back. He grabbed the truck with his chubby little hands and gave it a determined tug.

Joanie shot the boy's mother a nervous look. She wasn't sure what to do in situations like this, having never been in them before, but working for peace seemed a sensible thing to do. "Emily, honey, why don't you share your truck?" Joanie suggested, moving off the wooden park bench to referee the fracas in the sandbox.

"Aaron darling, please give Emily her truck back," the embarrassed mother—and hotel guest—said.

"No!" Aaron shouted, and tugged even harder.

Emily let out an outraged yell that could be heard, Joanie was certain, by the conference attendees streaming out of the hotel. Joanie glanced in that direction. Sure enough, Steve was with the group. He was flanked by Phoebe and Dennis, as well as several other college students. All had turned and were looking in the direction of the shrieking toddlers. He frowned in her direction, as did Phoebe Claterberry. She said something to Steve, who shook his head, then smiled and said something to the others. Pivoting, he headed back for the hotel and disappeared inside.

Meanwhile, the toddlers continued their argument. "Me play!" Aaron hollered.

"No, mine!" Emily screeched. Hand flat on Aaron's chest, Emily tried to push him away. Before Joanie could do much more than start to react, Aaron lost his balance and tumbled backward.

"Oh, my gosh! Emily!" Joanie reprimanded, scrambling to help the little boy up.

Red-faced and wailing, he pushed her away and ran to his mother. "I am so sorry," Joanie said.

"No, *I'm* sorry," the woman said. "Aaron knows better than to try and take someone else's toy."

"There's no reason why they couldn't share," Joanie said. She knelt in front of Emily, who was hugging her dump truck with both arms. "Emily, it's wrong to push someone. We don't do that. If you can't play nicely, we're going to have to go inside," she said gently but sternly.

"Maybe this will help," Steve said from behind them.

Joanie and Aaron's mother turned. Steve had two sandbox play kits in his hand. Joanie knew they'd come from the Bride's Bay gift shop.

He knelt in front of the kids. "Look what I have for you guys. Shovels and sieves and bright red buckets. And look, even funnels." He handed each child an identical net bag of toys.

"Aaron, what do you say?" his mother prodded.

"Thank you," Aaron said.

"Emily?" Joanie prodded.

"T'ank ooh," she echoed obediently.

As the two toddlers sat down in the sand and began working the toys out of the bags, Steve picked up the dump truck unobtrusively and hid it behind his back. "I'll just get this out of here," he whispered to Joanie, already gliding off as soundlessly as he had appeared.

Joanie watched Steve head back to rejoin the students. Phoebe glanced again at Emily, and then turned her attention back to Steve.

"Was that...who I thought it was?" Aaron's mother asked in awe.

"Yes. Steve Lantz, the Olympic athlete."

"He's a natural dad," the woman murmured.

"Yeah, I guess you're right," Joanie said, watching as Steve and Phoebe separated from the rest of the group and sat down beneath an umbrella at a poolside table. Clipboard in hand, Phoebe continued talking seriously to Steve. Both kept glancing almost surreptitiously at her and Emily as they talked.

Joanie knew they were probably discussing the events scheduled for the rest of the conference. Steve would be participating in some but not all of the activities, and he probably needed to be updated on any last-minute changes. At least Joanie hoped that was all it was, because she needed to be able to trust Steve on every level to even think of starting up with him again.

"NOT EATING AGAIN?" Steve asked Emily at dinner-time. He'd just walked into the employee cafeteria, where the grumpy toddler was seated in a high chair stubbornly ignoring her food.

Joanie said worriedly, "She's got to be hungry—she hasn't eaten anything in at least six hours."

"And we've tried just about everything," Columbia added.

Steve looked at the two women. "Have you tried frozen vanilla yogurt and pureed fruit?"

"No, but I'll give it a whirl." The head chef went back into the hotel kitchen.

"What made you think of that?" Joanie asked.

Steve shrugged and smiled, albeit a little mysteriously, Joanie thought. "Everyone likes milkshakes and fruit 'smoothees.' And if the new teeth Emily's got coming in are hurting her, they should feel soothing on her swollen gums."

"You're probably right," Joanie said, still sure something was up.

"You're right," Columbia said moments later, when Emily hungrily gulped the first spoonful of her shake, then opened her mouth for another bite. "That did hit the spot."

"I thought you didn't know much about babies," Joanie murmured.

"I'm learning," he said.

So it would seem, Joanie thought, noting how handsome he looked in the white long-sleeved shirt and khaki trousers. Just what she needed. Did he have to look so gorgeous and energetic at the end of a long business day?

"What are your plans for this evening?" he said casually, dropping into the chair beside her.

Joanie sighed and rubbed the flat of her hand across the crease in her white slacks. "Laundry. I had to purchase clothes from the gift shop for Emily just to make it through the day. Could you baby-sit her while I do the wash, or are you expected at the conference dinner tonight?"

"I have an open invitation to join the group at any time, but I begged off this evening so I could spend it with you and Emily. So. Where do you want to camp out?" Steve's gaze roved her sailor-collared navy sweater with its white knit tie. "Your place or mine?" He moved his gaze to hers.

She flushed at the approval she saw in his eyes. "Mine. That way if Emily gets sleepy, we can just put her to bed in her crib."

Steve watched as Emily finished the last of the yogurt shake. "No further word from Fiona, I guess?"

"No." Joanie regarded Emily wistfully as she washed her sticky fingers and face with a warm washcloth. Steve helped her get Emily out of the high chair. They dispensed with their dishes, then headed outside, past the pool and the playground to the staff quarters in the converted stables. Steve carried Emily in his arms, her head resting on one broad shoulder.

"And at this point," Joanie continued confidingly, her steps effortlessly matching Steve's, "I'm beginning to be afraid there won't be any word. On the other hand—" Joanie reached up to stroke Emily's tousled curls "—Emily is so cute and sweet and obviously so well loved, I can't imagine anyone leaving her for long."

"I know what you mean." Steve paused as Joanie unlocked the door to her unit. With his free hand, he opened the door and held it for her. "Do you think maybe we should take an ad out in the local papers?"

"Saying what?" Joanie asked as she gathered up the soiled baby clothes and a few of her own, and put them in a small wicker laundry basket.

"'Fiona, Emily needs you. We need you.' Something like that."

Joanie added a container of detergent and fabric softener to her basket. Steve had a good idea, to be sure, but it was also, Joanie felt certain, a waste of money, time and effort.

"What guarantee would there be that Fiona would see an ad, or if she did see it that it wouldn't somehow make her feel pressured and scare her off?" Joanie asked practically.

Steve shrugged. "None, but it's better than doing nothing."

Joanie picked up the laundry basket and balanced it on her hip. "We don't know for certain that Emily *has* been abandoned, Steve." Even though it was beginning to seem as if she had.

"But if we did know," he persisted softly, boxing her in and looking down at her in a way that made her pulse race, "would you want to raise her?"

It was an honest question, and it deserved a truthful answer. Slowly Joanie nodded. "Yes," she said. "I would."

THE PROBLEM WAS, Joanie thought as she put the baby clothes in the washer, added detergent, set the dials for warm water and switched on the machine, that she was not the person who should be bringing Emily up. Emily needed a mother and a father and a good home. Not a single parent who knew even less than someone like Steve—an avowed novice—about caring for children. And not someone who would be juggling work and baby and wondering all the time if she was doing the right thing.

Joanie knew Steve found this all very romantic and exciting, but the romance and the excitement would fade with time, and then what? Joanie recapped the detergent bottle. Would Steve turn to another woman as he had before? Would he lose interest in Emily, as well? And how would Emily handle that? After all she'd been through, the little girl didn't need to be abandoned on that score, too. Besides, she and Steve couldn't just pick up where they'd left off as if nothing had happened, could they?

"Ms. Griffin? I thought that was you."

Joanie whirled around to see Frances Flannagan standing in the open doorway of the staff laundry. As usual the white-haired guest from the Midwest looked a little lost, as if she still wasn't quite sure how to handle the idea of vacationing alone.

"Hi, Mrs. Flannagan," Joanie said. "How were those golf lessons I set up for you?"

"Oh, they were wonderful, thank you. I really like my instructor." Mrs. Flannagan transferred her old-fashioned pocketbook from one arm to the other. "I have another session set up for tomorrow. How's your day been? Did they ever find that little girl's family?"

Joanie smiled. It seemed the whole resort was talking about little Emily. "No, not yet," Joanie reported. "But we're working on it."

Mrs. Flannagan pressed a hand over her ample bosom. "I thought surely by now that the child and her family would've been reunited."

Joanie recapped the bottle of fabric softener. "Me, too."

"Where is she now?"

"Steve Lantz is baby-sitting her, although I don't know how much longer I'm going to be able to depend on him to shoulder a good deal of Emily's care. After all, he has his own work and responsibilities." And sooner or later her assistant, Jerry, was going to get tired of filling in for her.

Joanie paused, her next idea occurring in a flash. Certainly it wouldn't hurt to inquire. "I don't suppose you'd be interested in baby-sitting Emily?" she asked Mrs. Flannagan.

"Oh, dear, I'd like to, but to be perfectly honest I don't think it'd be wise." Mrs. Flannagan held up two rather arthritic-looking hands. "I'm not as fast or agile as I used to be, and children that age can be very active."

"I see your point." Joanie agreed. "Emily *is* quite a handful." She grinned, realizing in retrospect that her idea had been a little crazy, although she could still see the kindhearted but obviously lonely Mrs. Flannagan and the spirited little Emily getting on famously. "And we don't want you running out of energy on your vacation," Joanie concluded, reassuring the older woman.

Mrs. Flannagan waited while Joanie relocked the laundry door. "You off tonight?"

"Yes. What about you?" Joanie fell into step beside her. "Do you have plans?"

"I'm going to have dinner with some of the women I met at the bridge tournament." Mrs. Flannagan glanced at her watch. "Which reminds me, I better get going."

"Have a nice time." Joanie waved her off.

"You, too." Mrs. Flannagan headed in the direction of the hotel.

Joanie paused just outside her quarters and looked through the window. Emily was seated on the floor talking animatedly on her toy telephone. Steve was sprawled on the floor next to her, his back against the sofa, his long khaki-clad legs spread out in front of him. He had a paperback in his hand and was reading.

Both looked so happy and content Joanie found herself smiling. Maybe she was making too much of this, she thought, expecting happy endings right away. Maybe she should just accept what Fiona had done, in leaving Emily with Joanie, and take it one day at a time. After all, Emily's presence had shown her a whole new side of Steve and had given them something mutual to care about, to boot.

Still smiling, Joanie walked into her unit. To her surprise, Steve's hands were empty and he appeared to be doing nothing at all. That was strange, Joanie thought. She had just seen him reading. "Where's your book?" she asked.

A beat of silence was followed by his too-innocent look. "What book?" Steve asked.

Joanie knew that look. If she wanted to know what mischief he'd been up to, she would have to discover it for herself. She grinned, her own senses igniting, as she said, "The book you were reading just now. Where is it?"

Steve's brow furrowed. She knew he was feigning confusion.

Yes, something was up, something he'd rather she not know about. She gave him an admonishing look. "Steve, I saw you."

"Oh. Yeah. *The Cat in the Hat.*" He reached up to the sofa seat and brought the Dr. Seuss to his lap. "Yeah, I was looking at this a while ago," he said.

Joanie knew he'd been reading a thick paperbook, not Dr. Seuss when she glanced through the window. "Uh-huh." She sat down in the rocking chair opposite him, still trying to decide what to do.

"Want me to read it to you?" Steve offered. The laughter in his eyes charmed her, but she told herself sternly that she had to resist him. They were together now for Emily's sake. Nothing more. At least not yet. Not until she was sure she could trust him to actually be all he seemed. "Sure now?" he teased, in a parody of a Southern drawl. "I'm a very good reader."

Joanie shook her head and tried not to laugh. "No thanks."

Emily scrambled to her feet and toddled over to Joanie. She thrust her toy phone into Joanie's hand.

Joanie grinned and put it to her ear. "Hello! Hello!"

Emily giggled riotously and pulled the phone back. "'Lo! 'Lo!" she parroted into the receiver.

"Want me to go down and stay with the clothes while they finish?" Steve asked, bracing one strong arm over his bent knee.

Again Joanie shook her head. "The clothes are in the staff laundry room, which is accessible only by key. They'll be okay."

"Do you want to give Emily her bath now?"

"It's a little early yet." What Joanie really wanted to know was where he had put whatever it was he'd been reading. Inspired with a way to find out and simultaneously solve a problem she'd run into earlier, she got up from the rocker. "By the way, have you seen a puzzle piece that has a duck on it? Emily seems to have lost it."

"No, but it's got to be here somewhere," he replied.

While Steve looked beneath the end table and around the base of a potted plant, Joanie searched behind the pillows on the sofa. It wasn't there. She felt between the cushions. Not there, either. Nor was there any thick paperback book. "Would you mind looking beneath the sofa for me?" she asked.

"No problem," Steve got down on his hands and knees and lifted the sofa skirt. "Nothing here," he said.

"You sure?" Joanie got down on her hands and knees and looked, too. She scowled in frustration. She'd been sure that was where he'd stowed his book. Abruptly Steve grinned. He withdrew the missing puzzle piece from inside Emily's shape sorter. "Here you go."

"Thanks." Now what? She still hadn't found his paperback.

"Listen, if you don't mind—" Steve stood "—I want to go over and check on something in my place."

"No problem," Joanie said, watching as he pivoted and headed for the door. And it was then, as she noticed the hem of his shirt flapping over his belt, instead of tucked neatly inside it, that she knew where he'd put the book.

"Oh, Steve?" she said, dropping her voice to a come-hither whisper just as he got to the door.

"What?" He turned, his expression surprised but wary.

Joanie glided forward. She wrapped her arms about his waist, her fingers closing on the thick paperback book. "What's this?"

Eyes alight with mischief, he grinned, reaching behind him to capture her wrists, but that didn't stop her, because she already had a hold of the book. She tugged it out of the waistband of his khaki trousers. Before she could bring it around to look at it, he gripped her forearms and forced her hands back behind her, so that the length of her body was pressed against the length of his. The feeling was almost more than Joanie could bear. Ribbons of sensation shot through her.

"Let go," he said.

She shook her head even as she felt the traitorous weakening of her knees and the heavy thudding of his heart. He was affected by their sensual tussling, too.

"*You* let go," she said breathlessly, angling her head and chest back as best she could.

Unfortunately her movement only served to plant her hips more firmly against his. Her face burned at the evidence of first his desire and then her own. *Oh, no. No...*

"Joanie..." he said warningly.

She wasn't going to let him dissuade her. "I want to see the book."

She struggled to free her hands, but he tightened his grip, still holding both her wrists and the book behind her. "No."

"I—"

"No," he said more firmly, and then his lips came down on hers, and she was kissed into silence, seduced by the tender magnetism that had made her his in the first place.

Joanie groaned, as the bright, energizing sensations overwhelmed her, and then his kiss turned warm, gentle, coaxing. She melted against him, sure she must be dreaming, yet knowing this kiss...this man...this moment...was all too real. She wasn't merely resurrecting a memory from the past—she was making a new memory. A memory she sensed she would hold on to for a very long time to come.

Shaken by the thought of how hard and fast she was falling for him again, she caught her breath and drew away.

He drew her back. His lips fastened on hers once more, commandingly this time, assuming control. No longer important, the book slipped from her fingers and thudded to the floor. He let go of her wrists. She moved them up, over his chest, around his neck. She held him close, wanting so much more...

Steve felt her surrender in the way she opened her mouth to his, in the way she gave in to the passion with a soft sigh. Holding her in his arms was like coming home again, like *being* home, and he wanted only for it to go on and on and on. Feeling as if they'd waited too long, wasted too much time, he wove his hands through the silk of her hair and brought her closer yet. It felt so right, kissing her like this. It felt so right, holding her in his arms, feeling the eagerness of her body close to his.

Emily, tugging on their legs, brought them out of it. Slowly, wonderingly, they broke apart, looked at each other, then looked down.

Emily was watching them with a cheerful, inquisitive look. "'Lo, 'Lo?" she said brightly, then handed the phone up to Steve.

Steve used his free hand to accept the phone. He kept the other wrapped snugly around Joanie's waist. "Hello, yes, I'm here. Having a great time, thanks. Want to talk to Emily? No problem. It's for you, Emily." Pretending the call was urgent, he handed her phone back to her.

Emily giggled and putting the receiver to her face in a lopsided manner, toddled back to the sofa and began to chatter away again.

Meanwhile, Joanie looked down at the floor and caught sight of the book Steve had been working so hard to hide. Quickly she scanned the title. *"Parents' Encyclopedia of Child Care?"* she asked, amazed.

Steve nodded and thought that maybe he didn't need to devise ways to wrangle his way into her life, after all. There seemed a chance it would happen naturally. "I found it in town, in the book section of the general store."

She considered him a moment. "Why didn't you let me know you had it so I could read it, too?"

Steve shrugged, feeling even more inept. "Because if you'd had the book, you wouldn't have needed me," he said, caressing her shoulders gently as he pulled her close once again. He pulled her even closer for a brief, hard kiss. "And I wanted you to need me as much as I need you."

It took a moment for Joanie to take in what he'd said. Another before she could find her voice. "Oh, Steve..." Joanie said softly, searching his eyes and finding a confusion and desire that mirrored her own.

"I know." He shook his head, stunned at the lengths he would go to have her back in his life for good this time. "It doesn't make any sense. It's too soon. It's too late. It's too crazy. It's all of those things and more, and it's also the way I feel, Joanie—" he took her hand and placed it over his heart "—in here. I want to be with you," he whispered urgently. "I want to be Emily's daddy."

Joanie marveled. *Because you wouldn't have needed me...and I wanted you to need me as much as I need you.* She'd longed to hear those words from Steve for such a long time. She'd just never dreamed they would be paired with his request to be Emily's daddy. This situation was incredible. It was also impossible.

"Oh, Steve..." Joanie said again, waiting for her heart to flutter back into place.

"Don't say anything now." He placed a finger against her lips. "Just... think about what I've said."

And once again, they were interrupted. "Hungee!" Emily shouted, looking up at them and pointing at herself. "Hungee!"

"NOT EVEN TRUCK DRIVERS eat this much," Steve said half an hour later as Emily polished off some diced chicken, pureed peas, corn-bread stuffing, cooked pears, a homemade biscuit filled with strawberry jam and two small cups of milk.

Seeing Emily was finally finished, he wiped off her hands and face and lifted her out of the high chair he'd brought over to Joanie's unit.

Beside him, Joanie cleaned up the room-service tray that had held Emily's late supper. "I guess your encyclopedia is right. Children will eat when they're hungry. And eventually they all get hungry."

"Right. We just shouldn't make a big deal of it when she doesn't, I guess," Steve said.

"You're probably right," Joanie said with a smile. "Maybe if we did a little less hand-wringing, she'd be a little easier to please sometimes."

"Maybe," Steve said. Again their eyes met. Joanie felt the tension in him mirror her own. What would have happened if Emily hadn't been there to interrupt them when Steve was kissing her earlier? Would they have made love? Joanie wondered, her emotions in turmoil. Would it be wise if they did? Or was she being a fool about him all over again?

"Do you think the clothes are dry?" Steve asked.

Joanie wondered at how fast and easily the two of them had become a team. But she shrugged and said, "Probably. If you'll go down to the laundry room and get them, I'll put Emily in the bath."

"Be glad to," he replied.

Joanie had already run the water and put Emily in the tub when Steve returned. Halfway through her shampoo, Emily began to yawn. Figuring the little girl had to be exhausted, Joanie hurriedly finished her bath and got her out of the tub. Steve had a T-shirt, night-time diaper and some footed flannel pajamas still warm from the dryer waiting when Joanie carried the towel-wrapped Emily into her bedroom and set her down in the center of the double bed to put her in her pajamas.

"Fine gak Mama?" Emily said, her eyes troubled as she looked up first at Joanie, then at Steve. She struggled to sit up before they'd even finished diapering her. "Bye-bye now!" she announced querulously.

"No, honey, it's time for a story and then time for bed," Joanie said, efficiently finishing the last of the snaps on Emily's pajamas and then helping her to her feet.

"No." Tears gathered in Emily's eyes. Her bow-shaped lower lip thrust out in a pout. "Me fine!"

Wordlessly Steve disappeared into the other room. He returned with Emily's blanket and her teddy bear. "Here you go," he said.

Emily clutched both to her chest. She looked past them, then back at them. "Fine gak Mama!" she sobbed, rubbing her eyes.

"Any idea what she's saying?" Steve said as Emily gave up trying to communicate with them and began to wail in earnest.

Joanie shook her head. She only knew that the depth of Emily's distress was bringing tears to her own eyes. Her heart going out to her, she gathered Emily close and tried to comfort her. But Emily wiggled out of her grasp. She climbed off the bed and went to the window, dragging her blanket and teddy bear with her. Tears streaming down her face, she looked longingly out the window.

"Fine gak Mama!" she whimpered over and over again.

Steve got down on his knees beside her and held out his arms. For the first time, Emily refused to go into them. Undeterred, he patted her shoulder gently. "Emily, let's rock."

She shook her head and continued to stare longingly out the window. "Gak Mama...gak Mama..." she said.

Tears glistening in her own eyes, Joanie looked at Steve. "What are we going to do?" she whispered when again Emily shrugged off their attempts to comfort her.

Steve disappeared into the other room and came back with Emily's jacket, another blanket, and her cap. His expression was hopeful. "I've got an idea."

Chapter Seven

"I think she's finally asleep," Joanie whispered as Steve drove the golf cart sedately over the moonlit golf course. Emily cuddled against Joanie's chest, her blanket and teddy clutched tightly in her hands.

"Want me to turn back?" he asked.

Joanie guessed they were a fifteen-minute golf-cart ride from the converted stables. "I think you'd better."

As Joanie dried the last of Emily's tears with the hem of her blanket, she thought about the contentment she felt whenever she held the little girl in her arms. The contentment she felt whenever she was with Steve. Was this what it would be like to be married and have a child of her own? A lot had happened over the past few days. Tumult had entered her previously serene life, but strangely enough, she didn't want to undo any of those changes.

"Steve?"

"Yes?" He turned toward her in a drift of masculine cologne.

"What'll happen if we don't find Emily's mother?"

"You mean if she doesn't come back for her?"

"Yes." Joanie's voice trailed off as she cuddled Emily even closer. "I was thinking I'd adopt her myself."

"That's great." Steve steered the cart with his left hand and curved his right arm around her shoulders.

"There's only one problem." Joanie sighed and leaned into him. "Tonight has shown me that being a single mother wouldn't be easy." She buried her face in the warmth of his brawny shoulder. "It'd be one thing if I had parents I could rely on to help out, but I don't."

"You've got friends, though." Steve stopped the cart and turned toward her. "And people—like me—who'd be all too happy to help out."

That was true. But right now she had to think about Emily, Joanie told herself firmly, and the possibility that Fiona had left the precocious toddler's life for good. Why? Because Fiona thought, as did many other people, that Emily belonged with Joanie for now and perhaps forever. "So you think I should go for it—if it comes to that?" Joanie asked Steve uncertainly. "And publicly make Emily my own?"

Turning abruptly serious, he said, "Yes, I think you should do everything in your power to keep her."

Joanie sighed. She had the feeling all this sounded a lot easier than it ever would be to pull off. And yet she liked the idea. Emily needed her. And Steve, well, somehow he seemed to be a part of this equation, too.

But she didn't want to be too hasty. She'd gotten herself in trouble before by following her heart, instead of her head. "Assuming of course that Fiona doesn't come back for her," Joanie amended quickly.

Steve nodded, but it was clear from the skeptical curve of his lips that he didn't see that happening, not with the way events were unfolding. "You can count on me, Joanie. I promise you that."

He leaned forward to brush a light kiss across her lips, a kiss that seemed to say she *could* count on him, not just now, but for a long time to come. Shaken, Joanie drew away. Once again, he was moving too fast for her, but very much in a direction she wanted to go. She wanted a family of her own. She wanted Emily. *And Steve.*

Looking more content than Joanie had ever seen him, Steve started the cart up again.

As they rode in silence, past the golf-course clubhouse toward the staff quarters, the direction of her thoughts brought Joanie up short. Taking care of Emily with Steve was fun, challenging and satisfying in a way unlike any she had ever felt, but it wasn't a situation that was bound to continue for the long haul. Not like this, anyway. She had to remember that, she cautioned herself firmly, and not turn this into something more than what it was—a temporary crisis, generated by Fiona. Emily already had a home, a home she missed desperately, as evidenced by her crying jag tonight.

Unfortunately that knowledge did nothing to cut short Joanie's daydreams about the situation. Except that in her daydreams she was married to Steve, and Emily was not an orphan any longer but their child, free and clear of any gossip and scandal.

Oblivious of her secret thoughts and desires, Steve parked in front of Joanie's quarters. By the time they took Emily, her blanket and teddy bear inside and put Emily gently in her crib, Liz was at Joanie's door.

"What's up?" Joanie asked, almost glad of the interruption as she invited Liz in. Things were getting altogether too cozy for comfort between her and Steve.

Liz smiled affably. "I thought I'd baby-sit for Emily and give you two a break from the responsibility for a few hours."

Joanie looked at Steve. It was still early, only nine o'clock. Neither she nor Steve had to work the rest of the evening. Nevertheless, she wasn't sure she wanted to go off with Steve. She was already fantasizing enough about them as it was.

Joanie folded her arms. "That's really sweet of you, Liz—"

"Nonsense. I owe you many favors. Besides—" Liz released a beleaguered sigh "—I told my grandmother I'd be over here helping out with Emily."

"Problem?" Joanie guessed intuitively. She knew Liz loved, admired and respected her grandmother. She also resented the fact that Elizabeth Jermain had a tendency to want to run Liz's life with the same conviction and determination she had run Bride's Bay all those years. Liz, since taking over as manager of Bride's Bay recently, had to constantly struggle to keep her own identity as a woman separate from her grandmother's idea of what a Jermain woman should be.

Liz tossed off her suede-collared riding jacket and sank onto Joanie's sofa.

"So what have you been up to lately?" Joanie asked. Liz wasn't dressed to baby-sit. She was dressed for a midnight ride on Bride Bay's horse trails.

Steve surveyed the jodhpurs and boots Liz was wearing. "I'd like to know that, too."

Liz smiled at them mysteriously. "Never you mind about that. Besides, I came over here to get away from questions. You two just get going and have fun until midnight. I'll hold down the fort here."

Steve looked at Joanie, the corners of his mouth curving up. "Want to go over to the clubhouse?"

"Actually..." Joanie sighed, looking down at the rumpled business suit she had yet to have the opportunity to change out of. Getting into casual clothing and running shoes sounded like heaven to her. "I'd like to get some exercise."

His eyes glittered with anticipation. "You still run on the beach?"

"Every chance I get."

Steve stepped closer and her skin registered the heat. Hands on her shoulders, he grinned in a way that sent Joanie's pulse skyrocketing.

"Race you into your jogging clothes," he teased, guiding her toward her bedroom door.

Maybe she did need to run off some of this adrenaline, she thought. Scarcely breathing, she glided off.

When she went outside in a pink T-shirt and white shorts, Steve was already waiting for her. His muscles rippling beneath his plain gray T-shirt and matching shorts as he stretched out, he looked every inch the Olympic athlete he was.

"I won."

"Maybe, but I already stretched out inside," Joanie said, darting past him with a laugh.

He caught up with her in moments. They kept pace with each other as they jogged past the road that circled Jermain Island, through the grassy knoll beyond it and down to the beach. Moonlight shimmered on the water, waves lapped against the shore, a balmy breeze ruffled their hair. On and on they ran, past the beach spa and the wilderness preserve, all the way down to the southeastern end of the island, where the lighthouse rose above the shore in majestic splendor. The pace was a little faster than what Joanie ordinarily kept, and she was beginning to feel it.

Steve slowed and pointed to the lighthouse. "Does that belong to the hotel?"

"Yes."

He moved closer to her, all six foot six of him brimming with a curiosity that was distinctly male. And distinctly disturbing. "Can we go in?" he asked, the longing on his handsome face plain in the moonlight.

Joanie nodded, already reaching for the master key she routinely carried with her just in case. "If you want."

He caught her hand and said, "I want."

The sound of his voice sent a ripple up her spine. Joanie's breath was rasping in her chest as she unlocked the door, but, to her annoyance, Steve wasn't nearly as winded as she. He gave her a sympathetic look.

"Want to rest a minute before we tackle the stairs?" he said.

Joanie shook her head and bounded up the circular staircase as if she hadn't a care in the world. "Don't need to," she fibbed.

But when she reached the top, she knew she'd about had it. Her knees felt like rubber, and she had a stitch in her side that made her want to double over and groan. Struggling to get enough oxygen into her lungs, she opened the second door and stepped out onto the upper balcony. Heart pounding, she leaned against the wall and gestured at the sea. "The view is magnificent," she puffed, "isn't it?"

Steve nodded. "It's beautiful." He turned and looked down at her affectionately. "But you should have told me I was going too fast for you."

Her pride had her responding before she could think. "The day you're too fast for me is never going to come, Steve Lantz," she mocked with a toss of her hair, and planted her hands on her hips.

His eyes lit up. "Well, I'm mighty glad to hear that, Ms. Joanie Griffin," he drawled in a bad parody of John Wayne. Grinning, he stepped closer and continued,

"'Cause I want you comfortable when you're with me. Comfortable in every way."

His gaze traveled over her, the desire in his eyes unmistakable as he gathered her in his arms. "Steve..." Joanie cautioned, but she was already melting against him, her eyes fluttering closed with a sigh.

"One kiss," he whispered against her lips, his hands stroking her back persuasively. "That's all I ask, Joanie. Just one kiss. One long, lazy kiss. And then we'll head back."

But she didn't want to head back, she thought. Not yet. And then his lips met hers. She felt his need and his yearning, and hers. Again and again in that endless kiss they drew from each other, Joanie yielding to him one instant, taking control the next. Their mouths tasting and touching, embroiling them in smoldering passion and pleasure. He shifted closer, his tongue parting her lips, touching the edges of her teeth and then returning in a series of soft, drugging caresses that robbed her of the will and the ability to think. Desire was flowing through her, more potent and mesmerizing than ever before. And it was then, when he had thoroughly claimed her as his, when she had moaned low and deep in her throat, that his kiss slowly, reluctantly, came to a halt—just as he had initially promised.

When they drew apart, she noted with satisfaction that he looked every inch as unsteady and thoroughly loved as she felt. "Darned if your heart isn't beating even harder now," he teased her wickedly, gently pressing a hand to her breast.

Joanie's hands were splayed over his chest. Her lips curved in a smile. Yes, her heart was pounding, but she could feel the pounding of his beneath her fingertips. "Yours isn't so slow, either."

He smoothed a thumb in a semicircle across her cheek. His mouth was very close and very tempting. "Think our hearts are trying to tell us something?"

Joanie moved her shoulders helplessly... wanting everything... risking so much... and yet, when all was said and done, still feeling so painfully alone. "We know very little about each other," she reminded him, wishing he didn't look so handsome in the silvery light. Wishing he'd never given her reason to mistrust him. Wishing most of all that she didn't *want* to love him...

His eyes darkened soberly. He took a moment to answer. "What do you want to know?" Now he, too, seemed wary.

Joanie paused. Here was her chance, and she was going to take it. She drew a deep breath, marshaling her resolve. "Why you asked Elizabeth Jermain for a job, for one thing."

Steve stared at Joanie in amazement. "How do you know about that?" He had planned to tell her the good news himself when the time was right.

"The news hit the Bride's Bay grapevine as soon as you left Elizabeth Jermain's suite this morning. The unofficial word is that you will be starting next week, once the mentoring conference is over."

"It's true." Steve drew Joanie down onto the circular bench that rimmed the outer wall of the lighthouse balcony. "Elizabeth's given me a six-month trial."

Joanie swiveled to face him. "You'd have to live here on the island."

"Somehow I thought that would make you a little happier," Steve said.

"Maybe it would if you didn't have such a reputation as a lady-killer." She vaulted off the bench.

"I admit there've been plenty of women chasing me," he said. "Nothing like a couple of million dollars attached to your name to make you attractive to the babes." He got up and joined her at the rail. "But I'm not interested in being wanted for that reason, and so, as soon as I see it's the money a woman wants and not me, I'm out the door."

"No doubt those hasty exits have only added to your reputation as a lady-killer, " Joanie said dryly.

"And it's a reputation that has followed me since the Olympics," Steve agreed.

Joanie straightened to look at him, her blue eyes glimmering with a faintly accusing light. "And yet, you haven't exactly gone out of your way to fight the unfair rep."

Steve shrugged. "I figured any woman who was really interested in me would want to see past the tabloid stories to the real me."

"Are you looking to be married?" Joanie asked.

Steve wrapped his arms around her and held her close. He slid a hand beneath her chin and tilted her face up to his. He looked down at her intently, aware he was betting everything on the two of them. "Yes, I am, and when I do get married, I want it to last, and there's only one way that will happen," he said hoarsely.

"Which is?"

"One, if my wife has faith in me—no matter how things might look on the surface. And two, wants the same kind of normal, down-to-earth life I do. My jet-setting celebrity days are over, Joanie."

It was clear from the expression on her face that Joanie had no problem with that; she, too, wanted the same kind of life. As for trusting him...to Steve's disappointed resignation, she was still working on that.

Time would help fix that, he decided. And so would their getting to know each other better. He lifted her hand and traced the underside of her wrist with his thumb. "And as long as we're on the subject of past loves, don't you think it's time you told me about your failed engagement to Dylan?" he asked.

Joanie's lip trembled slightly as she looked away from their joined hands and out at the sea. Her face filled with remembered despair, and he could tell even before she spoke that she was still hurting inside, that for her the healing would not be complete until she opened herself to love again.

"What do you want to know?" she said.

"Everything you want to tell me about what happened."

She met and held his gaze. "Months after my... fling with you, right before I came to Bride's Bay, I made the mistake of getting involved with a very wealthy guest." She pressed her lips together in silent regret, then seemed to continue by rote, "Dylan had come to Myrtle Beach after turning his back on the life his blue-blooded family wanted for him—which was heading the family investment company—to follow his dream of becoming a novelist. He had plenty of money and took a room in the hotel where I was working. I thought we were in love. By the end of the summer we were engaged."

"Then what happened?"

A furrow appeared between her brows. "His parents tired of his literary hiatus and cut him off. Dylan swore it didn't matter, but I knew it did."

She pulled her hand from his and stared at the moonlight glimmering off the Atlantic. "After two months of scrounging around to make ends meet, he realized he missed his old life and went back to it."

"And that was that?" Steve couldn't imagine any man turning his back on Joanie. A more beautiful, giving, gentle woman he had never met.

She shrugged, as if her acceptance of the situation could take away the memories of her hurt. "He said that his returning to his previous life-style wouldn't change things, that he would come back for me once he had straightened things out with his parents and told them about me...but in the end he realized that it would never work. I wasn't part of that life, Steve. Nor, in his family's estimation—or his, given my very middle-class upbringing—could I ever be."

"His rejection must've really hurt," Steve said, wishing he could do more to help.

Joanie moved restlessly, her fingers trailing lightly over the rounded edges of the balcony rail. "It did hurt." She stared at her fingers and sighed. "Worse, I felt like a fool for believing our relationship ever had a chance, given our different backgrounds and life-styles."

"And since?" Steve closed the distance between them. *Tell me you're ready to find love with me.*

Joanie whirled and faced him with a street-smart smile. She tipped her head back, what Dylan's treachery had done to her was revealed. "Since, as you might very well imagine, I've only dated ordinary people like myself."

Steve shook his head at her. "There's nothing ordinary about you, Joanie," he said, taking her into his arms again. He sifted his fingers through her hair, tilting her face up to his and staring down into her eyes. "You," he whispered softly, already lowering his lips to hers, "are the most incredible woman I've ever known."

His lips came down on hers, soft and sure. A disquieting shiver ran through her. Her knees trembled. Her heart took a little leap, and then she was throwing caution to the wind, following her instinct, twining her arms about his neck.

Steve reacted in kind, and his next kiss forced her lips helplessly apart. His hands moved sensuously in her hair, then moved lower in long, smooth strokes over her shoulders, down her spine, to her hips then up to her breasts.

With a tenderness she'd never imagined, his mouth trailed a provocative path down her neck. Breathtaking hunger and soul-deep need—she felt both in his kiss. His hands were on her breasts, caressing and soothing until her nipples swelled and peaked. Tremors of desire shuddered through her, further weakening her knees.

He murmured her name and she moved toward the sound, blindly seeking the touch of his lips on her breasts, the stroke of his tongue across her nipples. Again and again, until a fire built within her and her skin sang with the heat.

Wordlessly he swept her up in his arms and carried her inside the lighthouse. There, on the uppermost floor, with the moonlight streaming in through the open door, he tugged off her clothes, then his. She had missed him so much, Joanie thought hazily as he clasped her to him and they kissed again and again. She had missed this closeness, the intimacy of being with him, the thrill of being in his arms.

Steve hadn't expected this, but he had wanted it, he thought with a satisfied shudder, just as he had wanted her, heart and soul. For months now, he'd felt lost as a man and so alone. No more. Joanie was back in his life and this time he was not going to let her go. She'd been his ever since they'd made love and she always would be. He could feel it in the way she shifted beneath him and in the ardent way she returned his kiss. Awed by the beauty of her, the perfection of her supple curves, he explored every inch of her with his hands and then his lips. Lingering in the vee between her legs, he felt her tense and moan. He shuddered in response. He'd never thought he could be so aroused without losing control.

Joanie couldn't contain the wild pleasure he was evoking. The passion in him demanded a response and she was helpless to contain it, helpless against her need to have him straining for more, too. Wanting to drive him as she was being driven, she urgently explored his hard, hot length, letting everything she felt pour into her deliberately tantalizing touch.

Steve moaned in response. The next thing she knew she was flat on her back, their discarded clothes a soft cotton bed beneath them. He was moving over her, cupping her hips in his hands, whispering her name and bringing her against him.

And then they were as one. Moaning again, she shifted, wanting him closer, deeper yet. He obliged her with long, deliberate thrusts and she met each one with an abandonment of her own. Desperate for more, unable to get enough of her, he kissed her with an intensity that took her breath away. And then there was no more thinking, no more talking, only feeling, only the slow, inexorable climb to the edge, and the lazy inevitable slide back to reality.

Looking as if he would never get enough of her, he framed her face with his hands and kissed her again. With a sigh of contentment, she gave herself over to it. Her body molded to his, her breasts rubbing against the steely muscles of his chest, her thighs sweeping heat into his.

When he finally ended the kiss, he kept her in his arms. Her body still throbbing with the aftereffects of their lovemaking, Joanie shook her head and lamented softly, "I knew this was going to happen if I spent any time at all with you."

"So did I." But Steve didn't sound upset.

Joanie rose above him. "We're moving too fast, you know."

"No we're not. According to my calculations, we're right on schedule."

Joanie groaned, remembering Liz and Emily. It was time for a reality check. "And speaking of schedules—" Joanie reluctantly began to dress "—it's almost midnight. We promised Liz we'd be back by then."

"Saved by the clock," he teased, and he, too, grabbed his clothes. Their eyes met, and she knew this wasn't the last for them. Rather, it was just the beginning....

They finished dressing and descended the spiral stairs. Joanie locked the lighthouse and pocketed the keys.

Suddenly she was anxious to get out of there, to forget the reckless way she had just given herself to him and the trouble she may have gotten herself into by giving her heart to him again.

"Let's run back," Joanie suggested. Anything to use up the adrenaline flowing through her. Anything to keep her from going back into that lighthouse and making wild, passionate love with him all over again.

Steve grinned, looking just as full of energy and love-making potential as she was. "You're on," he said.

They broke into a mad dash up the beach, then across the road to the staff quarters. Joanie wasn't surprised when Steve caught her just short of her portico, and tugged her into his arms.

"You forgot one thing," he said breathlessly as their bodies collided, length to length.

Her heart raced. "What?" As if she didn't know. As if Steve would let their evening together end any other way.

"A kiss good-night."

Her lips parted on a groan. Their mouths blended in the space of a heartbeat. He dominated, she surrendered. She asked, he gave. The sound of voices moving down the walk forced them apart.

Joanie looked up at him, saw the wealth of feeling in his eyes and knew she hadn't really given him a chance before this. She would now.

Chapter Eight

No sooner had Joanie reported to work at the concierge desk at seven the next morning than she realized she'd left in such a rush that she hadn't given Steve half the instructions she should've.

"I forgot to tell you I promised Emily she could go out and swing this morning after breakfast," Joanie told him on the phone.

"We were planning on doing just that."

Joanie shivered as the bell captain came in the front door and a blast of cool air hit her. "It's a bit nippy out this morning. She needs to wear a sweater and a hat. Maybe a windbreaker."

"We've got it covered," he reassured her.

"And be sure she has a balanced breakfast when you take her to the employee cafeteria," Joanie continued, glancing over her own To Do list for the day. "Fruit, cereal, milk and minced ham or scrambled egg."

He laughed. "You're sounding more and more like a mom."

"I can't help it." Joanie twisted the telephone cord between her fingers. "I feel responsible for her." Actually, Joanie wanted to be there when the two of them had breakfast. If they hadn't all overslept by nearly forty-five minutes and been running late this morning, she would've managed it, too.

"Not to worry," he soothed. "We'll see you when you get off."

The thought of being together again with Steve and Emily, of being a family, filled her with warmth. Was this what it would be like if she was married to Steve and they had a child of their own? Was this what it would be like if Fiona never came back and she and Steve decided to take care of Emily permanently? Joanie admitted the idea was appealing.

"Steve?"

"Yes?"

"I—" Joanie bit her lip. Even she knew she sounded ridiculous. Nothing bad was going to happen to them. Nothing was going to separate them. Hadn't the time they'd spent on the beach proved that? Plus, no one had yet come forward to claim Emily. That meant something, too. "Just take good care of her, okay?"

"You know I will."

Joanie looked up to see Phoebe Claterberry heading straight for the concierge desk. "Steve, I've got to go."

"I'll talk to you later." They hung up.

As she approached the desk, Phoebe asked, "Did the posters and books arrive for the press reception this afternoon?"

"Yes. I signed for them yesterday. They've been put in the old schoolhouse storage room."

"Great." Phoebe smiled. "We've got a photographer coming over on the ferry with the kids and their parents who've been invited to today's program. We're expecting them at two this afternoon. The reception will run till around five, at which point we'll have a cookout on the beach."

Joanie nodded. "Columbia's got everything under control. We'll have the kids and their parents fed in plenty of time to make the seven-o'clock ferry back to Charleston."

"Do you know if Steve Lantz will be joining us on the beach?"

Joanie shook her head. "You'll have to ask him."

"No problem. I'll do so when I see him."

"You've got a number of messages from Dennis Wright. In fact—" Joanie nodded toward the sweeping staircase "—there's Dennis now."

"Phoebe!" Dennis approached, looking as preppy as usual in pressed khaki trousers, loafers and an oxford shirt. "I've been looking all over for you. Why didn't you get back to me?"

"Well, I meant to, but..."

"But what?" Dennis replied quietly when she didn't finish. "I think I have a right to know why you've been ducking me since we arrived on Wednesday." He paused, the hurt he felt apparent. "It's not as if we get to see each other all the time."

"I know, but..." Phoebe began as Steve entered the hotel lobby, Emily in his arms. Phoebe glanced their way and immediately seemed to lose her train of thought. "I had some things to work out," she said. "I'm sorry, Dennis, but I need to talk to Steve." She rushed off without a backward glance.

"Maybe she's just tired," Joanie suggested to Dennis.

"It's not like her to be so distant," he insisted with a troubled scowl as he watched Phoebe fuss over Steve and Emily.

"Maybe she just needs space," Joanie said, but already her mind was leaping on ahead to other possibilities. Possibilities she was sure Dennis knew nothing about.

"Maybe," Dennis said. But he didn't look convinced. And neither was Joanie. Dennis was right. Something *was* going on with Phoebe. The question was what.

No sooner had Dennis left than Joanie walked over to join Steve, Emily and Phoebe. Though still in Steve's arms, Emily had both hands tangled in the soft cotton fabric of Phoebe's beach sweater. She was babbling unintelligibly.

"Well, just so you know you're welcome to attend the cookout," Phoebe said. "You can bring Emily, too."

"I'll try and put in an appearance," Steve promised.

"Hungee!" Emily announced.

"In the meantime, I'm off to feed my buddy here." Steve patted Emily on the back, then grinned at Joanie. "Now what am I supposed to feed the little tyke again?"

Joanie ran through instructions.

"Not to worry. I won't let her s-h-a-m-p-o-o her hair with jam again." Steve and Emily moved off.

Phoebe turned to Joanie, musing thoughtfully, "He's very good with Emily, isn't he?"

Joanie nodded. One day Steve would make some lucky child a wonderful father.

"Listen, I'm sorry Dennis and I put you in the middle of things," Phoebe continued. "I didn't mean to make a scene."

"But you *are* deliberately avoiding him," Joanie said, as she and Phoebe helped themselves to coffee from the cart set up in the room for the conference attendees.

Phoebe nodded.

"I suppose it's safe to assume that the two of you go back quite a ways then," Joanie said next.

Sighing, Phoebe nodded again and confided quietly, "We fell in love at a regional conference during our freshman year of college while we were both being trained to work with at-risk youth. Even though we went to different universities, we managed to see each other off and on throughout the year, but it was hard. There were so many weekends we both spent alone that the spring of our sophomore year it became too much for us and we broke up."

Phoebe paused, then went on, "I skipped the national conference last year, because I thought it'd be too painful to be around him, knowing how it had been and how it was. But then I saw him again last Christmas, at another mentoring thing, and we talked and it was nice and then we started writing letters and... well, I know from the last couple of letters that Dennis has sent me that he wants to pick up where we left off before, like nothing ever happened to break us up. But for me it's not that simple."

Phoebe held a hand over her heart. "I just have this feeling, if he ever finds out everything I've been doing the past two years, that he's *not* going to feel the same way about me. In fact, he's probably going to be mad as heck at me."

"And so this is why you've been avoiding Dennis?"

Phoebe nodded grimly. "Because I'm so confused. Anyway, thanks for listening, Ms. Griffin. It really helped."

Joanie watched Phoebe stride off.

Was it possible, Joanie wondered, that *Phoebe* was Emily's baby? Phoebe was about the size of the person in the trench coat, scarf and glasses. Was it possible Phoebe had given birth to Dennis's child and not told him? Was it possible Phoebe had brought Emily with her

to the conference, intending to tell Dennis the two of
them had a daughter, but then chickened out at the last
moment and in a panic left Emily with Joanie? And used
the name Fiona? Phoebe and Fiona. The names were
similar in sound.

Joanie wished she could ask Phoebe outright if this
was indeed the case, but she knew she couldn't. First, all
Bride's Bay guests were entitled to their privacy. Second,
Joanie didn't want anyone else to be the brunt of the wild
speculation and innuendo she herself had been the past
few days—especially on such a flimsy excuse. If Phoebe
was Emily's mother, it would become apparent by the
time the conference ended. If she wasn't... well, Joanie
would just have to keep looking and praying for a reso-
lution that left Emily with a mommy and a daddy, plenty
of love and a warm, wonderful home. In the meantime,
Joanie decided to keep a keen eye on Phoebe Claterberry and Dennis Wright.

JOANIE GOT OFF WORK at two and headed straight to her
quarters. She walked in the door to find Steve and Emily
sprawled on the floor playing with a set of wooden
blocks. A college-basketball game was on television.

She dropped her purse into a chair, shrugged out of her
navy blazer with the Bride's Bay pin above the breast
pocket and kicked off her pumps. "Having fun?" It
certainly looked as if they were.

"You bet," Steve said, grinning, looking handsome
and relaxed in a white T-shirt, pine green corduroy shirt,
thick sweat socks and jeans. He, too, had kicked off his
shoes. Lounging with his back against the sofa, he drew
one knee up and braced a forearm on his thigh. "So." He
looked her over, seeming very glad to see her, and Joan-

ie's heart took an excited leap. "How was your morning?"

Joanie was glad to see him, too. She smiled, liking the intimate atmosphere. "Busy, which is pretty usual when we have a conference going on."

"You look tired."

"I am." Wearily, Joanie sat in the chair beside him.

He grinned, taking one nylon-clad foot in his hands. "Maybe this'll help."

Joanie drew a shaky breath as his fingers worked their magic, gently massaging her ankle and the arch of her foot. "Feel good?" he asked.

Joanie nodded. Too good she thought, just as the basketball game cut to a commercial. But not just any commercial, she realized, stiffening reflexively. This was one of Steve's commercials. And it was a doozy.

In it, he was naked from the waist up. Shaving cream covered the lower half of his face. With a bevy of scantily clad beauties watching, the Steve on TV leisurely began to shave. The Steve sprawled on Joanie's floor groaned and looked deeply embarrassed. The Steve on TV looked as if he was enjoying himself immensely.

And so did the bevy of beauties who were now running their hands over Steve's shoulders, chest and freshly shaven face.

Just watching, Joanie was filled with a very potent, if highly irrational, jealousy. This commercial represented everything she'd ended up thinking about him. In it he looked like a man who enjoyed the limitless, varied attention from the opposite sex a man in his celebrity position often received. Was she such a fool not to believe that he, like so many other famous athletes, indulged in such attention privately, as well? She looked over at him, uncertainty rising in her like the tide.

His massage changed to a grip. He knew what she was thinking and detested it. "Joanie—"

Suddenly Emily yelled, "Daddy!" and toddled over to the television set. Leaning forward, she began kissing Steve's face on the screen. When the image faded, she lifted her hand in a wave. "Bye-bye, Daddy!" she shouted.

"Daddy?" Steve and Joanie echoed in unison, shocked. Surely Emily was wrong. Yet Joanie was acutely aware that Emily had never called anyone Daddy before.

Emily nodded. She hugged her teddy bear to her chest and pointed to the TV screen. "My Daddy!"

Steve turned to Joanie, a questioning look on his face as if this proved what he had wanted to believe all along—that Emily was, in fact, their child.

Joanie felt herself flush warmly. Once again she was forced to defend the indefensible. "Don't look at me," Joanie said, arrowing a thumb at her chest. "*I* didn't teach her that."

"Well, neither did I," Steve shot back. He levered himself up to sit on the sofa corner next to her chair, then captured her wrist and held it firmly when she would've pulled away. "Although," he continued grimly, "Emily's assertion does tie in to a certain theory of parentage you and I have already talked about and dismissed— perhaps too soon, I'm now beginning to think."

Joanie jerked her wrist from his grip. "There's no way you're going to get me to admit to being her mother, because it simply isn't true." She lurched to her feet.

"Then why did she say that just now?" Steve demanded, getting up and following her around the room.

"How would I know?" Joanie threw up her hands in frustration and whirled to face him. "You were the one who was with her all morning while I worked. Maybe you taught her to call you Daddy.''

He arched a brow. "For what reason if it's not true?"

"To use her to get closer to me, since you know I plan to try to adopt her if we don't find Fiona soon."

Silence fell between them.

He studied her, apparently drawing his own conclusions. "It's not just Emily calling me Daddy that's gotten to you. You're upset about the commercial, aren't you?"

What else? Especially when I add the way Phoebe Claterberry seems to be ditching Dennis to chase you and pay attention to Emily. "Let's just say the commercial reminded me of some things I shouldn't be so quick to forget." *Like the fact that women find you irresistible. Like the fact I once found a naked groupie in your bed.*

"What you saw was only an ad. That's not who I am in real life." His impatience was evident.

Joanie moved restlessly to the window as Emily resumed playing with her blocks. "I know that," Joanie declared irritably, folding her arms tightly beneath her breasts.

But even as she spoke, she was having second thoughts about their passionate lovemaking the evening before at the lighthouse. She'd given herself to him with every fiber of her being, thinking all the while that she was one of the few women he'd ever been close to in his life. Only to discover... what? That the TV ads and his reputation as a lady-killer extraordinaire were closer to the truth than she wanted to admit? That he might have sired a child with another woman, a child he knew nothing about? And hence, another woman in his life?

All this added up to heartbreak and scandal, the two things she wanted most in this world to avoid.

Steve placed his hands on her shoulders and looked down at her gently. It was all Joanie could do to keep up her defenses and not melt into his welcoming warmth. "What are you thinking?" he asked softly.

"Just what I said last night." Joanie blinked back the tears gathering in her eyes. "That we're getting involved too quickly. And I promised myself I wouldn't do that this time," she finished in a low, strangled voice. *For all the good it's done me. Whenever I'm with Steve, my common sense flies right out the window.*

His hands tightened possessively. "Forget what Emily said just now. There's nothing wrong with what we're feeling!" he said passionately.

Wasn't there? Then why was the air between them heavy with desperation? Why did he look as if he was afraid he was going to lose her? "Then why can't we slow down a bit?" she said.

He dropped his hands and searched her face. "Is that what you want?"

Joanie drew a calming breath, forcing herself to ignore her impulsively romantic nature. She wet her lips. "I think it would be wise, yes."

Steve's sensual lips curved downward in frustration. "It's not going to change anything," he warned. "I'll still feel the way I do and so will you."

But what if another woman came between them again? Joanie wondered, feeling all the more shaken and confused. Would she survive the hurt this time? She barely had the last. She put her hands out to ward him off. "Steve..."

Getting the message, he put several steps between them. "All right. I'll back off—for now. But be warned, Joanie." His eyes lasered into hers. "I'm not a patient man. And I have no intention of letting you slip away from me again.''

STEVE SAID GOODBYE to Emily, who was just about ready to take her afternoon nap, then headed next door. He frowned at the pale blue envelope taped to his door. His name was scrawled across the front. Inside was a note written in calligraphy. He read it quickly, then grimaced, unable to believe what was written there after the conversation he'd just had with Joanie on that very subject. It couldn't be true. Could it? And if it was... Damn it, he was tired of playing these games.

Note in hand, he strode furiously back to Joanie's door. He had to knock three times before she answered. She let him in, a silencing finger to her lips. ''I just put Emily down for her nap,'' she whispered, pointing back to the bedroom, where Emily's crib was.

''Fine. Then we'll whisper,'' Steve said.

''What's put the bee in your bonnet?'' Joanie demanded.

Steve handed her the letter, still struggling to comprehend the enormity of what he'd read. He'd never felt so deprived or so elated, never mind both at once. Joanie's frown deepened as she recognized the stationery. She slanted him a perplexed look. ''What are you doing with Emily's note?'' She clasped a hand to her chest. ''I thought I had it.''

Steve swore inwardly. ''It's a different note,'' he explained.

Joanie blinked. ''A different...'' Her eyes widening, she looked up at him in confusion. ''When did you get it?''

''When do you think? Just now.''

''What does it say?''

He exhaled impatiently. "Read it and find out."
Joanie did as instructed and read aloud:

"Dear Steve,
Love is like wildflowers. It's often found in the most
unlikely places. Please do right by her because *Emily is your child.*"

Joanie's mouth dropped open and she gaped up at
Steve in astonishment. "How is this possible?" she demanded in a hoarse, shaken voice.

"I think you know—Fiona." Steve wasn't the least bit
amused as he addressed her by her alter ego. He knew he
should've seen this coming.

Joanie's slender shoulders stiffened. "I am not Fiona."

Steve nodded grimly and moved closer. "Oh, really?"

Joanie flushed, obviously recognizing danger when she
saw it. She moved away. "Look, I don't know who left
this note or who Fiona is, but if Emily is your child—"
abruptly Joanie looked as if she was going to cry "—and
I guess she is, then I think you should do right by her,
too."

"For the record, Joanie, I would *never* desert my own
child, wife or family, the way my father deserted my
mother and me when I was six, no matter what the situation." Nor would he ever have lied and deceived Emily's mother the way she had deceived him.

But Joanie wasn't thinking about that as she addressed him. "I'm glad to hear that," she murmured,
reining in her feelings.

Steve stared at her, still shaken to the core. "Is that all
you have to say?" he asked incredulously.

Joanie shrugged. "Well, I guess we could move the crib
over to your place, although that might upset Emily."

Joanie shot a troubled look at her closed bedroom door and bit her lower lip. "She's gotten used to staying here."

"Don't tell me you're still denying we have a child together," Steve said with deceptive calm. It was all he could do not to shake some sense into her.

Joanie's chin took on a stubborn tilt. She folded her arms on her chest and held them there like a shield. She glared at him a long moment, then said, "I'm not even going to answer that."

"Why not?" Steve baited her. "Afraid?"

"Confused," Joanie corrected.

"Well, that makes two of us. Unless, of course," Steve taunted, "you intend to let me in on your plans."

Joanie threw up her hands in frustration and stalked away from him. "What plans?"

Steve followed, hard on her heels. "Your hopelessly misguided attempt to bogusly introduce Emily to the community as an orphan who needs your love."

"Why would I want to do that?" Joanie whirled around so suddenly she almost ran into him.

Steve shrugged. This situation had stopped making sense to him two days ago when Emily had first been found. "Maybe because the Jermains had enough scandal when their son Rafe was branded a traitor to his country and lost at sea," he said. "Maybe because they refuse to have anything else the least bit scandalous connected to Bride's Bay, and you're afraid of losing your job if they find out you and I had a child out of wedlock."

Joanie raked both hands through her hair, pushing the wildly curling mane off her face.

They glared at each other in silence, their emotions raw as the truth unfolded. Eventually Joanie blew out a weary breath. She shook her head in abject misery. "The fact remains Emily was apparently left with me by mistake," she stated flatly. "Fiona was probably the woman in the trench coat I saw trying to break into your quarters that day by removing a window screen. She probably just parked Emily's stroller in front of my door to keep her out of view while she opened up your place. Only I scared her away. Because Emily was still in front of my door, instead of yours, everyone jumped to the wrong conclusions."

Steve felt the kind of pain he hadn't felt since the day his dad had abandoned him. As much as he hated to admit it, Joanie's theory made sense. If it was true, it meant Emily wasn't their child. Only his. And that fact could drive them apart as easily as it had once brought them together.

"At any rate, if she is your baby," Joanie continued numbly, "then you must know who the mother is, or at least who the biological possibilities are."

How much easier it would have been for him if he could have told her there was no one else. He turned away from her as regret washed over him. He paused for a long moment. "There's only one. Irene Martin, a sports reporter for *Swimmers' World* magazine. She interviewed me over Christmas break the winter I met you."

"So it was just a couple of weeks..." Joanie whispered, looking stricken as she put it all together.

"Before we met, yes," Steve finished grimly, when she didn't go on.

"I see." Joanie's voice was dull with hurt, and she turned away.

Suddenly Steve was desperate to explain. He caught her arm and swung her back around to face him. "While Irene was in Connecticut interviewing me, she got word that her parents had just been killed in a car crash in

Grand Rapids, Michigan, where they lived.'' He paused, remembering the horror of that night and how it had re-kindled his own feelings of loss where a parent was concerned. Looking deep into Joanie's eyes, he went on, ''Irene couldn't get a flight back to Michigan until the following morning. And she was devastated, as you might well imagine. I didn't know what else to do, so I stayed with her all through the night, and I made sure she got to the airport the next morning. During that time, I comforted her as best I could.''

Joanie regarded him in silence for a moment, then said, ''By making love to her?'' Her words were icy with disdain.

''She was crazy with grief, Joanie.'' Steve knew that it sounded like a lame excuse, and yet, given the same situation, he knew he would do what he had again. Irene had needed him, and on some level he had needed her. They had both been single, consenting adults, with no commitments to anyone else. And in the end it had only been a way to survive. He wondered if Joanie would ever understand that. He wondered if Joanie would ever *let* herself understand that.

''And then what happened?'' Joanie asked him, holding herself very, very still. ''The morning after?''

Steve tensed at the disbelief her sarcastic tone implied. Keeping his expression carefully implacable, he pushed on matter-of-factly, ''The next morning, we both knew it was a mistake, one we had no desire to repeat.'' He held Joanie's gaze as the world around them came to a complete and utter standstill. ''I put her on the plane home. And with the exception of one postcard from Irene, thanking me for my kindness, and the sympathy card and flowers I sent to her via the magazine, we never communicated again.''

Joanie hesitated. Steve could see she wanted to believe him; she just wasn't sure she should. And for that he damned her, too. "Then who is Fiona?" she whispered.

Steve wished he could say he didn't know. He shrugged helplessly. "Fiona could be Irene. Or she could be a friend of Irene's." Steve sighed. "I just don't know."

Joanie turned away. He moved behind her, his hands lightly cupping her arms, his voice low and urgent as he said, "You're upset with me, aren't you?"

Upset? Try devastated, confused, disappointed. She blinked back the tears gathering in her eyes and tried not to lean into his embrace. "I won't pretend that the thought of you with another woman, any woman, doesn't upset me," she replied, "because it does, Steve." And he needed to know that, just as she needed to know it would never happen again—not if the two of them were going to be together.

"Joanie, that was in December." Steve's voice was gentle as he turned her to face him. "You and I didn't even *meet* until January. I agree—making love with a virtual stranger isn't the wisest thing I've ever done—but I repeat, I have nothing to feel guilty about."

Joanie flattened her palms against his chest. "I understand, on an intellectual level at least, how and why you ended up in bed with Irene that night."

"But you're still upset with me," he guessed, stroking her hair.

"It's more complicated than that," she admitted. Just the fact Steve had been with Irene reminded Joanie of the night she'd found a groupie in his bed. She wanted to believe there was nothing to that. She wanted him to tell her that *all* those awful things she believed about him were not true.

"Tell me what you're thinking." Steve touched her arm, and when she didn't resist, he drew her fully into his embrace.

"That I want Emily not to be your child, so another woman will not come between us." Joanie leaned her head against his shoulder. The corduroy of his shirt was soft and warm against her face. "And yet, I don't want to lose Emily, and if Emily isn't your child—" Joanie drew back to look at him "—and I know she isn't mine, then chances are we will lose her, Steve." Sadly Joanie contemplated the future. Her eyes grew even more troubled. "Either way, it looks like there's heartbreak for at least one of us at the end of the line."

"Unless Emily has been permanently abandoned and just needs a home. In which case we could still give her one together," Steve said.

Joanie considered that for a moment, her feelings in turmoil. She did not want to give Emily back to Fiona at this point any more than Steve apparently did, but that did not mean Emily was theirs to keep. Maybe she was just Steve's child now. Or maybe she was Steve and Irene's. Maybe Fiona was trying to help the three of them—Steve, Irene and Emily—become a family. What then?

Steve held her against him as he waited tensely for her reply. And Joanie knew she didn't want to let Steve go any more than she wanted to let Emily go.

Finally she sighed. "The possibility of our keeping Emily with us permanently is a long shot, Steve. But you're right," she said softly. "Either way, we have to know the truth about who Emily's parents are. The sooner the better."

Chapter Nine

"I talked to the authorities," Joanie said as she let herself into Steve's quarters half an hour later. "I told them about the misunderstanding regarding the first note. They agreed to give us another three or four days to see what we can learn. What about you? Any luck?"

Steve nodded as he continued buttoning up the starched blue dress shirt he was planning to wear to the press reception that afternoon. "*Swimmers' World* magazine said Irene quit her job there two years ago February. They have no idea where she ended up. At the time she left, she was planning to take some time off to recuperate from the loss of her parents and straighten out their estate, maybe do some free-lancing."

Joanie sat on his sofa and watched Steve put on his tie. "Was Irene pregnant when she left?"

Steve sighed and sat down beside Joanie, stretching his legs out in front of him. "Not that her boss knew. In fact, he said she'd been losing weight that winter because she was under so much stress."

Pregnant women usually gained weight, not lost it, Joanie thought. Were they chasing down a dead end? And why did it matter to Joanie if they were? She'd known all along that Emily wasn't hers. Now Steve knew it, too. What Joanie hadn't bargained on was the possibility that Emily was Steve's child—with another woman yet!—or how shut out that made her feel. Soon Steve wouldn't need her at all. Nor would Emily.

Joanie pushed the troubling thoughts away. The future would come soon enough. She needed to concentrate on the present, as did Steve. Their situation, Emily's situation, had to be resolved. She faced Steve. "Now what?"

"I'll keep looking for Irene of course." Steve cupped her chin in his hand and studied her expression. "This bothers you, doesn't it?"

Joanie shrugged while the question settled over her and then decided to speak her mind. "I can't help but wonder what's going to happen when you find Irene."

Steve dropped his hand. His lips thinned unhappily. "I'm not in love with her. I never was. I thought I'd made that clear."

"What if mother and baby are a package deal?" Joanie was grateful her voice could sound so calm when her insides were knotted. "What if she wants you as Emily's daddy?"

"I can be that without being married to her," Steve said, taking her hand in his.

Joanie withdrew her hand from the tantalizing warmth of his. She was in too deep here, far too deep. "Are you sure?"

Silence fell between them as his confidence that everything would work out quickly and simply began to fade. He threaded his fingers through the rumpled layers of his burnished-gold hair and released an exasperated sigh.

"Look, let's just take it one step at a time, okay?"

The longer Joanie looked into Steve's eyes the more she knew he was right. There was no use borrowing trouble. If she was going to get her heart broken, that would happen soon enough.

"You're right, of course," Joanie said, drawing a deep, steadying breath. "Anyway, I was thinking if Irene did drop Emily off, or had a hand in it, she might be somewhere nearby. So I'm going to go up and check the central hotel reservation system for Irene Martin's name, and then all the home rentals in the area, here and on the mainland."

"What about Emily?" The chiseled contours of his face becoming more pronounced, he watched as she vaulted to her feet and began to pace.

"Liz agreed to come over and stay with her while she finishes her nap. She's with her now."

Steve nodded, stood and shrugged on a navy blue blazer. "I'm due over at the old schoolhouse for the press reception." He caught her hand and turned it over in his. Slowly, inevitably, their eyes met, held. "So you know where to find me if anything comes up."

Yes, she did. For now. But how long would that be the case if what he expected was true and he'd had a child with another woman?

THE PRESS RECEPTION went without a hitch. Recent graduates of the Charleston mentoring program and their parents, joined with the tutor/mentors in talking to the press. Cookies and punch were served while Steve autographed both posters of himself and copies of his biography, detailing his own struggle out of poverty, then posed for pictures with the kids invited to the celebration.

Once or twice, he saw Joanie dart in to check on how things were going, but he was so busy they didn't have time to talk. Finally, though, the press had left and the party had moved down to the beach. Only he and Phoebe Claterberry were left, and they, too, would be gone as soon as Steve had finished straightening up.

"You know, we could leave this for the housekeeping staff," Phoebe said, as Steve took off his jacket and rolled up his sleeves.

"I don't mind. Besides, it'll only take a minute. But you go on ahead," Steve said. "Join the others on the beach."

"No, I'll stay and help." Phoebe began stacking punch cups as he gathered up empty book and poster boxes, and flattened them for recycling. She was wearing a long, floral-print dress that fell well past her knees. "Actually it's kind of good that we're alone," she said.

It was? Steve thought, wondering if there was something to Joanie's jealousy, after all.

"Because I need to ask your advice," Phoebe continued pragmatically, in a way that immediately put him at ease.

Since winning a gold medal, strangers approached him all the time, and that number had doubled and then quadrupled with the second medal and endorsement contracts. Steve didn't know why people felt he had all the answers, but they did. "You're a swimmer then?" Finished with the boxes, Steve began rearranging the desks.

"No. I just need to talk to someone who really has it all together. Plus, I know you of all people must understand what it's like to be ambitious almost to a fault."

Steve grinned at Phoebe's on-target assessment of him. "That I do."

Phoebe came closer and, briefly forgetting all about cleaning up, sat down on the edge of a desk. Her feet dangled over the side in a way that made her look terribly young. "So here's my problem," she began, leaning forward earnestly. "I've had this dream for a long time, and I really, really want it come true. Unfortunately to fulfill this dream I'm probably going to have to leave someone I love behind."

Steve studied her briefly, then continued rearranging the desks into neat orderly rows. "I can see where that would be upsetting," he said.

Phoebe toyed with the ends of her long, blond hair. "With my graduation from college coming up next year, I'm going to have to make a decision about what to do with my future very soon."

"And you're torn about what this decision should be," Steve guessed, having gone through some of the same turmoil himself both while in college and after his first and second Olympics.

"Yes." Phoebe clasped her hands together in her lap. "You see, I want it all—husband, great job, a couple of kids. But there's no room in my life for the career I want now and my pursuit of a family at the same time."

Finished, Steve leaned against the chalkboard. He had worked with enough kids Phoebe's age to know they were prone to exaggeration. "Are you sure about this?" he asked.

"Positive. And there's a second problem, too," Phoebe continued, her guileless blue eyes looking all the more distressed. "Someone I love is going to be very hurt if he finds out what I've been keeping from him. I mean, I've known all along that I should have told him about what was happening to me, but I just couldn't. Not when he lives such a public life. I mean, if what I've been keeping from him the past two years, the way I've been kind of skulking around behind his back, came out, it could be a major scandal."

Steve wondered if Phoebe was seeing another guy on the side, whom the "someone" she loved didn't know about. She was talking so cryptically it was impossible to figure out what she meant, which was, he supposed with perplexed weariness, the way she wanted it.

Aware she was waiting for his answer, Steve pushed away from the chalkboard. "Well, here's what I believe. A person's family and loved ones ought to come first always, above everything else."

"Even if it means sacrificing what might be an absolutely stupendous career?" Phoebe asked.

"Phoebe, if your career means that much to you, maybe you're just not ready to get married and settle down. You're still very young. There's no law that says you have to get married at the same time you graduate from college."

"I know that." Phoebe jumped down from her perch and sauntered closer. "I'm just afraid that everyone else, from my parents on down to this person I love, are going to feel otherwise."

"Ah, parental pressure," Steve said.

Phoebe shrugged. "And spousal, or however you'd say it when you're talking about two people who aren't married. Not yet, anyway."

"Well, I think you should follow your heart," Steve said firmly. If he had done that and followed Joanie when she first turned her back on him, he thought, the two of them wouldn't still be at odds. Hell, they might even be married and raising their own family by now. And if he and Joanie were married, this situation with Irene and Emily might be a lot easier to manage.

"You really mean it?" Phoebe asked excitedly, moving nearer still.

"Sure I do," he said, pausing and looking down at her kindly. Phoebe smiled, looking for a second as if he'd just handed her a gold medal.

Just then there was the sound of the door opening. "Oh, gosh," said Phoebe, "there's Ms. Griffin, and she looks like she wants to talk to you. I guess I better head on down to the beach now." The student walked to the door, pausing momentarily to exchange pleasantries with Joanie, then sauntered off.

Joanie came closer. To Steve's annoyance, she seemed to have jumped to conclusions again at finding him alone in the old schoolhouse with Phoebe long after the others had left. But they were conclusions that could easily be put to rest. The question was, though, should he make explanations? Or insist she start trusting him implicitly, even without explanations, now?

JOANIE APPROACHED Steve, doing her best to hide the kick in the gut she'd felt when she saw him talking so intimately with the pretty college coed.

She knew she shouldn't be jealous. She was. She knew he'd given her no reason in the past few days to mistrust him. Part of her—the part of her that recalled their infamous past—mistrusted him, anyway. And that in turn made her angry at herself.

"What's up?" Steve asked.

Joanie worked to keep her emotions under control. "There's no Irene Martin staying anywhere on Jermain Island. Nor are there any Martins or any Irenes."

"What about the mainland hotels?"

"Nothing there, either. And I checked every place within a hundred miles on the system."

Steve studied her. "Any other messages for me?"

"No." Joanie noted he had some chalk from the blackboard smudged across the front of his shirt. "But I've been thinking…" She reached out and rubbed at the smudge that angled across his chest and one shoulder. "Has it occurred to you we may be chasing down the wrong woman?"

Steve grew very still beneath the light ministrations of her fingers. "What do you mean?"

Joanie reluctantly dropped her hand from the firm muscles of Steve's chest and shoulder. She gestured helplessly. "If anyone at the resort has been acting like someone who has just deserted a baby, it's Phoebe."

"Wait a minute." Steve caught Joanie's wrist. "We know from the note that the baby is mine. Assuming that's true, Emily can't be Phoebe's child, as well."

Joanie paused. "Then there was never anything, well, personal between you and Phoebe?"

Steve released his hold on Joanie abruptly. He looked irritated by her persistent questioning. "How could there have been? I didn't even remember her at first."

"And yet she stayed behind to talk to you alone."

"I'm a motivational speaker. That happens all the time." Steve crossed to one of the narrow windows and closed it. "People think that because I won a couple of medals I can tell them some secret that'll help them take charge of their life, too."

She watched as he picked up his blazer and shrugged it back on. "And can you?"

He gave her a penetrating look. "I can talk about working hard to fulfill a dream." His voice dropped a notch. "I can talk about going after something one slow, deliberate step at a time."

He closed the distance between them. He put one hand on the wall next to her ear and leaned in close. With his free hand, he touched her face, lightly brushing his knuckles from cheek to chin. The gentleness she saw in his eyes was enough to send her senses into a tailspin.

"You okay?" he asked, staring down at her.

"I don't know." Joanie jerked in a breath and raked her teeth across her lower lip. "This whole situation is making me a little crazy." She was having all sorts of weird thoughts. And that wasn't like her. In fact, she hadn't felt this way since the last time Steve was in her life.

He nodded. "The not knowing for sure what's going on is making me a little crazy, too," he admitted frankly. "If someone is going to slap a paternity claim on me, I wish they'd quit worrying about my reaction or anyone else's and just come forward." He leaned down to kiss Joanie's temple. "It would save us all a lot of grief."

Joanie splayed her fingers across Steve's chest, loving his warmth and his strength even as she was caught on the thin edge between temptation and common sense. "Maybe Emily's mother can't," she replied.

"Why not?"

Joanie swallowed around the sudden dryness in her throat. Aware this was something that had to be faced, like it or not, she lifted her gaze to his and forced herself to go on. "There could be tons of reasons. The potential scandal of it. Your reaction. Maybe Emily's mother left Emily with you the way she did so you'd have a chance to get used to being a father before she confronted you with what she'd done—I mean hiding her pregnancy from you."

Steve's eyes darkened to pewter. "You seem to have a lot of sympathy for this mystery woman," he noted.

Joanie lowered her gaze again and stared at his strong, corded throat. "I've had a lot of time to think about it," she defended herself. When she made to step past him, he laid his other hand against the wall on the other side of her. She was trapped in the cage of his arms, her back to the wall. His eyes roved her upturned face, lingered on the pulse beating madly in her throat, before returning to her face.

"Right now all I know for certain is that I want to get this matter settled so we can pick up where we left off," he whispered in a matter-of-fact voice that sent frissons of desire rippling down her spine, "and make plans to live happily ever after."

She felt breathless and confused. "Steve..."

He was taking way too much for granted. That Irene would be found, admit maternity and step aside. That the two of them would fall in love all over again and get married.

"What?" His hands fell to her shoulders. His grip wasn't gentle and his breath wasn't steady.

"Don't—"

"I have to do something to make you see how I feel," he said fervently, pulling her close.

Her heart skipped a beat as he lowered his mouth to hers. He took her lips with a rush of passion, kissing her long and hard and deep. She clung to him, reveling in the euphoric sensations sweeping through her. Only Steve had ever made her feel this loved and desired. Only Steve had made her feel that as long as they were together, they had everything.

Slowly they drew apart. Joanie knew that had they been anywhere else, anywhere safe and private, they would have made love again. That was the way it always was with Steve—as if she was caught up in a whirlwind.

But whirlwinds could be very destructive, she reminded herself sternly, and if he made love to her again and they were forced to part—for whatever reason—she would not walk away unscathed.

She went to move away, only to find herself held close again. She buried her face against his shoulder as she struggled to regain what little equilibrium she had left. His body was like a solid wall of support and understanding.

"Steve, please, this isn't a good idea," she murmured.

"Your newfound doubts about me are because of Phoebe, aren't they?" he asked.

Joanie lifted her head. Embarrassed, angry color filled her cheeks. "I admit that seeing her with you brought back a lot of old doubts."

"I can't help it that strangers admire me or want to talk to me," he murmured soothingly, stroking her hair.

"I know."

He caressed her cheek with the back of his hand. "Groupies and fans are part of any Olympic athlete's life. With time no one will know who I am, no one will care, and that will all fade."

But his good looks and his sex appeal wouldn't, not for a very long time, if ever, she thought. "Haven't you heard?" she asked shakily, turning her back on his tender touch. "Women age. Men just get better with time."

He closed his arms around her and brought her back against his chest. He buried his face in her hair, then turned her to face him. "You've got nothing to worry about, Joanie. My days in the limelight are over. I asked Elizabeth Jermain for a job here because I want a normal life for myself."

A normal life. How nice that sounded. Joanie closed her eyes. "I want that for you, too. But in the meantime, I need a little time." She swallowed and looked up at him. "I need some space." She needed to be able to think, while not noticing constantly how handsome he was, while not feeling the tender evocativeness of his touch or seeing the gentleness in his eyes.

He tightened his hands on her upper arms. There was no denying the possessiveness of his touch as he gave her a quelling look, rife with determination. "I'm not going to let you run away from me again, Joanie."

She knew how far Steve had gone to be with her, and she wanted it to work out, too. But she was afraid she was kidding herself with her hopelessly romantic notions. She was afraid she didn't know the real Steve versus the public gold-medal-winning Steve at all. And she was afraid that fear wasn't ever going to go away.

JOANIE MIGHT STILL BE there physically, Steve thought, but emotionally, intellectually, at least part of her was already running away from him again. He headed back to his quarters and changed into clothes suitable for the beach cookout, where he'd promised to make an appearance.

As he headed for the beach, he wondered if Joanie would ever let her guard down long enough to trust him completely. He knew that because of the way he'd grown up, his father's abandonment, that he could not live with Joanie if she had one foot out the door and was forever on the verge of leaving him. No, when he married, it had to be for keeps.

When Steve arrived, the barbecue was in full swing. Phoebe Claterberry was deep in conversation with Dennis Wright. Dennis had his arm around Phoebe's shoulders.

Columbia Haynes joined Steve briefly. "Think those two will work things out?" she asked.

Steve hadn't a clue. "One can only hope," he said. He knew it would put Joanie's mind at ease if Dennis and Phoebe were a "couple" again by the time they left.

Mindful of the time, Steve signed a few more autographs, gave words of encouragement here and there, then returned to the front desk in the main building to check his messages. To his surprise, Joanie was at the concierge desk.

"You're working again tonight?" He knew she hadn't been scheduled.

"I need to make up for the time I've missed the past few days." She smiled, the picture of cool efficiency. "You don't mind baby-sitting Em, do you?"

As if she even had to ask, Steve thought, irked. "Of course not," he said, knowing an excuse when he heard one. Joanie was avoiding him. Because of the way he'd kissed her in the old schoolhouse? Or because she just couldn't bring herself to trust him, not now and not ever. He pushed aside his uneasiness.

"So where's Emily now?" he asked.

Joanie gave him another smile, brighter and more efficient and more coolly impersonal than the first. "Liz took her to the staff cafeteria for some supper."

Steve straightened. He knew he should leave. He just didn't want to. He crossed his arms and lounged against the concierge desk. "Liz's really getting into this baby-sitting business, isn't she?"

"We all are," Joanie said, the new wash of ever deepening color in her cheeks belying the rounded perfection of her tone. "But then maybe that's not surprising." Her eyes met his. "Emily is an adorable child."

Steve was about to reply when Shad Teach stopped by the desk. He handed Joanie a key. "Cottage 3 is available again. Housekeeping's cleaning it now."

Joanie frowned. "What happened to Mrs. Flannagan?" she asked Shad.

"She checked out earlier today. One of the bellboys saw her to the ferry."

Joanie paused. "Was there some family emergency?"

"I don't know." Shad shrugged. "But when I talked to her on the phone, she didn't sound upset." He looked up to see several guests coming in the front door, bags in hand. "I'll talk to you later, Joanie." Shad hurried off to assist them.

"Something must be wrong," Joanie said to Steve, apparently forgetting for a moment her decision to put some distance between them.

Steve followed her into her private office, which was behind the front desk. "What makes you think that?"

Joanie sat down behind her computer. She pressed a number of buttons as she booted up the file on Mrs. Flannagan.

"For starters, Mrs. Flannagan had reservations for three more days. She was taking golf lessons and was enrolled in a bridge tournament that's still ongoing."

"So?" Steve shrugged and pulled up a chair next to Joanie, then turned it around and straddled it. "A lot of people cut their vacations short for one reason or another."

Joanie shook her head. "Not Mrs. Flannagan. She's a widow, Steve. She told me at the beginning this vacation was going to be hard for her, because she'd never vacationed alone before." Joanie sighed, clearly troubled. "And I could tell by the way she kept stopping by the desk and asking about the different things that were going on that she was really lonely. So I set up golf lessons for her with the pro and got her into a bridge tournament. Last night I suggested she enroll in the beachcombing seminar, and she seemed very excited about it. For her to leave without even saying goodbye to me is very strange."

"Maybe she was just embarrassed about cutting out when you'd done so much for her."

"No," Joanie said. "I still think something's wrong. And if Mrs. Flannagan was annoyed or felt the resort was lacking in any way, then we need to know about it so we can correct the problem." Joanie typed into the computer and pulled up Mrs. Flannagan's Kansas City address and phone number.

She dialed and waited. Finally she frowned and hung up. "No answer. I'll try again tomorrow." She scrawled a note to remind herself.

"Are you this much a perfectionist about everything or just about your work?" Steve teased.

"Everything meaning?"

"Your personal life."

Joanie stuck the note on the desk calendar next to the phone. She straightened, her expression grim. "You don't do yourself any favors by compromising on what you want in a lifelong mate."

"Are you speaking from experience?"

She shrugged. "In a roundabout way. I realized early in life that my mother really loved my father, but my father didn't really love my mother, and as a consequence he wasn't faithful to her. But they stayed together for my sake."

Steve's own childhood had been less than perfect, too. He knew how hard it was to live without the two terrific parents every kid secretly yearned for.

"That sounds tough," he said sympathetically.

"It was." Joanie drew a deep breath and let it out on a sigh. "We were all miserable."

Steve could almost see her barriers rising. He sensed that to try to touch her at this moment would be a mistake. "That's not going to happen to you, Joanie," he said. *I won't let it.*

"You're right. It won't." She sat back and crossed her arms. "Because I'll never marry without true love on both sides."

Steve realized he had his work cut out for him if he was going to win Joanie's heart. He also realized there were good reasons for her wariness and difficulty in trusting men. So maybe it was time he put his own hang-ups aside and cut her some slack.

Joanie closed her computer file. There were shadows beneath her eyes that not even the careful application of makeup could hide. She looked unbearably weary, and he longed to put his arms around her.

"I've got to get back to the concierge desk," she said.

"When do you break for dinner?" Steve asked, already thinking ahead to what he could do to get her spirits up.

"I don't." Joanie sighed again. "I promised Jerry and Liz the entire evening off for the way I've inconvenienced them both the past few days. I'm going to work straight through until ten."

Steve held his own disappointment in check. Joanie would survive the long hours. She wouldn't survive the loss of love. "Want me to bring Emily over so you can see her before she goes to bed?'' He had an inkling of how much Joanie would like that.

She smiled at him. "Please."

NO SOONER had Steve left than Phoebe Claterberry appeared. "Hi, Ms. Griffin. I want to sign up for the Frisbee-throwing contest at the beach tomorrow afternoon."

Joanie got out the sheet and showed Phoebe where to sign her name. "You look awfully chipper this evening, Phoebe." *You look the way I wished I felt,* Joanie thought.

"It's on account of my talk with Steve this afternoon," Phoebe confided.

A chill went down Joanie's spine. "Oh?"

"He's really cool." Phoebe sighed. "You just look into his eyes and you know he understands you. Of course—" Phoebe paused to sign the sheet "—I already knew that because we've talked intimately before."

"Oh, really," Joanie said casually, noting that Phoebe's handwriting was an awful lot like the handwriting on the notes that had been left in regard to Emily. "When?"

"It was about two and a half years ago."

"Which would have been late in the fall, your freshman year of college," Joanie guessed. *No, no, this can't be. If it were so, Steve would have told me.*

"Right," Phoebe continued. "When Steve actually came to give a motivational talk about goal-setting at Cornell, I was on the student committee that hosted him. We took him out for drinks and dinner afterward, and then I drove him back to his hotel, which was when we talked. But I don't think he remembers much about that evening. Of course, I can hardly blame him. He was awfully tired and he's traveled so much and met so many people he can't recall everyone. But I know I'll never forget that night," Phoebe finished, her hand over her heart.

"You should mention it to him," Joanie prodded, "if it was that important to you. I'm sure he'd like to know," she emphasized.

"Oh, I couldn't," Phoebe retorted shyly. She glanced at her watch and made a face. "I better hurry if I don't want to miss the evening seminars." She paused. "Do me a favor, Ms. Griffin? Don't say anything to Steve about...that evening, because it would really embarrass me."

"I won't," Joanie promised, albeit reluctantly.

"Thanks. See you later, Ms. Griffin."

Joanie watched Phoebe run off to the meeting room. Was Phoebe one of Steve's conquests? Was Phoebe Emily's mom and not Irene, and Steve just didn't recall? Joanie wondered miserably. And if so, what kind of man did that make Steve? Was she a fool to be falling in love with Steve all over again?

She had no answers for that. All she knew was that every time she saw Steve with Emily or spent time with him herself, she gave a little more of her heart....

"Is SOMETHING bothering you?" Steve asked, when Joanie saw him later that evening.

Joanie had forced herself not to jump to any conclusions about Phoebe and Steve. For all she knew, Phoebe could be involved with Emily's appearance in a very oblique way—she could be acting on someone else's behalf, someone like Irene Martin. Or she could just be acting funny because she was hiding something that had nothing to do with either Steve or Emily or Irene. Just because Phoebe seemed to have a schoolgirl crush on

Steve did not mean they'd had a child together. It could, however, mean that Phoebe wanted Steve to take her child—her illegitimate child by another man—and raise it as his own. For many women, Steve would be a dream father.

As for her handwriting, anyone who knew calligraphy would write in the exact same manner. And plenty of people knew calligraphy.

"Why would you ask that?" Joanie looked at Steve, pleased and touched that he had tidied her unit after putting Emily to bed for the evening and even had a room-service table with covered silver chafing dishes waiting.

"You seem ... distracted," he said.

And uneasy and scared that I'm following in my mother's footsteps and falling in love with the wrong man, Joanie thought. "I'm just tired," she said.

"You want to call it a night?" His disappointment was obvious.

She knew he'd planned a late-night supper for two. Perhaps some kisses and intimate talk, too. But Joanie didn't want to face where those kisses and intimate talks might lead. Not tonight.

"Would you mind?" Joanie asked. Ignoring the probing light in his eyes, she fibbed, "I've got to be up early to check on the setup for the Frisbee tournament tomorrow morning."

Chapter Ten

Joanie looked at the sofa cushions in consternation. "I know your shoes were right here a second ago."

Emily giggled and toddled into the bedroom.

Joanie followed, planting her hands on her hips as she surveyed the living quarters that had once been neat as a pin but were now strewn with baby things. "Emily, where are your shoes?" Joanie asked in amused exasperation. Saturday mornings were always busy at Bride's Bay. Even more so when a conference was being held.

Emily pushed a chair up to Joanie's bed and climbed onto the sleep-rumpled sheets. She danced across the center, plopping down onto the pillows. "Night-night!" she called playfully, squeezing her eyes shut.

A knock sounded on the door. Joanie pivoted and went to let Steve in. He was wearing a soft blue cotton shirt, open at the throat, with a white T-shirt beneath. Jeans and loafers completed the ensemble. Joanie inhaled the woodsy scent of after-shave that clung to his jaw and said hi.

He smiled at her, their gazes locking, electricity sizzling through them both.

His glance strayed to the hotel high chair one of the busboys had brought over on his break. He frowned. "You had breakfast already?"

"A major mistake. I thought it would be easier than taking Emily to the employee cafeteria and allow us to get a faster start this morning, but all I did was give her enough fuel to play pranks on me." She turned and called, "Emily, Steve's here." Breathtakingly aware of him right behind her, Joanie led the way into the bedroom.

Emily had been sitting up, but as soon as she caught a glimpse of them, she lay back down and again squeezed her eyes shut.

"Looks like Emily's asleep," Steve said loudly.

She giggled.

"Yes, I guess Emily is asleep," Joanie said equally loudly. "The problem is we can't find her shoes, and if we can't find her shoes we can't take her to the beach to watch the Frisbee-throwing contest this morning."

Emily scrambled to a sitting position as the excitement of an outing dawned on her.

"Want to go on a walk, Em?" Steve asked. Emily nodded soberly. "Then help us find your shoes," he said.

"No shoes!" Emily shouted.

"No shoes, no walk," Steve replied. He bent down to look under the bed. Joanie looked behind the bathroom door and in the tub. Emily giggled at both of them.

"Guess that means we're cold," Steve said, brushing against Joanie as they passed.

Cold was not how Joanie would have described herself; she tingled from even that slight contact. Intent on their mission, however, she looked in the crib. Back out in the living room. On the closet floor with her own shoes. Steve checked out the laundry hamper and the wastebasket.

Then Joanie looked beneath the still-mussy covers on her bed. "Aha!" She extracted first one shoe and then the other.

Emily's gleeful expression turned to one of trepidation. "No!" she said, curling her feet up under her, so it was impossible for them to put her shoes on. "No owie!"

"I think she's trying to tell us something," Steve asked, his brow furrowing in concern.

Joanie nodded soberly. "Like maybe these shoes are hurting her feet? Is that it, Emily?" Joanie sat down beside Emily on the rumpled covers. "Your shoes are hurting your feet?"

In response, Emily grabbed her teddy and blanket and held them close to her chest. Steve sat down on the other side of Emily and compared the bottom of the shoe to the bottom of the girl's foot. Sure enough, the shoes were looking a little small.

"I think we're going to have to go shopping again, Emily," Steve said. He glanced at Joanie. "Is there any place on the island to buy shoes?"

"The general store in the village. They don't have a big selection, but what is there is good quality."

"All right. New shoes it is." Steve shifted Emily onto his lap. "Em, want to go to the store?"

"Beach!" Emily said. Leaning forward, she tried to put her shoes on herself.

"I really should check on the Frisbee contest," Joanie said, watching as Emily cuddled against Steve. "And make sure everything's going as scheduled."

Steve looked up. "I thought you had the morning off."

"I do."

"Then why?"

Because Phoebe and Dennis had entered the contest, Joanie thought, and Joanie wanted to put Phoebe to the test with Emily, see what her reaction was to Emily when Dennis was watching.

"I just thought it would be fun to see how it was going," Joanie fibbed, not wanting to voice her suspicions to Steve until she had a little more proof. "And I thought it might amuse Emily to see them tossing the Frisbees."

Steve helped Emily put on her tiny pink-and-white windbreaker, then helped Joanie into hers. They put Emily in the stroller and were off. The day was beautiful—sunny and clear with a strong ocean breeze. As Joanie suspected, Phoebe and Dennis were among the couples practicing furiously in the half hour before the contest began. They were also arguing politics.

"Senator Hatchworth's economic model was by far the best," Phoebe said, giving Dennis a saucy look.

"The heck it was!" Dennis argued back, giving Phoebe an appreciative look. "The plan my father introduced to the Senate is way better, Phoebe."

Phoebe frowned. Looking over and seeing Joanie, Emily and Steve, she tossed the Frisbee back to Dennis, then ran over to join them.

"Hi!" Phoebe grinned amicably up at Steve, then over at Joanie and down at Emily. "Are you two entered in the contest, too?"

"No. We just thought we'd stop by on our way to the village. We're going shoe shopping for Emily."

"Oh, neat!" Phoebe knelt down in front of Emily's stroller as gulls swooped overhead. "Hi, sweetie. How are you?" Phoebe asked Emily softly. "Are you having a good time on the island even without your mama and daddy?"

Emily perked up. She leaned toward Phoebe and captured a lock of her long blond hair. "Gi me gake gah Mama," she said.

Phoebe laughed in delight. "Gi me goo goo gah gah," she said while beside her Dennis Wright scowled in boredom.

Emily giggled and mimicked her the best she could. But Joanie noted, not sure whether she was happy or relieved, that there seemed no mother-daughter bond between the two.

"Not really into babies, are you?" Steve remarked to Dennis.

Dennis shook his head. "Can't say I am, at least not right now."

"But Steve is, aren't you, Steve?" Phoebe said, straightening.

Which was another reason, Joanie thought, for Phoebe to abandon Emily to Steve.

Steve nodded. "Into babies, and very much into Emily."

Phoebe smiled, a little wistfully this time. Hunkering down beside Emily one more time, she kissed her little hand. "You are one lucky kid, you know that?" Phoebe said. Then, aware Dennis was waiting on her, she said goodbye to the group and trotted off to resume practicing for the competition.

Emily squirmed restlessly in her stroller. "Ready to head for the village?" Steve asked Joanie.

She nodded.

Again, she noted that Emily was not the least bit upset to leave Phoebe or Dennis or the beach. Which meant that if Emily was Phoebe's daughter, there was not much of a bond between mother and child. Otherwise, Emily would be crying to stay with Phoebe. Unless Emily didn't know Phoebe at all, because Emily had been brought up so far by the mysterious Fiona . . .

Joanie sighed. If that was the case, maybe Phoebe was right to abandon Emily. Maybe Phoebe thought Emily needed more mature parents. Maybe Phoebe just wanted to pursue her own education and establish herself in her career before tackling motherhood. Phoebe certainly looked up to Steve and admired him. Was it possible Emily was really Dennis's child and Phoebe had just selected Steve to be the father because she thought Steve was a good guy and would be a good father? And because Fiona, for whatever reason, could no longer care for Emily?

Joanie had to find out the truth. If Phoebe *was* Emily's mother, Joanie was going to have to get Phoebe to own up to that because Emily deserved that much, and more.

"You've been awfully quiet," Steve said as they approached the general store.

Joanie didn't know if she should tell him about her suspicions regarding Phoebe and Dennis or just wait for Phoebe to do the right thing on her own. "That's because I have a lot on my mind," she said.

"Such as?" Steve held open the door.

"For starters, should we get Emily traditional white-leather high-top shoes, like the ones she's got now that are too small, or running shoes, which might be a little more practical for the island?"

"Why not get her both?" Steve said. "Unless," Steve continued to the clerk who came forward to help them, "there's some reason a toddler shouldn't wear running shoes."

"Running shoes are fine as long as they have the proper support and ours all do," the clerk said with a smile.

Fifteen minutes later, Emily was wearing her new shoes.

"What do you say?" Steve asked, casting a glance around at the vast array of goods in the children's section of the store. "Should we pick up a few more outfits for Emily as long as we're here?"

"Emily could use a few things," Joanie agreed. With Steve's help, she picked out a sweatshirt embroidered with the resort logo and another pair of sturdy denim overalls and coordinating turtleneck pullover. "These will be great for playing outdoors in, and—" she found a sun hat "—this will keep her head from getting sunburned."

"How about some more pajamas?" Steve said, picking out a pink flannel sleeper, with Snoopy on the front. "And some sunglasses—" he added a pair to the pile growing on the counter "—so Emily can look cool?"

Joanie sighed, looking at the pile. "I think that's enough," she said.

Steve wanted to buy out the whole store. He handed over his credit card. Joanie walked Emily around while their purchases were rung up.

Watching them, Steve thought he'd never seen a more perfect-looking mother and daughter. The biology of the situation aside, he sensed Joanie knew it, too.

Finished, they headed out into the spring sunshine once again. Emily protested when Joanie went to put her into the stroller. She raised her arms for Steve to pick her up.

He complied. "Want to do a little window-shopping and then stop for lunch?" he suggested, taking Joanie's hand with his free one.

Joanie's hair gleamed gold in the sunshine. Color crept into her cheeks, and her eyes were alight with pleasure and excitement. "There aren't many shops," she said, laughing.

"Who cares? Not me, when I have two such beautiful ladies for company."

Steve spied the upscale sandwich shop/bakery down the street. The delicious aroma of freshly baked bread wafted toward them. "Hey. Let's have lunch now. That place looks great. Smells even better. What do you say?"

"Cookie!" Emily hollered.

"Well, that certainly answers my question."

"All this stroller seems to be good for is stowing packages," Joanie said, pushing it ahead of her.

Steve strode along feeling as if the three of them had done this a hundred times before. His dreams seemed to be coming true.

Ye Olde Sandwich Shop had a self-serve counter and a daily menu written on a chalkboard. There were four very small tables with two chairs each and a gingham-curtained bay window that fronted the street.

Minutes later, Joanie carried two trays of sandwiches and drinks back to the table, while Steve looked around for a high chair. There wasn't one. "No problem," he said. "Emily can sit on my lap and eat her lunch, can't you, Emily?"

The shop was beginning to fill up as other tourists came in for lunch. Joanie watched a woman with a baby in a stroller, her arms laden with packages, come in.

"I can't imagine trying to do this alone," she murmured as Emily reached for her.

"Being a single parent would be difficult," he agreed, placing Emily on Joanie's lap. "Whenever possible, I think a child should have two parents," he said firmly.

Joanie stroked Emily's hair, restoring order to the wispy halo of golden curls. "You're thinking about the way you grew up, aren't you?"

Steve nodded, wishing everything was already settled, that Joanie was already his wife. "My father's deserting us had a big impact on me—a very negative one," Steve confessed. "I don't want my own child to suffer the same. And speaking of that, we need to talk about the future."

For a moment, Joanie wasn't sure she'd heard right. "Here? Now?" she whispered, stunned he had chosen such a public place for a private discussion.

"Don't tell me you're not thinking about it," he said intimately, his eyes roving her fondly as she cuddled Emily on her lap.

"Of course I'm thinking about Emily's future," Joanie said, blushing.

"Not just Emily's future. I'm talking about *our* future, Joanie." He reached for her left hand and brought it to his lips. "Yours, mine and Emily's."

"Emily was really left with you, Steve, not me," she said a great deal more casually than she felt. "The second note told us that. My having her at all was a giant mistake."

Steve leaned forward. "I doubt Emily would call it that. She's obviously come to love you, Joanie. And you can't tell me you don't love her, too," he said huskily.

She stared down at the table. "Of course I do." It was impossible not to love the vivacious toddler.

"We need you in our lives, Joanie. Emily and I both do. And we want you with us."

Need you. Want you. Not love you. She met his eyes and saw herself, and all she was, reflected in them. "But I have no legal claim to her," Joanie protested softly.

"But I do, and I want you in my life." He covered her hand with his. "I want you in *our* life."

He was only doing this because of Emily, because he wanted her to have the sort of family he'd never had.

Joanie studied him as a kaleidoscope of emotions twisted through her. "The only thing I want you to do right now is find Irene." Because only then, if she saw for herself how Steve felt about the woman, would she know in her heart what the future held for her and Steve. "Have you been able to locate her?"

"I talked to my former coach and got a list of editors from every sports magazine in the country last night. I called them all after Emily went to sleep. Not one of the magazines has had any contact with Irene in the past year."

"You didn't tell me."

"You were tired when you got off work."

"But this morning—"

"It was a fruitless search. I didn't see any reason to disappoint you on such a beautiful morning."

What else hadn't he told her? Joanie wondered. "You don't really want to find her, do you?" she guessed, her heart breaking a little at the knowledge.

He gave her a frank, unapologetic look. "Not if it means a custody fight over Emily or trouble in my romance with you, no."

Was that what they were having? Joanie wondered fifteen minutes later as they packed a now sleepy Emily up in her stroller and headed back toward Bride's Bay hotel. A romance? Or was Steve simply in search of a good, loving mother for the child he suddenly found himself saddled with? He had said he couldn't imagine taking sole care of Emily and working, too. And Steve was the kind of goal-oriented man who needed to work. Plus, the job he'd accepted at Bride's Bay involved some travel. He would need someone to care for Emily while he was on the road.

Pushing the stroller with one hand, Steve wrapped his free arm around her waist. "But just for the record, I did hire a private detective yesterday to aid us in tracking Irene down."

So he was doing the decent thing, Joanie thought, relieved. "Good." But even as Joanie lauded his efforts, she knew she didn't really mean it. She didn't want Irene in their lives any more than Steve did.

"I want to close the book on Irene and move on," Steve continued, stopping the stroller on a deserted section of the walking path under a live oak dripping with Spanish moss.

"And suppose you find that Irene wants the three of you to be a family?" Joanie challenged, resting against the tree, her hands behind her.

Bracing himself with one arm against the tree, Steve leaned in close. "Is this some kind of test to measure exactly how committed I am to you?" he asked softly, probing her upturned face.

Joanie couldn't deny she still had her doubts, although they were dwindling so fast she had to struggle to hang on to them. "Maybe," she said, aware her heart was suddenly pounding against her ribs and her knees felt weak. She wanted to forget all that kept them apart, rush headlong into his arms and inhale the fresh, masculine scent of his skin. She wanted him to kiss her and make wild, passionate love to her until they forgot all that kept them apart.

And he did look as if he wanted very much to kiss her then and there. But instead, he acted with restraint. "I can see I still have to prove myself to you."

Ignoring the unchecked passion swirling around in her, Joanie angled her chin up at him. "I guess you do at that," she retorted.

He smiled at her gently, then stepped back. The absence of a kiss left Joanie feeling oddly bereft.

Steve shrugged with amiable intent. "Then I better get moving on it. I'll start by checking in with that detective I hired just as soon as we get back to the resort."

Back at their quarters, Joanie put the still-sleeping Emily down in her crib while Steve called his detective.

"Irene quit magazine writing altogether to work at some newspaper in the Midwest," Steve reported a few minutes later.

Part of Joanie didn't want Irene to be found. She was enjoying being Emily's mama even temporarily. She was enjoying being the woman—the only woman—in Steve's life. But realistically how long could that last? Sooner or later, someone would come forward with the truth about Emily.

"So we're getting closer to tracking her down," Joanie said.

"Yes." Steve looked at her with grim optimism. "According to the detective, we should have all the answers we need very soon."

"IS THIS WHERE you pick up the applications for summer employment?" Phoebe Claterberry asked.

Steve looked up from the desk in his new office. Although he didn't officially start until the following week, he'd wanted to get a head start filling out the paperwork involved with starting a new job.

"No, you'll have to talk to Elizabeth Jermain or her granddaughter about that." Able to see there was something on Phoebe's mind, Steve put down his pen and continued affably, "Do you want to apply for a job?"

"I'm thinking about it," Phoebe admitted as she edged closer. "I'd love to summer here."

"But—" Steve sensed some reservation in her voice and attitude, almost as if she was hiding something.

Phoebe shrugged. "I've already got another job offer," she admitted without much enthusiasm.

"But there are problems with this other offer?"

Phoebe nodded. Sighing, she walked all the way into the room and sat. "There are plenty of reasons I shouldn't take this other offer, the primary one being the loss of my—"

She stopped as Dennis Wright appeared in the doorway. He gave Phoebe a stunned look. "Is it true, Phoebe? Shad Teach told me you were going to try to find a summer job here."

Phoebe nodded reluctantly. "Yes."

"What about the jobs I've already secured for us?" he asked.

Phoebe raked both hands through her hair. "I've thought about it and changed my mind."

"Without telling me?" Dennis asked, hurt.

"I was going to," Phoebe said.

"Yeah, right." Disbelief glistening in his eyes, Dennis bolted from the room. Phoebe got up and rushed out after him.

"What happened?" Joanie asked seconds later, coming in. She looked elegant and flawlessly beautiful in her pale yellow business suit.

Steve stood. "They had a lovers' quarrel. At least I think that's what happened. I'm not really sure."

"Oh." Joanie looked relieved.

Steve saw the manila envelope in her hand. "Something up?"

"Yes. This came for you at the front desk." She handed it to him. "Since I was headed back to see you, anyway, I told them I'd bring it to you."

Steve ripped open the seal and looked inside. He smiled with satisfaction. His surprise was intact. Pocketing the envelope and its contents without revealing anything to an obviously curious Joanie, he said, "Where's Emily?"

Joanie smiled. "She was invited upstairs to visit Elizabeth and the judge in their private quarters. One of Liz's brothers stopped by with his two-year-old son, Troy, and they thought he and Emily might have a good time playing together. I just went up and checked on her. She had no desire whatsoever to come with me at the moment. Elizabeth and the judge both want her to stay and play with Elizabeth's great-grandson. I said it was okay and that I would pick Emily up at three this afternoon."

"Which kind of leaves you at loose ends in the interim," Steve noted casually, determined not to give his plan away.

"Yes." Joanie nodded. "With two hours, twenty-three minutes and forty-nine seconds to spare."

Steve caught the fragrant floral scent of her hair and skin as he neared. "Not that this mothering business has gotten under your skin," he teased.

"Oh, heavens no." Joanie rolled her eyes. "I'm completely calm and cool about it at all times."

Grinning, he tucked his hand beneath her elbow. "Got time to run an errand with me in one of the hotel minivans?" He could finish the paperwork, what little of it remained, tonight.

"Sure," Joanie said, falling into step beside him as easily as if they took off together on a whim every day. "Where are we going?"

He took her hand in his and just grinned.

FROM THE WAY Steve was behaving, Joanie had the feeling this was not going to be just an ordinary Saturday afternoon.

"Why are we stopping here?" she asked as Steve parked the minivan in the drive of one of the private estates.

He switched off the engine and removed the keys from the ignition. Smiling, he turned to face her. "Don't you like it?"

"I love it." The place had sprawling grounds and a magnificent ocean view, and was wildly expensive. "But I don't think anyone's living here at the moment. Last I heard it was for sale or lease."

"Not anymore." Steve opened the manila envelope and extracted a key and lease. "Starting now, it's all mine."

Joanie stared at him, wondering what this all meant. "How long did you lease it for?"

"Six months. If it works out okay, I've got an option to buy." He climbed out of the van and walked around to open her door. "Want to take a look around inside?"

"It's as beautiful inside as it is out," Joanie said, admiring the sophisticated kitchen with its black granite countertops and state-of-the-art appliances. The parquet floors were covered with area rugs and polished to a high sheen. Living room, dining room and kitchen all featured floor-to-ceiling windows and ocean views. Beyond was a screened-in porch, also facing the ocean and complete with cushioned white wicker furniture, a ceiling fan and myriad plants and flowers.

"And back this way are five bedrooms and four baths," Steve said.

"There's plenty of room for a crib in here," Steve said, showing her the first room, a child's nursery with plenty of built-in shelves and a window seat. "Come see the master bedroom."

Unlike the other bedrooms, this room had an ocean view. A stone fireplace was at one end, a Jacuzzi next to it. A quilted blue-and-white bedspread in an island print covered the king-size bed. The tub, shower and twin sinks in the adjacent bathroom were done in pearl white marble and gold-plated fixtures. There was plenty of bathroom cabinet space, two walk-in closets and a separate vanity.

"It's beautiful, like something out of a fantasy," Joanie said breathlessly.

Steve came up behind her. He wrapped both arms around her and drew her back against him. "Yet you look sad."

"For purely selfish reasons, I assure you." Staying safely in his arms, she turned to face him. "I'm going to miss having you next door to me in the staff quarters."

Steve tightened his hold on her possessively. "I'm going to miss you, too. But the staff quarters are no place to raise a child. Emily deserves a real home. After all the years on the road, going from one competition to the next and then fulfilling my endorsement contracts, I want a home, too. A real home."

What he said made sense. "I can understand that," she said softly, struggling against the more immediate sense of loss. "That's one of the reasons I took the job at

Bride's Bay, because I thought I could make a real home here for myself.''

She turned away from him, aware that suddenly there was a lump in her throat. It was ridiculous, but she felt as if she was losing him all over again, as if he was already walking away. She hugged herself as a chill went through her. Struggling to hold on to her equilibrium, she asked, "When did you rent the place?"

"My second day here." His voice was very low and very close.

Joanie's eyes widened and she spun around in surprise. "But you didn't know that Emily was yours yet."

"But I knew the most important thing—that I was falling in love with you all over again, just as helplessly as before. Only this time, when I came to you, I wanted to have something concrete to offer you." He took her in his arms and held her close. "A home, marriage, family. Everything you've always wanted, Joanie. Everything we've both always wanted."

Chapter Eleven

"My, don't the two of you look happy," Elizabeth Jermain commented when Steve and Joanie arrived to pick up Emily. Troy and Emily were sitting on the sofa side by side watching a Barney video.

"Yes, they're positively glowing," Cameron Bradshaw agreed with a smile.

Joanie felt herself grow even warmer. Was it that obvious she had completely fallen in love with Steve?

The judge regarded Steve with a twinkle in his eyes as he ambled toward them. "So, Steve, I heard you leased a home?" he said in his distinct Southern drawl.

Steve acknowledged this with a dip of his head. "Word travels fast."

Judge Bradshaw's grandfatherly face split in a smile. "It's a small island. Elizabeth and I like to think nothing on it escapes our attention. When are you planning to move?"

"Not for a few days."

Joanie felt relieved. She still was not anxious to see him go, even if he'd be only a mile or so away.

"I've got some personal stuff being shipped in," Steve continued amiably, bending down to gather up Emily's jacket and diaper bag. "I think I'll wait until it arrives before moving in."

"You're wise to take your time," Elizabeth said, handing Steve one of the storybooks Emily had brought with her. "Although there's also something to be said for not letting the best opportunities go by." She glanced at Joanie, adding, "Sometimes you have to follow your heart and act quickly, regardless of all the expert advice to the contrary. Isn't that right, Cameron?" Elizabeth reached out and took the judge's hand.

"Absolutely," he said, smiling at his wife.

The video ended with a flourish. Emily and Troy were quickly off the couch, singing and dancing to their own largely unintelligible version of the Barney theme song.

Five minutes later Emily was in her jacket, and thank-yous and goodbyes were said. Joanie and Steve, a happy Emily in his arms, headed down the sweeping staircase and out the rear doors of the hotel toward the staff quarters.

"Do you think Elizabeth was trying to tell us something?" Joanie asked, falling into step beside Steve.

He tilted his head as if it really didn't matter to him either way and answered thoughtfully, "I think Elizabeth and the judge can tell how we feel about each other," he said, reaching out with his free hand to grasp hers and pull her close to his side. "I think they can see it in our eyes every time we look at each other."

Joanie squeezed his hand, aware how happy he had made her in so short a time. "Oh, Steve," she whispered, "I want this to work out. But there's so much still standing in our way."

"Don't think about it." He threw his arm around her shoulder and shushed her with a kiss. "For now it's one day, one hour, one moment at a time."

"STORY!" EMILY DEMANDED a short time later as Joanie finished changing her diaper.

Steve smiled down at Emily fondly. "Okay. I'll read you a story before your nap. You pick out which one, though." Steve offered an array of books.

Emily pointed to a book with Kermit the Frog on the front, then toddled over to the rocking chair. Clearly this was where she wanted to be read to.

Before Steve and Emily could settle into it, there was a commotion outside. Joanie and Steve exchanged puzzled glances. *Now what?* Joanie wondered.

Joanie went to the door and edged it open. Beyond the low wall that edged the converted stables, she could see Phoebe Claterberry and Dennis Wright emerging from the formal gardens. Phoebe, who appeared to be crying, stumbled away from Dennis. He was dogging her every step. "You are such a jerk!" she shouted. "I don't know what I ever saw in you!"

"Well, that makes two of us!" he shouted back. "Because I sure as hell never expected you to lie to me, and especially not about something this important! Damn it all, Phoebe, how could you betray me and my family this way? Don't you have any heart at all?"

Phoebe planted her hands on her hips and regarded Dennis with an exasperation that seemed to grow fiercer with every second. "Of course I have a heart, but I have to do what I believe is right, and that's what I've done!" she shot back.

"What you have done," Dennis countered, "is betray me and my family. I don't think I'm ever going to be able to forgive you for this, Phoebe, particularly when I realize how long the deception has been going on." He glared at her. "Seeing you in there with Steve Lantz today really opened my eyes!"

"What do I have to do with any of this?" Steve murmured to Joanie, amazed.

Unfortunately Joanie thought she knew.

But this was no way for Steve to find out who Emily's real mother was. He and Emily both deserved better than that. It was up to her, Joanie thought, to talk some sense into Phoebe before this situation exploded before their eyes. Hurriedly she grabbed her blazer and looked around for her shoes.

"You keep Steve Lantz out of this!" Phoebe shouted back at Dennis.

"I will when you start leveling with me!" Dennis returned.

"Maybe I better go break this up and calm everyone down before they disturb the guests," Steve said.

Joanie glanced in the direction of the main hotel and hoped that the Jermains weren't hearing what she was, or Dennis and Phoebe would find themselves off the island by morning. Scenes like this were not tolerated at Bride's Bay.

Joanie reached for her pumps and put them on. She could already see that one of the bellboys had come out onto the porch and was peering over at the gardens. "Not a good idea, Steve."

"Why not?"

Because there'd be even more of a scene, Joanie thought. She clutched Steve's arm. "Dennis is obviously jealous of you. Besides, I think this needs a woman's touch." She paused to kiss Emily and Steve. "I'll be back as soon as I can," she promised.

Joanie slipped out the door and, waving the curious bellboy back inside, hurried toward Phoebe and Dennis. They were still arguing bitterly as she neared them, albeit a little more quietly.

When Dennis glanced up and saw her, he turned back to Phoebe and got in one last parting shot. "I'm never going to forgive you for this," he vowed. "Never!" He stormed off.

Phoebe burst into tears and launched herself into Joanie's sympathetic arms. For the next few minutes Phoebe sobbed as if her heart would break. Finally she lifted her head and dabbed her eyes. "I'm so s-sorry, Ms. Griffin. I tried not to make a s-scene."

"Let's sit down over here." Patting her arm reassuringly, Joanie guided Phoebe to one of the stone benches in the center of the garden.

"Dennis is furious with me for keeping something from him."

Here it was, Joanie thought, the chance she'd been waiting for. "Maybe it's time you started leveling with everyone," Joanie said.

Phoebe tugged her sundress over her knees and then dug in her purse for a tissue. "What do you mean?"

"Maybe you should tell Steve what you've done before someone else does."

Phoebe peered at Joanie in confusion. Her lashes were drenched with tears. "Why would he care?"

Phoebe, Phoebe, you have so much to learn. "I think you're underestimating him," Joanie pushed on calmly. Phoebe dabbed her eyes with the tissue as Joanie persisted, "I think Steve has a right to know what you've been up to the past couple of years."

Phoebe looked confused. Finally she drew a quavering breath and asked, "What does Steve have to do with the Republican Party?"

It was Joanie's turn to blink.

Phoebe leaned forward confidentially, her hand to her heart. "Dennis is mad at me because he just found out that after two years of seriously and secretly flirting with the idea I've joined the Republican Party."

Joanie was so stunned by the revelation she nearly fell off the bench, but it was clear Phoebe was dead serious. "That's it? That...that's all?" Joanie stammered. "That's what you've been hiding?"

Phoebe nodded soberly.

Joanie didn't know whether to laugh or cry. "Phoebe, surely a person's politics are rather trivial in the greater scheme of things."

"Not to Dennis," Phoebe said bleakly as she fished in her purse for another tissue. "Dennis's father is a senator and a member of the Democrat Party. His father is up for reelection next fall. I was offered the job as the youth coordinator for Senator Wright's Republican *opponent*. Now do you get it?"

"Oh, my," Joanie said.

"It gets worse," Phoebe went on. "Dennis is heading up the youth campaign for his father. Which means if I took the job we'd be pitted against each other and wouldn't be able to see each other at all, not without being branded traitors and spies by our own bosses and political parties."

"Which would make things even more miserable for the two of you."

"Right. It'd be adding injury to insult. Anyway, I was supposed to help Dennis this summer, and I even thought about giving up my own opportunity for the sake of our romance, but the bottom line is that I don't believe in Dennis's father's politics, so I can't do it." Phoebe heaved a weary sigh.

"Which is why you were contemplating working at Bride's Bay this summer," Joanie said, relieved as everything began to fall into place.

Phoebe lifted her shoulders in an aimless shrug. "It seemed like a good idea—for about five minutes. Because then I would've been able to save my romance with Dennis. But then I thought about it and I talked to Steve about it, and I realized that I had my own goals and dreams to pursue, my own convictions to follow. If I give up this job, I know I'll always regret it. And besides, this job I want to take is something I believe in passionately. Getting college-age kids to register and vote is important, Ms. Griffin."

Yes, Joanie thought, it was. "Maybe when Dennis calms down he'll understand that," Joanie said.

"No." Phoebe shook her head, her mood dismal. "As far as Dennis is concerned, I'm already the enemy."

Joanie could see that was true, too. "What about Steve? Where does he fit into all this?"

"Dennis is just jealous of Steve, although he has no reason to be. There's never been anything remotely personal between us. I just think Steve's a wonderful guy, a role model for us younger people, because he's accomplished so much in his own life. Which is why I went to him for advice—he's one guy who seems to have it all together."

Phoebe glanced at her watch. "I need to get back."

Joanie knew Steve was waiting for her, too. She stood reluctantly. Her heart went out to Phoebe. Being in love with someone at any age was not easy. "If you need anything, please let me know," Joanie offered.

Phoebe smiled tightly. "Thanks, but there's nothing you or anyone can do," she said softly, looking thoroughly dejected as she moved off.

Joanie returned to her quarters and slipped inside. Emily was cuddled on Steve's lap, sleeping soundly, her halo of curls pressed against his chest, her cherubic face bearing blissful contentment, even in her sleep. Steve looked equally happy. Joanie wished it could always be that way.

He gestured toward Joanie's bedroom, silently asking her to assist him in putting Emily down for her afternoon nap. She went in and lowered the side of the crib. He carried Emily in and laid her gently on the mattress. Joanie put her teddy bear in next to her and covered her with her blanket.

Steve looped an arm around Joanie's shoulders, and as they stood together watching Emily sleep, Joanie felt a rush of tenderness. If only the three of them were a family, she thought yearningly. If only she didn't have to worry about losing Emily and Steve both, should Emily's mother appear and want Emily back.

Mistaking the reason behind Joanie's worried expression, Steve took her hand and led her out into the living room. He shut the bedroom door, so their voices wouldn't disturb Emily.

"What happened out there?" he asked, inclining his head toward the window.

Briefly Joanie explained Phoebe's deception. "You seem awfully relieved," Steve remarked after a pause.

"That's because I thought maybe Phoebe was Emily's mother. She was acting so strange, and the two of you had known each other before . . ."

Steve released a long sigh. ". . . and you jumped to one conclusion and came up with five," Steve finished for her.

Joanie shivered at the hurt she saw in his eyes. She took an involuntary step back. "I'm sorry, Steve," she said, holding his gaze. "I let my imagination run away with me in thinking the two of you might have had a one-night stand."

Steve frowned. "I won't say I'm happy you jumped to conclusions again. It was your jumping to conclusions that separated us before, if you recall," he reminded her.

Joanie was filled with guilt. She knew she'd severely misjudged the situation and him. She wished there was a way to make it up to him. "I promise not to do it again," she said.

He drew her to him, and wrapped his arms tightly around her, his erratic heartbeat pressed against her own. "I'm going to hold you to that promise, Joanie."

He kissed her and the kiss felt like a commitment, like a bridge to their future. And Joanie knew if they made love again, things between them would be changed irrevocably. There would be no going back, no pretending it was all a mistake, made out of haste. She was giving him her heart this time. She was giving him her soul and taking his in return.

"Tell me you want me." His splayed fingertips tantalized the pebble-hard tips of her breasts.

Already trembling with need, she threaded her fingers through his hair. "I want you."

"Tell me you need me." Undressing her, he lowered her to the floor.

"I need you."

He stretched out beside her and drew her into his arms, then urged hoarsely, "Tell me you won't ever leave me again."

Tears sparkled in her eyes. She forced back the rising lump in her throat and, along with that, how close she'd just come to losing him again. "I won't leave you," she promised.

His arms tightened around her possessively, and his expression showed both fierce satisfaction and wonderment. He touched a finger to her face, trailing it from cheekbone to chin.

Joanie needed to touch him, too. To make sure that this was all real, that the notion of them as a couple wasn't going away. Ever so gently, her palms smoothed up his back, down again, worked beneath the hem of his shirt. Then she traced the shape of his arousal inside his slacks.

"I want to please you," she whispered. "So very much."

He kissed her, hard and sweet, knowing that she pleased him just by being. "You do," he said.

"No." She shook her head, reminding him that she had never been the aggressor with him, the way he sensed she could be, maybe even wanted to be. "But I will," she promised.

She looked so beautiful in her passion, he thought, as she finished undressing herself and started disrobing him. So wanton, with her cheeks flushed, her hair flowing down around her shoulders, that he felt himself responding wildly. "Joanie—"

She silenced him with a finger to his lips. "Let me," she said, trailing her fingertips over him, teasing his hard masculine flesh.

"I'm not sure..." He groaned as she straddled him. They'd barely started and he was near climax already. "...that I..." He drew a ragged breath as she moved enticingly over him. "...can wait."

"It doesn't matter." Shifting lower, she dropped kisses in an evocative circle around his navel, the inside of her thighs brushing the outside of his with warm, featherlike touches.

Steve's lower half flamed like a raging inferno. "It does to me," he said in a strangled voice.

She placed a hand on the insides of his thighs, rubbed them up and down, covering all the erogenous zones. Except one.

What she was doing was unprecedented and outrageous. Sensual almost beyond bearing. And far too compelling to stop. He yearned to be touched, the way he knew she would touch him—again. And going by the ardent mischief in her eyes, she knew it, too.

"Joanie . . ." His voice carried a warning. He couldn't take much more of this playing around. He wanted to make love to her now.

"What?" she asked as she closed her hands around him in a safe and familiar way. Delicately she moved her fingertips over the tip. Heat flowed through him, fierce, unrelenting and as rawly emotional as the passion roiling within him. He cupped a hand behind her neck, wanting to feel all of her against all of him. "Come here again."

Watching him with bright, merry eyes, Joanie playfully ignored his summons and rested her hands on either side of him. "I *am* here," she whispered, as if daring him to try to change things.

Her capriciousness was something new. Steve liked it. He liked it a lot. As a matter of fact, it was filling him with ideas of his own. Two could play these games, and she was already intoxicating him more than she knew. He reached for her, sliding his hands across her waist, then down her hips. Ignoring her soft, sweet intake of breath, he stroked his way across the jutting peaks of her breasts to her shoulders.

"Come here so I can kiss you," he bargained softly, running his hands up and down her bare arms.

Smiling, she leaned forward and studied his amused expression. Deciding apparently that it was safe to proceed at whim, she first obligingly began, then deepened, the kiss. Steve was cooperative to be sure, but only to a point. He let her rest against him, but didn't lift his body to better mesh with hers. He let her kiss him, but didn't move to aid in the tangling of tongues and mouths in any way.

Frowning against his lips, but not giving up, she strained upward slightly, seeking a better angle. And it was then that he made his move, clamping his arm around her middle, flipping her onto her back so that she lay flat beneath him.

"No fair," she complained breathlessly.

Steve grinned. She didn't look the least bit mad. Maybe it was the rogue-filled history of the island getting to him, but right now he felt a little like a pirate who'd just captured the feisty, fair maiden of his dreams. "All's fair in love and war," he teased, kissing her temple and knowing he couldn't have won himself a better prize. "Remember?"

"But this wasn't in the plan," Joanie protested on a ragged breath as he anchored her against him.

"Ah, yes," he said, kissing and caressing the curves of her breasts, "but the plan's been changed, and for the better."

"Better?" Joanie echoed, keeping her voice deadpan with considerable effort. "I don't know about... ahhh... that." She gasped as his tongue found her center, teasing and tormenting until she fell apart in his arms. Pleasure swept through him, just as fierce.

"I do," Steve said, sliding back up and over her, his lips meeting hers as he slowly and completely filled her and let the passion take hold. And this time he knew they were going to do much more than simply make love to each other. This time they were going to pledge each other their futures. And very gently, very tenderly, he set about doing just that.

"I DON'T KNOW if I should sit in on this meeting," Joanie told Steve several hours later, shortly before the private investigator arrived.

"I want you here with me," Steve said, drawing her close.

Minutes later they were getting down to business, while Emily—who'd awakened refreshed and happy after her afternoon nap—played quietly on the floor beside them.

"Irene's last job was at a Topeka, Kansas, newspaper," the private investigator began. A young man in his twenties, he was well dressed, very sharp and not one to waste a second. "I spoke to the managing editor. Irene quit a little more than a year ago to move back to Kansas City to be near her grandmother. Just as you suspected, she had a baby daughter who was about six months old at the time."

"Which means Irene's baby would be eighteen months old now," Joanie concluded. *"Emily's age."*

"Right." The private investigator accepted the cup of coffee Joanie handed him.

"Were you able to find a birth certificate?" Steve asked.

The PI handed over a photocopy. "Emily Fiona Martin. As you can see," he noted, "there's no father listed."

But, Steve thought, Emily was born almost nine months to the day after he and Irene had made love. That was pretty conclusive in and of itself, especially when combined with the fact that Irene was not the type of woman prone to casual affairs.

"What about Irene's grandmother?" Steve asked. "Is her first name Fiona?"

"Can't say. All I know for certain so far is that the grandmother lived in Kansas City."

Joanie leaned forward urgently. "Have you been able to locate any other next of kin?"

"Not yet, although I've telephoned every Martin in the book. None professes to know Irene."

"And she didn't write for the newspapers in Kansas City?" Steve queried, perplexed. He shot a glance at Emily, who was playing with her blocks nearby.

"Not so much as one free-lance article."

"Maybe her grandmother was on her mother's side of the family and had a different last name," Joanie suggested.

Good point, Steve thought. "Have you checked the obit for Irene's parents in the Grand Rapids newspaper?"

The PI nodded. "It simply says that Mr. and Mrs. Martin were survived by two people, their daughter, Irene, and Mrs. Martin's mother, in Kansas City."

Which left them exactly nowhere, Steve thought, his frustration growing. "What about friends of Irene Martin's parents in Grand Rapids?" Steve pressed.

"I'm working on it." The PI began putting notes back into his briefcase. He clicked it shut. "I should have an answer soon. Meanwhile, I still have to follow up on the physician, George Riley, who delivered Irene's baby. It's possible he'll know something."

"All right," Steve said.

"I'll get back to you as soon as I know something more," the PI promised, getting up to leave.

While Joanie showed him to the door, Steve picked up the phone and dialed information. "Topeka, Kansas, please. A Dr. George Riley." He wrote down the number given him and dialed again. Told Dr. Riley was with a patient, he left his number for the doctor to call back.

"You think Emily is yours and Irene's now, don't you?" Joanie asked quietly, returning to his side.

Steve nodded. He hooked his arm around Joanie's waist. Drawing her near, he buried his face in the fragrant softness of her hair for a long, thoughtful moment. "I'm sorry I didn't believe you initially. I just wanted so badly for her to be our child."

Joanie turned to face him. Splaying her hands across his chest, she tilted her chin. She paused as tears welled up in her eyes. "And maybe it's time we started facing that."

Steve knew a Dear John talk coming when he heard one. He tightened his fingers on her waist. "What do you mean?"

Joanie drew a shaky breath. "Simply that when you find Irene, our situation may change."

Steve knew what Joanie was hinting at, but he was not going to let her go without a fight. He would do everything in his power to get her to stay. "I don't love Irene. I never did."

She gazed up at him solemnly. "Nevertheless, the two of you have a child. It's obvious Irene felt you needed to be a part of Emily's life."

"And I will be," Steve said firmly, his devotion to Emily unchanged. "That doesn't mean things won't work out between you and me," he continued.

Joanie shook her head sadly. "I think you're being overly optimistic."

Maybe he was, Steve thought, but he didn't know what else to do. Painfully aware of his need for her, of his love for her, he kissed Joanie's temple. "Joanie, I love you."

"And I love you." The tears that had welled up in her eyes brimmed over and fell down her cheeks. "But nothing can be decided until we find out what's happened with Irene. What made her turn Emily over to you in such a potentially traumatic way." Joanie looked at Emily, who had just put the last block on top of a very ambitious creation.

Joanie gripped his arms. "You're going to have to trust me on this, Steve," she whispered, shaking her head miserably as she cast yet another adoring look at Emily. She stepped closer and wrapped her arms around his waist. "No mother would leave a toddler on a stranger's doorstep under normal circumstances, even if that stranger was the father."

Steve frowned and took Joanie fully into his arms. He didn't know how it had happened, but once again his life with Joanie was turning into a disaster waiting to happen. He stroked her hair and held back a sigh.

"I have the feeling the news, whatever it is, is going to be bad, too."

JOANIE HAD no sooner clocked in for her Saturday-evening shift than she was told Elizabeth Jermain wanted to see her. Asking Jerry to watch the concierge desk just a little longer, she climbed the sweeping staircase to Elizabeth Jermain's suite.

As usual, when asking for updates on hotel activities, Elizabeth opened her leather notebook and got straight to the point. "I understand two of our guests, Phoebe Claterberry and Senator Wright's son, Dennis, caused a scene in the garden this afternoon, in which you acted as peacekeeper and referee."

"That's right," Joanie said.

Elizabeth frowned. "Can we expect any more problems from those two?"

"Actually I don't think they're speaking to each other at the moment."

"I'd like you to do what you can to insure that situation remains defused," Elizabeth cautioned.

"I'll do whatever I can," Joanie said.

"Now, are there any problems you would like to discuss with me?" Elizabeth asked with a smile.

"Just one. A guest, Mrs. Frances Flannagan, checked out several days early, with no explanation, when she had already rented a cottage for an entire week. I've tried to follow up to determine what the problem was, but so far I haven't been able to get in touch with her."

Elizabeth looked worried. "Please keep trying. As you know, I don't want any of our guests to go away unhappy."

Joanie nodded in agreement. Their business concluded, she stood. "I set up a lot of activities for her while she was here. I'll talk to the people she was with. Maybe one of them will have a clue as to why she left the way she did," Joanie said.

Twenty minutes later the Bride's Bay golf pro told Joanie, "Mrs. Flannagan canceled her lessons with me."

"What do you mean she canceled them?" Joanie repeated incredulously. "She told me they were going well."

The pro shrugged. "Maybe she thought it would hurt your feelings if you found out she'd changed her mind."

"I suppose that could be it."

Joanie ran into Liz outside the clubhouse. "I heard you're asking questions about Mrs. Flannagan," Liz said.

Joanie nodded as together she and Liz headed for the main hotel. "Turn up anything?" Liz continued.

Joanie shook her head as they walked past the marina, where a variety of rainbow-colored sailboats peppered the bay. "Not yet. I can't shake the feeling that something was wrong, though."

Liz shot Joanie a concerned glance. "With the service at Bride's Bay?" she asked, looking equally concerned.

"It's possible." Joanie shoved her hands into her pockets as they strolled through the formal gardens and waved at the judge, who was out checking over his precious roses. She knew that as hard as she'd tried to keep up with her job, she'd been distracted the past few days. Caring for Emily and repairing her relationship with Steve had taken precedence.

"Maybe Mrs. Flannagan just got homesick and decided to go home on the spur of the moment," Liz suggested as they breezed past the fountain in the center of the garden.

"Maybe." Joanie pushed her hand through her hair. "In the meantime, though, I'm going to keep trying to track her down." When she and Liz mounted the steps to the hotel and walked into the lobby, Elizabeth Jermain was seated behind the counter registering several guests while Shad Teach saw to their luggage. Joanie's assistant, Jerry, was equally busy at the concierge desk.

Without warning, Steve appeared at Joanie's elbow. "May I speak with you a moment?"

"I'll lend my grandmother and Jerry a hand," Liz said.

"I'll just be a minute," Joanie said. She led Steve into her office and shut the door behind her. He was dressed in a suit. She knew by the serious look on his face that he had some news. "What's up?" she asked.

He paused as if he didn't know where to begin. "Irene's Topeka physician put me in touch with another physician in Kansas City," he began reluctantly. He was pale, his gray eyes unrelentingly grim.

"And?" Joanie's heart pounded.

He swallowed hard, then said, "Irene is dead, Joanie. She died six months ago."

Chapter Twelve

"I don't understand," Joanie began, reeling in shock. She looked into Steve's face. "Then where was Emily all that time?"

Steve sat on the edge of Joanie's desk, looking as if he had the weight of the whole world on his shoulders. "With her only living relative, her sixty-nine-year-old grandmother, Frances Fiona Flannagan."

"So it was Mrs. Flannagan who left Emily on my doorstep," Joanie cleared a space on her desk so she could sit next to him.

Steve nodded, running a hand agitatedly through his hair. "Apparently."

"I tried to call Mrs. Flannagan at her Kansas City home a few minutes ago. There was still no answer."

A variety of emotions moved across Steve's face. "I know," he replied wearily, seeming distant. He hesitated. "Her physician referred me to a neighbor, who told me that Fiona expected to be away at least another week or two, and that, as much as it broke her heart, she would not be coming back with the baby. The neighbor thought, however, Fiona would change her mind. Hire a nurse. Anything to keep her granddaughter with her. Apparently Fiona was quite attached to Emily."

"And no wonder," Joanie said thickly. "She's such a lovable little girl." Joanie could feel the tears welling up in her eyes. She pinched the bridge of her nose to keep them from falling. Steve needed her to be strong now. She wanted him to know he could count on her in times of hardship, as well as happiness.

"Well, this explains a lot," Joanie went on evenly. "Why Mrs. Flannagan, or Fiona, hung around, asking so many questions, why she appeared to be hanging out around the staff quarters the night I did Emily's laundry, why she delivered a second note telling you that you were the father when she knew we thought Emily had been left with me, not you."

"The question is, what are Mrs. Flannagan's intentions now?" Steve asked, the worried furrow between his brows deepening. "There's still a lot to be worked out legally."

And what are your intentions, Steve? If Mrs. Flannagan has changed her mind, will you fight her for custody of Emily? Or simply share in the care of your child? And where do I fit in this picture? Will you still need me?

"And to do that we have to have Mrs. Flannagan here now," Steve continued, tucking Joanie's hand in his. He traced the inside of her wrist meditatively before releasing his grip. "I've got the detective checking the bus, plane and train stations right now, but I have the feeling she may not be as far away as she'd like us to think."

"It's possible she may have just gone over to a mainland hotel." Joanie slipped off the desk and into her chair. She turned to her computer and reached for her phone. "I'll get on it right away.

"In the meantime, maybe her partners in the bridge tournament know something," Joanie suggested.

"Can't hurt to ask," Steve said.

"Especially since the Saturday-afternoon games haven't wrapped up quite yet," Joanie said.

"SO NONE OF YOU knew Mrs. Flannagan was leaving early?" Joanie asked the bridge players.

"No, but it wasn't that big a surprise," one said.

"She said she was homesick for a loved one," another added.

The only "loved one" Mrs. Flannagan had now was Emily, Joanie thought. As she looked at Steve, she knew he was thinking the same thing. He, too, was worried they were going to lose Emily.

"She hadn't imagined she could miss her loved one so much," the first woman continued.

"Yes," her partner confirmed. "And that made her have second thoughts about going so far away like this again."

Joanie swallowed, realizing that what they were saying could mean that Mrs. Flannagan had changed her mind about relinquishing custody of Emily to Steve. "Did she say who the loved one was?"

"No, in fact she was downright coy about revealing it," still another bridge player said. "But I had the feeling it wasn't a beau she was talking about."

Joanie glanced at Steve. The bridge players might not know, but she and Steve knew who the loved one was that Fiona had been talking about. Emily.

They thanked the guests and walked out into the hall.

"Are you thinking what I'm thinking?" Joanie asked.

Steve nodded, the tension in him almost palpable. "Whatever happens, it's not going to be as simple and uncomplicated as we'd hoped." He took her hand in his and looked into her eyes. "I'm going to need you more than ever."

Joanie launched herself into his arms and held tight. "I'll be here for you. I promise."

STEVE'S SPEECH ended to a standing ovation and thunderous applause. A few minutes later the conference attendees began streaming out of the banquet hall. Joanie threaded her way into the hall, hearing comments as she went.

"Wow, what a speech!"

"Steve Lantz could motivate a stone into doing what he wanted!"

Phoebe Claterberry paused in front of Joanie. She was wearing a short, black-jersey tube dress that made her seem several years older than she was. Her hair was in a beguiling French twist. Still looking a little starry-eyed, Phoebe smiled at Joanie.

"I always knew what we did in the mentoring project was a good thing," she said, "but Steve made all the sacrifices we make to be with the kids seem noble somehow. Like if we do it right it's going to benefit us almost more than them."

"Too bad he doesn't have the solution to our problems," Dennis Wright interjected, coming up to stand beside Phoebe.

"I'd hoped the two of you would've resolved your differences by now," Joanie commented, trying her best to avert another emotional scene between the two college students.

Phoebe's lip took on a pouty thrust. "I tried talking to him, Ms. Griffin. *I* think we should be the next James Carville and Mary Matalin—you know, opposing campaign managers who are romantically involved. But Dennis here refused."

"I told you," Dennis reminded Phoebe impatiently, "at this point in my life, my first loyalty has to be to my father and my political party."

"See what I'm dealing with?" Phoebe said with an annoyed toss of her head. She whirled on her ex-boyfriend. "You haven't got a romantic bone in your body, Dennis Wright!"

"And you, Phoebe, haven't got a practical one in yours!" Exasperated, Dennis yanked at his tie and hurried off rudely.

Phoebe looked as if she was going to burst into tears.

"Are you all right?" Joanie asked, touching her arm.

Phoebe pulled herself together with visible effort. She gently blotted the tears sparkling on her lashes with the tips of her fingers. "Yes. But I need to talk to Steve."

Joanie turned to see Steve heading for them, still signing autographs for the students as he went. Phoebe broke into a smile. She pushed through the crowd to his side and latched on to his arm the way a drowning person reached for a life preserver.

"Steve! I'm so glad I caught you before you left. I really, *really* need to talk to you."

So do I, Joanie thought. But what could she say? She was an employee of the hotel. She couldn't put her own needs above those of a Bride's Bay guest, even if the guest's demands were outrageously personal.

Steve looked at Joanie. "We'll talk later," she promised with a smile, knowing that he was as hamstrung as to what he could say and do as she was at the moment.

"Where are you going to be?" he asked, leaning forward and speaking into her ear so only she could hear.

"My quarters."

"I'll be there as soon as I can."

"Do what you have to do," Joanie said, reassuring Steve with a look that said it was all right, she understood his dilemma. She turned on her heel and left.

When he arrived fifteen minutes later, Joanie had just finished rocking Emily to sleep. He let himself in. Together, as was their custom, they settled Emily in her crib for the night and went back into the living room, closing the door behind them.

"That was fast," Joanie said. "I figured Phoebe would talk your ear off all evening."

Steve acknowledged her comment with the quietly accepting shrug of one long accustomed to dealing with the complications set forth by adoring female fans.

"I like her, but she's just a kid."

"With one hell of a crush on you," Joanie murmured.

Steve's brows lifted inquiringly at the jealousy in her voice. Flushing beneath his close scrutiny, Joanie turned away.

"You noticed, hm?" he said wearily.

Joanie paced to the front window and drew the blinds. Crossing back to the small refrigerator, she struggled to get control of her feelings. It wasn't easy; she was definitely feeling possessive tonight when it came to Steve.

"It would have been hard not to notice," she said calmly. "In fact, that's half the problem with her and Dennis Wright now. He sees her feelings for you, too." And he felt just as jealous and insecure as Joanie did right now. Lord, that irritated her. She'd thought she'd put those days of feeling jealous and insecure where her relationship with Steve was concerned behind her.

"If Dennis cares about Phoebe as much as I think he does," Steve said, "he'll realize that his jealousy isn't helping anyone and he'll start trusting and believing in

Phoebe again. Fortunately they'll both be out of here tomorrow.''

He accepted the chilled water Joanie handed him and paused to take a sip. His reflective glance remained on her face as he changed the subject skillfully. "Any luck in finding Fiona?''

Joanie shook her head, glad to talk about something else. "There's no Frances or Fiona Flannagan registered in any of the hotels in the central reservations system."

Steve drained his glass and put it down with a thud. "I suppose it's possible she registered under another name."

"Or is staying at one of the bed-and-breakfast places or hotels not on the CRS network."

He folded his arms and regarded her with a cool, unswerving gaze. "Are there a lot of them?"

"Approximately a hundred. So far, I've only managed to check about twenty-five." Aware of his eyes upon her, Joanie went to the phone. "We could start again now if you want."

"No." Moving with surprising speed, Steve caught her wrist before she could pick up the receiver and tugged her to his side. "I'll turn it over to the detective," he murmured decisively. "He can follow through for us from here."

Joanie tried to protest, the need in her to see things settled becoming unbearable. She didn't want to have to keep worrying about anyone or anything coming between them.

But Steve had other plans. Hands on her shoulders, he turned her to him, so they were standing face-to-face.

"I don't want to think about that tonight, Joanie," he said. His arms tightening like an iron band about her waist, he drew her closer, so they were touching in one long electric line from knee to breast. His lips dipping possessively to hers, he kissed her, at first deliberately and surely, then with an increasing edge of desperation. Joanie knew she shouldn't let him distract her this way, but she could not quite muster up the will to fight him, either.

"Damn it, Steve, you're not playing fair," she moaned, and felt her whole body soften in surrender as his tongue flicked softly between her lips.

"I never play fair." He paused to shrug out of his shirt and toss it aside. "I thought you knew that."

Joanie watched with disturbing hunger as he stripped off the rest of his clothes with the easy familiarity of a man who had made incredible love to her before and planned to make incredible love to her again. A man who knew he already had her heart.

"I do," she began, "but—"

Wearing only his boxers, he closed the distance between them. "Tonight, I want to think about us, Joanie. And only us."

That wouldn't be hard to do, Joanie thought, acknowledging his victory over her when he was standing before her, looking so unselfconsciously handsome, virile and athletic.

Gripping her upper arms, he pulled her against his hard length. He stared down at her, the look in his eyes potent and extremely sexual, as he murmured persuasively, "Tell me it's what you want, too."

As much as it would have served her purpose, she couldn't deny this was so. It was much easier to seek out love than go searching for trouble. "It's what I want, too," she admitted with a soft sigh, her voice a ragged whisper of need as she wound her arms about his neck.

"Good," Steve said, shifting his mouth back to hers again in a sensual, seeking kiss. No longer able to deny her own relentless desire, unable to resist touching him, she caressed the crisp hairs on his chest and the smooth muscles beneath. He was so strong, so sure of himself, so sure of them.

His lips forged a burning trail down her body, following the path of easily undone buttons and snaps, before moving to the rosy buds of her taut breasts, covering them with butterfly-light kisses that made her tremble. She slid her arms back around his neck and wound her fingers into his hair. Eyes closed, her head thrown back, she luxuriated in the nuzzling of his lips on her bare skin. Everything inside her was quaking, yearning. They had just started, but she didn't know how much longer she could wait.

"I want you," she whispered, holding him close, arching her hips in response, as her love for him flowed through her. "I want you so much."

"Then show me," he said hoarsely, trembling, too. "Show me how you feel."

"Like this?" Feeling more daring and wanton than she could have imagined possible, she slipped her hands inside his boxers, knelt to tug them down and off. On her knees in front of him, she caressed him intimately, even as her own body flooded with warmth.

"Yes," he said, surging and pulsing in her hands, his whole body tensing, his heart pounding in his chest. He stood it as long as he could, then reached for her and drew her up into his arms.

She had never seen Steve as needing anyone—not like this—but he needed her now, tonight. She could feel it, see it, and she was only too glad to be there for him. Her breath locked in her lungs as he guided her against him, his hands stroking her body up and down, moving between her thighs, over her breasts, again and again until her muscles felt as lax and golden as honey. She moaned, reveling in the fire storm, yearning to feel him as part of her very soul. She knew their lives were far from settled, but she couldn't bear the thought of losing him...losing this. She couldn't bear not making love with him....

Steve knew the second the doubts began crowding in on her again. He saw the pain, the confusion on her face, the fleeting reflection of all they had to lose. He knew, because he felt it, too. And it was killing him inside, even as he vowed to overcome it.

"It's not going to happen," he whispered softly, between deep, soulful kisses, as he lowered her slowly to the floor. "Nothing's going to separate us. Not again. Not this time."

"How do you know?" she asked, trembling, seeking reassurance.

He smoothed the golden curls from her face, his determination as deep and profound as her fear. "Because I won't let it," he promised, covering her body with his. His desire to protect her had never been stronger.

"But..."

His blood running hot and quick, he braced his arms on either side of her. "We belong together, Joanie. You and I. Now." He nudged her knees apart and settled himself heavily between her thighs, wanting more than ever to possess her. "And for all time. Nothing's going to come between us. Do you hear me?" He touched her until she was weak with longing, burning from within. "Nothing."

"Oh, Steve..." Joanie moaned as he kissed her eyes, her ears, her throat, then took her mouth again, plundering again and again, until she was moving shamelessly, wantonly against him. Shaking, she wrapped her legs and arms around him.

"Now?" he said, smiling down at her.

"Now." They kissed again as he drew her up against him and surged slowly, deeply into her. She sighed exultantly as he moved rhythmically within her, burying himself to the hilt. She heard herself whispering her pleasure. She felt his response. And then all was lost in the long, slow climb and the shuddering pleasure.

Afterward, lying close to his side, Joanie shut her eyes and clung to him, knowing now more than ever that the simple act of coming together like this would never be enough for her. She wanted more. She wanted marriage. Commitment. Children. Family. She wanted it all, and she wanted it with Steve.

Right now they weren't free and clear of trouble yet. But they would be soon. And once Emily's situation was secure, then she and Steve could—and would—concentrate on their own future.

"IT'S NOT EASY being green," Kermit the Frog sang on TV, early the next morning.

Emily jumped up. "'Mit song! 'Mit song!" she shouted excitedly.

"...the color of the leaves..."

So this was what Emily had been demanding they sing to her, Joanie thought with a smile as she joined in the singing of the *Sesame Street* song, as did Emily and Steve.

Watching Joanie dress Emily, Steve realized that Joanie had given him a sense of family, of being deeply, irrevocably loved in a way he had never been before. This was what he had been looking for, the happiness that had eluded him. With a frown, he wondered how his own father had ever walked away from him and his mother. He would *never* do the same to his wife and child.

He walked over to help Joanie put on Emily's shoes. "Busy day today?" he asked as he tied one tiny sneaker, Joanie the other.

Joanie nodded. "The kids from the mentoring conference are checking out. So I've got to go to the desk and help handle the rush." She paused to kiss Emily's cheek, then looked at Steve. "Can you watch Emily?"

Happy to comply, Steve nodded. "I've got errands to do on the mainland, but Emily can go with me."

Just then the phone rang and Joanie moved to answer it.

"Hello. Yes, he's here. Just a minute, please." Her eyes met Steve's as she handed him the receiver. "It's the detective. He says he has some important news for you."

Joanie watched as Steve hung up the phone a few minutes later. He looked more worried than she'd ever seen him. "What's going on?" she asked.

"Mrs. Flannagan and Emily are both booked to head back to Kansas one week from today on American Airlines."

Joanie swallowed. "What do you think that means?"

"I wish I knew." Steve sighed and raked both hands through his hair.

Joanie drew a deep breath and let it out slowly. "Do you think she's had a change of heart...about leaving her with you?"

Steve cast a fond look at Emily. In a Bride's Bay sweatshirt and jeans, her wispy blond hair standing up in curls, she'd never looked cuter. "It would be understandable if she did."

But it would break his heart, too, Joanie knew. She closed the distance between them and gently touched his arm. "What are you going to do?"

"I don't know. Part of me says I should wait and let the situation work itself out." His lips thinned. "The more cautious part tells me to get a lawyer—now."

"ALMOST DONE," Liz said a couple of hours later as Shad Teach and his crew of bellboys ferried the last of the luggage out to the waiting minivans that would take the departing conference attendees down to the ferry.

"Including Phoebe Claterberry and Dennis Wright," Joanie said, going over her own list.

"Oh, yeah, can you believe it? They were actually holding hands when they left."

Joanie blinked. "You're kidding!"

"Nope. Whatever Steve said to her last night after his speech must have had some impact. Of course, I saw him talking to Dennis, too."

"He played matchmaker for them?" Joanie was amazed.

"Apparently." Liz typed room numbers into the computer for the hotel maid service.

"Well, good for him," Joanie murmured. And to think she'd worried about Steve succumbing to the enamored Phoebe. She should have known better. "Do you mind if I clock out now? I've got some personal business to take care of."

"No problem," Liz said, "as long as you cover for me on short notice when I need it. I have a feeling I may be asking a lot of you in the next couple of months. Get going now," she said, shooing Joanie toward the door.

Figuring she would find out what was going on in Liz's personal life soon enough, Joanie took off. Back at her unit, she quickly went down the list of bed-and-breakfast inns she'd compiled. Thirteen phone calls later, she found the information Steve wanted. Mrs. Flannagan was registered at Holloway House, but she'd already gone out for the morning. The owner didn't know when to expect her back. Joanie did not leave a message. She would be waiting for Fiona when she did return.

Unfortunately Joanie's plan to act as emissary between Steve and Fiona was a total washout. By suppertime, she knew her day-long wait at Holloway House was all for naught. Leaving a message for Fiona to call her when she got in, Joanie took the ferry back to Jermain Island.

She went straight to her quarters. To her consternation, Steve and Emily weren't there, nor were they in his quarters.

Joanie went back to the main building and checked with the bell captain. "Have you seen Steve and Emily?" she asked Shad.

"I haven't seen them since around two this afternoon," he replied.

Joanie could only hope they'd had more success than she had. "If you see Steve, will you please tell him I'm looking for him?"

"You bet," Shad promised with a devilish wink.

In the meantime, Joanie thought, she'd check out the home Steve had leased. It was highly possible he and Emily had gone over there.

Her heart racing in anticipation of seeing Steve again, she got the keys to a minivan and dashed out the front door. Minutes later she was walking up the sidewalk of his newly leased home.

He met her at the door.

"Joanie, I'm glad you're here. I found Mrs. Flannagan—she's Fiona to her friends, she tells me—and she has something to tell us both."

STEVE GAVE JOANIE a hug, then led her to the living room, where Frances Fiona Flannagan was sitting.

"Gake geh mama!" Emily declared, pointing at Fiona. "Geh Mama!"

"All this time, she was saying grandmama," Joanie mused.

"Or great-grandmama," Fiona said, as Emily scrambled up on her lap for a hug.

"I'm glad you're here, Joanie," Fiona said earnestly. "I want you to know why and how everything happened the way it did."

Steve looked at Joanie. "Irene tried to contact me when she realized she was going to have a baby, but none of her messages caught up with me."

"Irene said if she couldn't get the father of her baby to return her calls, she doubted she could get him to participate in child-rearing, so she decided to go it alone. I was against that," Fiona continued seriously. "I thought my granddaughter should tell the baby's father face-to-face, but she refused to do so, and she would not tell me who the father of her child was, either. Instead, she moved back to Kansas to be closer to me and took a job in Topeka, which was only an hour or so away. And she visited frequently. When Emily was six months old, Irene discovered she had a rare but fatal form of cancer. And there was no hope. She moved in with me. Not until after she died did I find out that she had named me, and not Emily's father, sole guardian of Emily. The will stated I was to care for Emily until I was no longer able and then I was to return to the attorney and get a second letter of instruction.

"That letter told me to leave Emily with Steve for a period of one week, after which it would be clear if he wanted Emily with him and would be a responsible father. To prepare Emily and familiarize her with Steve, Irene had left me a video cassette of Steve—at the Olympics and doing a television commercial for the shaving cream he endorsed."

"That's why Emily kissed the TV screen and called him Daddy," Joanie said.

Fiona nodded. Emily perked up at the mention of her name and ran to where Joanie and Steve were sitting on the sofa. "I didn't want to leave Emily on Steve's doorstep, of course, but I also felt I had no choice but to honor Irene's last wishes. My attorney found out Steve would be here at Bride's Bay for a conference. So I followed Steve to the island, took the stroller over and parked it in the shade. I was trying to figure out how to get Steve's door open when you happened along, Joanie, and thought I was breaking in."

"So you were the woman in the trench coat and scarf." Joanie glanced down as Emily took a handful of her blazer in one tiny fist and Steve's shirt in her other.

"Right. I had left a letter in an envelope addressed to Steve, taped to Emily's shirt. She was sleeping. But Emily apparently woke up and opened the letter—the puppy absconded with the discarded envelope. When I realized everyone thought Emily had been left with Joanie, I had to leave a second note—that's the one I taped to Steve's door. I left the island early because I was afraid I would run into the three of you and that Emily would give me away before Steve got to know her better."

"And the round-trip airline tickets back to Kansas?" Joanie asked as Emily leaned her head on her shoulder and propped her feet on Steve's lap.

"That was just in case everything didn't work out as Irene had hoped," Fiona said. "But now that they have, we're going to have to go back, anyway. We have legal matters to take care of there."

"What about getting things straightened out here?" Joanie wondered.

"I called the local authorities soon after Fiona arrived this afternoon," Steve said to her. "I told them that Fiona's agreed to let me have custody of Emily, and that I, in turn, would like her to live with us, so that Emily can spend as much time with her as possible."

"My attorney in Kansas assures me it can all be done rather quickly," Fiona said. "All we have to do is get there."

"D'ink!" Emily said, tugging on the knee of Fiona's slacks. "D'ink p'ease!"

"There's apple juice and milk in the fridge," Steve said.

"I'll get it." Fiona was already on her feet. "You two have a lot to talk out, I'm sure."

When they were alone again, Steve turned to Joanie. "The media are going to have a field day with this. But Emily and I have to go back to Kansas City and face this, get the story out, have it a matter of public record and then go on from there."

I... not we.... He doesn't want me to go with him...

"Then you and I can pick up where we left off last night, start planning for our future."

Joanie felt like the wind had been knocked out of her. For both their sakes, she tried to stay calm. "You want me to stay here?"

Steve nodded seriously. "I think it would be best. Don't you?"

"I THOUGHT you might be here," Steve said several hours later as he sat down beside Joanie on the bench that rimmed the upper floor of the lighthouse. Stars sparkled overhead. A cool wind was blowing off the ocean. It should have been an incredibly romantic moment, but all Joanie could think about was the heartbreak that lay ahead.

Joanie glanced at Steve, who covered her hand with his. Outwardly, she knew she looked calm if a little windblown from her two-mile run, but inside, she felt numb. "Did you talk to Elizabeth Jermain?" she asked. When she'd left Steve, that's where he'd been headed. Emily had been with Fiona at Steve's island home.

"Yes. I told Elizabeth I still wanted to be the marketing director for Bride's Bay, but that I didn't want any scandal connected to me somehow connected to them. And right now, there's no telling what the public reaction is going to be to this."

He was right about that, Joanie thought. Public response could go either way. That was probably why he didn't want her with him. He was afraid she'd tip the balance the other way. "What did Elizabeth say?"

"That she'll hold the position open for me for a couple of weeks and then we'll see what things look like and reevaluate."

In other words, he's created an escape hatch for himself and Emily. "Oh." Joanie pulled her hand out from under his. She put her sneaker-clad feet on the bench and brought her knees up to her chest, clasping her arms around them. She hadn't realized the thought of losing him could hurt so much. And to lose Emily, too…it was almost more than she could take.

"I'm still hoping to take the position here, Joanie."

"And if you can't?" Joanie murmured, her voice muffled against her knees.

"Then I can't," Steve said. He studied her in silence, his own feelings kept carefully in check. "Why did you take off like that without telling me where you were going?" he asked softly at last.

Joanie lifted her head, able to be honest about that much. "I needed to run off some steam."

Steve stared at her in gritty silence, beginning to sense that something was very wrong. "And did you?" he asked in obvious trepidation.

"Not really, no."

He ran a hand from her ankle to her knee. "Which is why you're sitting up here all alone."

"I have a lot to think about," she said sadly, wondering if the pain inside her could get any worse. She pulled her leg from his gentle grip and scooted away from him.

"We both do." His gaze roved her tense posture as he continued cautiously, "I talked to Fiona, Joanie. I told her how I felt about you. I told her I wanted you to be a part of Emily's life, too."

Joanie didn't know whether to laugh or cry. The truth was she was on the verge of doing both—simultaneously. If that happened, she knew it would not be a pretty sight. She straightened her legs out in front of her and studied the toe of her sneaker.

"And what did Fiona say?"

"That she approves." He clasped her shoulders gently, forcing her to look at him. "I want you to marry me, Joanie, as soon as possible."

The words that would have, under any other circumstances, made her ecstatic, rang flat. She blinked back tears and stood.

"Hey, what's wrong?" he asked.

Joanie pushed a trembling hand through her hair. It was time for her to let him off the hook. To accept the fact that she did not fit comfortably into the fishbowl existence of his celebrity and never would, which meant they could never be happy together, not for the long haul, because his fame was not going to go away. "Steve, the fact of the matter is that you don't know how the public will react to Emily. And the fact that you're involved with me won't help the situation. The media is bound to find out about us—it's bound to get ugly." Seeing he was about to protest, she continued determinedly, "In the end, Bride's Bay is going to be exposed. I can't let that happen. The Jermains have been through enough. So has Emily. And you have to do what is best for her—even if it means staying in Kansas City."

He closed in on her, not stopping until they were mere inches apart. "I know a public scandal is inevitable, but I promise I'll find a way to keep you and Bride's Bay out of it—"

Joanie held up a palm, knowing she couldn't bear to hear him say anything more, or she really would burst into tears. "I can't marry you, Steve."

He blinked at her in what seemed to be genuine astonishment. "What?"

Feeling sick inside at all she was losing, Joanie moved into the dimly lit interior of the lighthouse.

More angry than exasperated now, he caught her wrists and stopped her flight toward the stairs, then backed her against the wall. He studied her grimly as he caught her shoulders in a warm, possessive grip. "Joanie, we can work it out," he said in desperation. "I'll contact the press agent who arranged publicity for me during the Olympics. Just please," he said vehemently, his voice dropping another persuasive notch as he caressed her shoulders gently, "don't be foolish. Don't throw this all away."

Joanie stared at him in stony silence. Then she said, "I'd hoped we could build a family together, but because of your celebrity, you'll always be vulnerable to scandal, and you're right to think I can't live that way—not in Kansas, and not here at Bride's Bay." Desperate to get out of the closed space, she tried to step by him.

Steve put out a hand and wouldn't let her.

Tears slipping down her face, Joanie pushed him aside. She headed for the stairs and rushed down them, aware he was hard on her heels the entire way.

"Damn it, Joanie, don't leave me...don't leave Emily," Steve pleaded as they stepped outside onto the beach.

Joanie knew, even if Steve—like Dylan—couldn't admit it yet, that it was going to happen, anyway. So why put off the inevitable?

"It's the only way," Joanie insisted as the waves crashed against the shore, echoing the slamming of her heart against her ribs.

"No, it's not." Steve stepped forward until they were so close they were almost touching. "And if you would just give me time to pave the way for us, it'll all work out. I'll make sure it does."

Dylan had said much the same thing to her. Only to realize eventually that she did not fit into his world and never would. Joanie's eyes filled with hot tears as she swept her hair back off her face. "Why can't you just face it? We can't be together, Steve."

Steve recoiled as if she'd struck him. "And that's it?" he echoed in a harsh tone. "That's all the chance I get?"

"What's the point in dragging it out?" Joanie cried in a strangled voice, her heart aching unbearably. "It hurts enough already."

Chapter Thirteen

"Congratulations on booking the South Carolina Bar Association conference, Steve," Liz remarked as he entered the hotel one morning four weeks later.

"Thanks." Steve bypassed the front desk and headed for his office.

"Working round the clock won't solve your problems, though," Liz continued, following dutifully at his heels.

The last thing Steve needed was someone else telling him he'd made the biggest mistake of his life, blowing it with Joanie again. "I haven't been working round the clock," Steve said as he set his briefcase on his desk.

"No, you're right," Liz agreed, dropping into a chair. "You have been spending quite a bit of time with Emily."

Yes, he had. But, dear God, he missed Joanie, missed her with a hunger and a desperation so great he could hardly fathom it. Joanie, who he would love for the rest of his life. Not, he lectured himself sternly, that this was likely to do him any good. No, some things were just not meant to be. She did not want to be part of his life. He would just have to accept that.

"So. How's the new nanny working out?"

Steve opened his briefcase and removed the specs for the new Bride's Bay sales brochure he'd been working on with a Charleston advertising agency. "Fine. She comes in during the day to help Fiona with Emily. Evenings, when I'm around, it's just the two of us with Emily."

Liz regarded Steve curiously. "You don't regret asking Fiona to move in with you?"

Steve handed the specs to Liz for her approval and sat down. "Not at all." He knew in that respect he'd gained more family. "Emily loves her great-grandmother every bit as much as Fiona loves her. And with five bedrooms, we've got plenty of room."

"How about your heart?" Liz asked. "Do you have room in there for a little forgiveness where Joanie is concerned?"

Steve did not want to be reminded of the single greatest loss he'd ever experienced. He gave Liz an irritated glance. "Joanie made her choice."

"Joanie reacted emotionally," Liz said.

Yes, Steve thought. Joanie had acted from the heart. Her deepest feelings and fears were ones he couldn't fight. "That's what hurts the most. Knowing that Joanie didn't believe in me," Steve told Liz, aware that her attempts to reconcile him and Joanie were only making his frustration and unhappiness worse.

Liz sighed. "Please, Steve. Won't you give Joanie another chance?"

And put his heart on the line again? Steve shook his head. "Sorry," he said. "No can do."

"MY GRANDDAUGHTER tells me you're thinking of leaving the island," Elizabeth said to Joanie as the two of them sat down to have tea in Elizabeth's suite.

Joanie watched as Elizabeth poured tea for the two of them. "Liz is right. It seems the sensible thing to do."

"Does it?" Elizabeth smiled benignly as she handed Joanie a bone-china cup. "I was under the impression you were very much in love with Steve Lantz and equally enamored of his daughter, Emily."

"Very much in love" didn't begin to cover it, Joanie thought. She adored Steve, and she adored Emily. And she had personally demolished both relationships, big time.

"I care about them, yes." She took a deep breath. Much more and she'd burst into tears, embarrassing them both. She set her cup aside with a hand that shook. "I don't think I can discuss this."

It had been bad enough watching Steve handle the news about Emily like the pro he was. Rather than try to withhold the story altogether or give it out in bits and pieces as reporters uncovered it, he'd been straightforward; he'd held a press conference to introduce Emily and Fiona to the world. Irene's memory was honored and all the legal details were promptly taken care of.

The public appreciated both Steve's candor and his affection for his newfound family. Hence the story was over almost as soon as it had broken. Which in turn had made it possible for him to return to Bride's Bay, where he'd settled in and worked diligently ever since.

Elizabeth lifted a quelling hand. "Sit down, Joanie. Please."

Able to see that Elizabeth was simply trying to help, Joanie complied. She just didn't have the heart to tell Elizabeth that nothing was going to change the way Steve felt about her. Not after what she'd done. Because if there'd been even a glimmer of hope, the slightest chance, he would have come after her by now. Steve was the kind of man who was used to fighting incredible obstacles to reach his goals. He was the kind of man who fought for what he believed in. Obviously he no longer believed the two of them were meant to be together. And after the ridiculously insecure way she had acted, she could hardly blame him. She'd been a fool.

With a gentle smile, Elizabeth tried again, "Loving someone is not easy. I know that from personal experience. But it's an endeavor that is well worth the effort, Joanie."

"I know that..."

"But?"

Joanie shook her head. "I've made such a mess of things." She had gone into her relationship with him with a suspicious heart. Partly because of what had happened before, and partly because of her fear of getting hurt again. So she had held back. And at the first instant of doubt, she'd done what she always did when she felt threatened—she'd looked for a way out.

As ugly as that final scene had been, breaking up with him had been the easy part. Going on without him was what was hard. Because she knew now that she had changed. She had realized it took two people, both doing their level best, to make a relationship thrive. Steve had given her a hundred percent of himself. She had not. And now, too late, she realized she had so much more to give. But that wasn't about to happen. Not after the way she'd jumped to conclusions—again.

"Then go to him and tell him you were wrong," Elizabeth persisted.

No. It was over. Much as Joanie didn't want to face that, she knew she must. She shook her head sadly, wishing desperately there was some way for her to make it up to Steve. "He'll never forgive me," she whispered.

Elizabeth smiled. "How will you know, dear," she asked gently, "unless you try?"

JOANIE FOUND HIM jogging along a deserted stretch of beach. He was wearing shorts and a T-shirt that showed off his swimmer's build. He'd never looked better, and a tingle of awareness swept through her as he slowed to confront her.

Joanie could tell by the wary look in his pewter eyes that this was not going to be easy. But then, nothing worthwhile ever came without a lot of effort, she reminded herself sternly. Heart racing, she slid her trembling hands into the pockets of her Bride's Bay blazer and edged nearer. The woodsy scent of his cologne clung to his jaw, inundating her with memories of their brief passionate affair.

"Can we talk?" she said.

Steve stared at her for a long moment, then murmured his assent. He sat down on the stairs of the lifeguard stand. Suddenly he cuffed a hand around her waist and hauled her down onto his lap. Breathing deeply, he buried his face in the fragrant softness of her hair.

"If you're here to tell me you're quitting, you can forget it," he said fiercely.

The rough possessiveness in his voice sent her heart slamming against her ribs. Almost afraid to hope that meant what she thought it did, she drew back to look at his face. Reading her mind, he repeated gruffly, "I said I'm not going to let you quit."

Joanie looked into his eyes and realized this was a good sign. "I wasn't aware you had anything to say about it."

"I have plenty to say." He kissed her thoroughly, then said hoarsely, "I'm at fault here, too, Joanie. I know that in here." He pointed to his head. "And in here, too." He pointed to his heart. "I should have taken you to Kansas with me."

Joanie shook her head emotionally. "No, Steve, you were right. I didn't have the experience to do what you did." Her voice caught. "Besides, I know now you were just trying to protect me."

"I still should have given you a choice." Silence.

Tears spilled over Joanie's lashes and caught on the corners of her smile. "If you felt this way, then why didn't you tell me?"

He shrugged negligently, then pressed a kiss to her trembling lips. "Call it an aversion of failure. I'd already struck out with you two times. I was afraid if I came to you too soon, before we'd had a chance to recuperate from all that happened, that I'd strike out again and be out of the game permanently."

Joanie paused. "You're telling me you have regrets, too?"

"Plenty of them." Steve sighed, still holding her close. "The first and foremost of which is in not chasing you down and proving to you that there was nothing between me and that groupie the first time you and I broke up."

Joanie frowned as she recalled that troubled time. So much heartbreak could have been averted if only he had. "Why didn't you?"

Steve lifted her hand to his mouth and kissed her knuckles gently. "I think it goes back to when I was a kid. I didn't want to be left again by someone I loved. You walking out, well, that hurt. When you wouldn't return my letters or phone calls, that hurt even more. So I put our love aside and moved on—only I never could forget you. You were right when you first accused me of having ulterior motives for taking this job. I wanted to see if what we had was as good as I remembered. I wanted to see if the love we'd felt could be resurrected."

"And was it?" she asked, looking deep into his eyes for her answer.

"Oh, yeah, in spades."

Joanie sighed contentedly, then said, "Emily's presence complicated things."

"Enormously," Steve agreed. "But they turned out to be great complications for all of us."

Joanie wreathed her arms about his neck and kissed him thoroughly, letting all that she felt pour into the lingering caress. "I do love you, Steve, so much."

Steve's arms tightened around her. He held her as if he never wanted to let her go. "You're sure this time?" He couldn't bear her walking out on him again.

She nodded, then traced aimless patterns on his chest. "I think the real reason I ran from you—from us—both times was that I was afraid things just wouldn't work out, that I wouldn't adapt well enough to the kind of fishbowl existence a world-famous celebrity like you lives in, and we'd grow to resent each other, like my parents did. I couldn't handle that." She swallowed hard. "My feelings for you were so strong they frightened me."

"Do they still frighten you?"

"No." She silenced his doubts and her own with another long, lingering kiss. "I know now that love happens when you least expect it, and that loving someone, building a relationship with that person that will last, is never going to be easy."

"But the trouble is worth it in the end," Steve said.

"Oh, yes." As they shared another kiss, one full of promise, Joanie knew she was exactly where she wanted to be—not just for the moment, but for the next fifty or sixty years. Contentment sizzled through her and was mirrored in the expression on his face. "Especially if it means we end up together."

Steve smiled. "With everything we always dreamed. And to that end, Joanie," he said confidently. I have a suggestion...."

"I'M SO HAPPY for you," Fiona Flannagan said several hours later. Steve and Joanie had just told her they'd patched things up between them. "The two of you make a wonderful couple."

"Thank you," Joanie said as she and Steve linked hands and smiled into each other's eyes. "We think so, too."

"Hi! Hi!" Abruptly realizing they had company, Emily left the wooden puzzle she'd been reassembling on the living room floor and toddled forward. Chortling happily, she launched herself into Joanie's arms.

Joanie's eyes misted over as she held Emily to her, drinking in the baby-fresh scent of her skin and hair. "Oh, I missed you, honey," she whispered fiercely.

Fiona looked from Joanie to Steve. "So, does this visit mean what I think it means?"

"I asked her to marry me again today," Steve confided.

Unable to contain her happiness, Joanie smiled. "And I accepted."

"Wonderful!" Fiona said, clapping her hands in joy.

Emily clapped her hands, too. "Love you!" she said.

Joanie and Steve hugged her warmly. "We love you, too."

Epilogue

The strains of "It Had to Be You," played by the small orchestra Elizabeth had hired to mark the occasion, filled the formal gardens. Emily toddled down the carpet strewing flowers, just as she'd been taught. Elizabeth's great-grandson, Troy, followed with a velvet pillow held aloft in his hands.

Her heart bursting with the happiness she felt, Joanie glided toward Steve.

He had never seen her look more beautiful than she did that day, in a long, white gown and veil.

As they reached the altar, Steve took her hand in his. Together they recited their vows.

"To have and to hold from this day forward...for richer, for poorer, in sickness and in health...as long as we both shall live."

"You may kiss the bride," the minister said.

And Steve did.

HARLEQUIN®

AMERICAN ❖ ROMANCE®

COMING NEXT MONTH

#617 THE BOUNTY HUNTER'S BABY by Jule McBride
New Arrivals

Remy Lafitte was charismatic—a tracker of men, seducer of women, a Cajun healer. But one steamy New Orleans night, plain Jayne Wright won his heart. When she vanished before her wedding, Remy was hired to retrieve her. But their one-time tryst couldn't be ignored, not when the bad-boy bounty hunter discovered she was pregnant—with *his* baby!

#618 THE COWBOY AND THE CENTERFOLD by Debbi Rawlins

In trying to keep a low profile, Rainy Daye had unwittingly landed in a small town filled with gossipmongers. And having a gorgeous, emerald-eyed cowboy as a boss didn't help, either. Somehow, Rainy had to keep *Midnight Fantasy* from hitting the Maybe, Texas, newsstands...and blowing her cover sky-high!

#619 FLYBOY by Rosemary Grace

Brave, built and with blue eyes to die for, Captain Rodger ("Blackjack") McConnell had the right stuff. Only one thing scared the flyboy—love! When he found himself falling for Sue Rigger, he ejected from her as fast as from one of his planes. But he didn't know they had a son.... Would the daredevil pilot take a chance at fatherhood—and a second chance with Sue?

#620 THE BEWITCHING BACHELOR by Charlotte Maclay

Erich Langlois was dark and dangerous—sexier than any man Julianne Olson had ever known. But what was he doing coming out of her armoire in the middle of the night? "Witchcraft," the townspeople whispered, and Julianne had to admit that when she was under the spell of his burning gaze, she could deny him nothing.

AVAILABLE THIS MONTH:

Meet "Hurricane" Mitchell. Born in the middle of a raging storm, Cane has been raising hell ever since. This Texas rogue is all wrong for Bernadette...but love has a way of taming a man. Sometimes.

THE STORMCHASER
by Rita Clay Estrada

All men are not created equal. Some are rough around the edges. Tough-minded but tenderhearted. Incredibly sexy. The tempting fulfillment of every woman's fantasy.

When it's time to fight for what they believe in, to win that special woman, our Rebels and Rogues are heroes at heart.

Look for #573 THE STORMCHASER in February 1996 wherever Harlequin books are sold.

IT'S A BABY BOOM!

NEW ARRIVALS

We're expecting—again! Join us for the New Arrivals promotion, in which special American Romance authors invite you to read about equally special heroines—all of whom are on a nine-month adventure! We expect each mom-to-be will find the man of her dreams—and a daddy in the bargain!

Watch for the newest arrival. Due date: next month...

#617 THE BOUNTY HUNTER'S BABY
by Jule McBride
February 1996

What do women really want to know?

Only the world's largest publisher of romance fiction could possibly attempt an answer.

HARLEQUIN ULTIMATE GUIDES™

How to Talk to a Naked Man,

Make the Most of Your Love Life, and Live Happily Ever After

The editors of Harlequin and Silhouette are definitely experts on love, men and relationships. And now they're ready to share that expertise with women everywhere.

Jam-packed with vital, indispensable, lighthearted tips to improve every area of your romantic life—even how to get one! So don't just sit around and wonder why, how or where—run to your nearest bookstore for your copy now!

Available this February, at your favorite retail outlet.

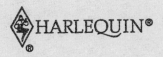

This Valentine's Day, take your pick of the four extraspecial heroes who are coming your way. Or why not take *all* of them?

Four of the most fearless, strong and sexy men are brought to their knees by the undeniable power of love. And it all happens next month in

Valentine's MEN

Don't miss any of these:

#617 THE BOUNTY HUNTER'S BABY
by Jule McBride

#618 THE COWBOY AND THE CENTERFOLD
by Debbi Rawlins

#619 FLYBOY
by Rosemary Grace

#620 THE BEWITCHING BACHELOR
by Charlotte Maclay

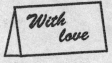

From HARLEQUIN AMERICAN ROMANCE

INTRODUCING...  WINNER'S CIRCLE

A collection of award-winning books by award-winning authors! From Harlequin and Silhouette.

VALENTINE'S NIGHT
by Penny Jordan

VOTED BESTSELLING
HARLEQUIN PRESENTS!

Let award-winning Penny Jordan bring you a Valentine you won't forget. *Valentine's Night* is full of sparks as our heroine finds herself snowed in, stranded and sharing a bed with an attractive stranger who makes thoughts of her fiancé fly out the window.

"Women everywhere will find pieces of themselves in Jordan's characters."
—*Publishers Weekly*

Available this February wherever Harlequin books are sold.

This February, watch how
three tough guys handle the

Lieutenant Jake Cameron, Detective Cole Bennett and
Agent Seth Norris fight crime and put their lives on the
line every day. Now they're changing diapers, talking
baby talk and wheeling strollers.

Nobody told them there'd be days like this....

Three complete novels by some of your favorite
authors—in one special collection!

TIGERS BY NIGHT by Sandra Canfield
SOMEONE'S BABY by Sandra Kitt
COME HOME TO ME by Marisa Carroll

Available wherever Harlequin and Silhouette books are sold.

When desires run wild,

can be deadly

JoAnn Ross

The shocking murder of a senator's beautiful wife has shaken the town of Whiskey River. Town sheriff Trace Callihan gets more than he bargained for when the victim's estranged sister, Mariah Swann, insists on being involved with the investigation.

As the black sheep of the family returning from Hollywood, Mariah has her heart set on more than just solving her sister's death, and Trace, a former big-city cop, has more on his mind than law and order.

What will transpire when dark secrets and suppressed desires are unearthed by this unlikely pair? Because nothing is as it seems in Whiskey River—and everyone is a suspect.

Look for *Confessions* at your favorite retail outlet this January.

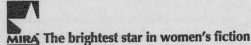